TERRIFIED, CHRISTINA COULD BARELY SEE NICK COME TOWARD HER IN THE DARKENED ROOM.

His mouth plundered hers in a tantalizing way that brought tingles to her sensitive skin. He ran his tongue along the edge of her mouth until the sensation became unbearable.

Nick reached for the lantern and hung it from a hook on the ceiling above him, casting a soft, glowing light on them both. Christina could not stifle the gasp that escaped her when she saw his face. Gone were the eyepatch and the disfiguring scar. In their place were two sparkling gray-black eyes, alight with humor.

"So you like me better this way?"

Dear Reader,

We, the editors of Tapestry Romances, are committed to bringing you two outstanding original romantic historical novels each and every month.

From Kentucky in the 1850s to the court of Louis XIII, from the deck of a pirate ship within sight of Gibraltar to a mining camp high in the Sierra Nevadas, our heroines experience life and love, romance and adventure.

Our aim is to give you the kind of historical romances that you want to read. We would enjoy hearing your thoughts about this book and all future Tapestry Romances. Please write to us at the address below.

The Editors
Tapestry Romances
POCKET BOOKS
1230 Avenue of the Americas
Box TAP
New York, N.Y. 10020

Libertine Lady

Janet Joyce

A TAPESTRY BOOK
PUBLISHED BY POCKET BOOKS NEW YORK

An *Original* publication of TAPESTRY BOOKS

 A Tapestry Book published by
POCKET BOOKS, a Simon & Schuster division of
GULF & WESTERN CORPORATION
1230 Avenue of the Americas, New York, N.Y. 10020

ISBN: 0-671-46292-X

First Tapestry Books printing March, 1983

10 9 8 7 6 5 4 3 2 1

Dedicated to
IRENE GOODMAN,
who makes dreams become reality.

Chapter One

Off the coast of Spain, 1817

A NOONDAY SUN IN THE CLOUDLESS AZURE SKY above the Mediterranean cast brilliant light upon the rough planked decks of the *Madelaine*. Christina Anne Bristol turned her face to catch the slight breeze that barely billowed the yards of white canvas above her head. She brushed away a damp amber tendril that teased across her face and gazed into the inviting blue water of the sea as it slid past the starboard bow. The heavily laden merchant ship lumbered through the calm sea, set on a course from Malaga, Spain, through the Strait of Gibraltar to England. As soon as they passed by the limestone cliffs of Gibraltar, they would enter the Atlantic where the winds would be stronger and the temperature lower. Though Christina would welcome the cooler weather, she did not look forward to the high winds which would hasten her journey. She had no wish to reach London and begin the new life her father had planned for her.

The Dominican priory at Malaga, where she had been confined for the last three years, may have been restricting, but the simple life was free of her father's domination and the teaching sisters had been sympathetic to her plight. In the convent school, she had found peace, a loving atmosphere that had soothed her. There would be no understanding or affection forthcoming from her father, Benjamin Bristol. She had learned what she could expect from him the first time they met. A shudder ran through her petite frame and she closed her eyes as the memory returned.

Once again, it was that terrible day three years ago when she had huddled behind the heavy gold drapes in the salon at Briar Park, her maternal grandparents' estate in Yorkshire. It was one day after her mother's funeral and her grandparents were arguing with a man she had never seen before. Their raised voices filled the room. She was too terrified to move from her hiding place while the stranger threatened the frail old couple.

Benjamin Bristol, the father Christina had been led to believe was dead, had arrived without prior warning to assume the guardianship of Christina. From shortly after her birth, she had lived with her mother and grandparents. Whenever she had asked about her father, her mother had gently explained that he was gone and would not be coming back. A closed sad look would always creep across her mother's beautiful face and as Christina grew older, she interpreted her mother's expression as one of grief for the loss of her beloved husband. Not wanting to cause her mother further pain, Christina eventually stopped asking about him and imagined him as a dashing war hero who had fallen before Napoleon's sword. This romantic image and the fact that her mother had apparently hidden herself away from society and the attentions of men on a remote estate had seemed proof that her father's death had broken her mother's heart.

She peeped out from behind the drape and her eyes grew wide with horror. The man who claimed her as his daughter overwhelmed the room with his forbidding presence, looking nothing like the young, handsome father of her dreams. His eyes, within the folds of his florid porcine face, were gray and cold as the North Sea. He spied her and his mouth thinned cruelly, slashing across his beefy face to connect his shaking jowls. He turned to the short, thin man who had accompanied him from London. "She is much worse than I expected, Morrison. Take this dowdy chit out to the hall while I have her belongings collected." He turned to Christina's grandmother. "See to it, woman! You should be glad I am taking her off your hands. She has been allowed to run wild, but, no longer. She is fourteen and should have acquired the manners of a young woman of quality and breeding." His gravelly voice dripped sarcasm. "I am surprised that my dear, departed wife allowed her such latitude. Propriety was always so important to Elizabeth."

Caroline Harris looked pleadingly at her husband. Squire Harris placed a comforting arm around his wife, lifting his elegant silver head and straightening his spine. In an emotion-roughened voice he attempted one last argument. "You have no right to her, Bristol!"

A humorless chortle interrupted the plea. "I have every right. The chit bears *my* name, does she not?"

The slump of George Harris's proud shoulders signified his defeat. He tightened his arm around his weeping wife. "There is nothing we can do if he wishes to take her, Caroline."

A short while later, the two elderly people watched with tear-streaked faces as Christina was placed inside Bristol's closed carriage. He had no patience with their emotional farewells and quickly ordered the driver to start. At first, Christina cried piteously to be taken back to Briar Park, but Bristol had slapped her soundly until she was silent. She cowered in the corner of the large Berlin carriage and watched the familiar countryside rush past the glass panes as the tears rolled silently down her cheeks. Her life among people who loved her and her care-free existence on the windswept moors had come to an end. By the time they arrived in London, Christina's arms were bruised from the shaking she had received along with Bristol's ultimatum concerning her future. "You will behave as a young lady of fashion if it takes years of training. You will be an asset to me, much as your dimwitted mother was before you. The Dominican sisters in Spain will see to it."

A weak voice calling her name snapped Christina out of her reverie. She turned away from the rail to smile at the woman who was gingerly making her way across the *Madelaine*'s swaying decks. Annette Harcourt could not muster the energy to return the smile. Her large blue eyes were dulled and shadowed and her thin face was tinged slightly green from the effects of *mal de mer*. "When I was hired to escort you back to England, I did not realize that I could not withstand the motion of the sea." Christina steadied the older woman who was grasping the rail with shaking hands.

"I wish you felt better, Annette. I am quite sick of my own company. The Castilian Spanish the sisters taught me is not understood by the crew." She lifted her shoulder in a sardonic shrug. "It is unfortunate that King Ferdinand or a member of his court is not our captain. Then, at least, I could discuss the weather."

Annette laughed weakly, then sobered. "It is better for you not to speak to these men anyway. The rough sailors that man this ship are not fit company for a young lady." She paused and viewed her charge, seeing the lovely oval face framing large, blue-green eyes. Christina's burnished red hair and soft curves would indeed attract the attention of the men on board the merchant vessel. Christina's deep green broadcloth frock was suitably modest with a crisp habit shirt of white poplin tucked in a deep square décolletage. The highwaisted skirt fell to her ankles in many gores and the long narrow undersleeves of white poplin reached from the short puffs of dark green at her shoulder to her wrists. The simple lines enhanced the fullness of her young breasts and the slimness of her hips. Though her hair was caught up beneath a straw "Gypsy" hat securely held by a long narrow silk scarf tied beneath her chin, loose silken curls peeped beneath its edges. She was far too tempting· a sight for any man and Annette cursed her own malaise for preventing her from being in Christina's constant company in order to ward off any attentions from the rough crewmen. Forcing a frown in an effort to emphasize the seriousness of her warning, she continued, "Your betrothed would not approve of your associating with this rabble. I cannot understand why your father booked passage aboard this lowly vessel and failed to send his agent along with us for further protection."

"It doesn't matter, no one has made undue advances. I believe the captain has warned off his crew, Annette." Christina's lips twisted. "My own well-being is not my concern." Hearing Annette's sharp intake, she continued. "My thoughts are with my grandparents. I know that my arrival in London and compliance with my father's wishes will rid them of whatever hold he has on them. I am curious to learn what sort of settlement my father demanded in return for my hand. It must have been a huge sum. He has hidden me away in that convent school since my mother's death without any communication. Suddenly, he sent you to fetch me and to have an elaborate wardrobe prepared. Am I to be paraded before the lofty Benton family for their approval?" She ignored Annette's astonished expression. "My father sent only enough money to the sisters to pay the most meager expenses. I wore the drab attire of a novitiate during my years at Santa Demetria's, just as the girls from the poorest families who were sent there to take their vows. The young ladies of 'quality', whom my esteemed parent wished me to emulate, were attired in the dark blue uniform of the school. When I inquired if it were my father's intention that I enter the order, Sor Margareta informed me as gently as that dear lady could that he had not sent funds to cover the expense of the proper uniforms."

The fleeting look of remembered pain that crossed Christina's beautiful features tore at Annette's heart. The older woman could well imagine the cruel taunting and embarrassment her charge must have suffered from her classmates at the school. Young ladies could be heartless and Annette could well imagine the miserable existence Christina had been forced to endure. She placed a comforting arm around Christina's shoulders. "Do not worry, my lamb, I am sure that your betrothed will be instantly enamored of you, and would be even without the fine trappings your father has provided." Thinking to soften Christina's harsh estimation of her father's motives for ordering her stylish wardrobe, she offered, "Whatever his reasons, he spared no cost for your trousseau and you need never worry that your appearance is not befitting the future wife of the viscount of Larleigh."

A shudder ran through Christina's body. "Just how repugnant is the man my father has sold me to?"

"Oh Tina, dear, I have not seen Nicholas Benton, but I have heard it on good authority that he is a sensational catch. He is reported to be young and wealthy."

"If he is considered such a 'catch' as you say, then why has he agreed to marry me, sight unseen? Either no one else would have him, or he is indeed a simpleton!"

"If the viscount is a simpleton, it could be a stroke of luck. You are an intelligent young woman and shall have no trouble dealing with him."

Christina's natural curiosity was piqued by the distant look on Annette's face. "Were you happily married?"

"Yes, for the short time we had together. I was widowed less than a year after my marriage."

Christina wondered why Annette had never remarried. Though now past middle years, her figure no longer youthful, there was still evidence that she had been comely in her youth. Her gray hair had once been a luxurious black, framing an oval face. "I know what you are thinking," Annette began. "But, I was left quite enough funds for my needs and I enjoy my duties as a young lady's companion." A sad look came over Annette's face and her large blue eyes clouded.

In a soft voice that was more a statement than a question, Christina said, "You still miss him, don't you?" There was a moment's pause before Annette answered. With a barely perceptible sigh, she turned her gaze toward the glimmering waters. "Yes."

Sensing that Annette would not reveal more, Christina suggested, "Perhaps we should return to our cabin."

"I believe that would be best for me. However, there is no need for you to go down to that stuffy little hole assigned to us." Her voice had returned to its usual authoritative tone. "There is not a breath of fresh air below decks, but I am better off in my berth than up here where I can see the cause of my distress." She gave Christina's hand a squeeze. "Listen to me, Tina. You must remember not to encourage any notice from the members of this crew." Her sharp eyes and stern gaze forced an agreement from Christina and she took her companion's arm and helped the older woman to the hatch that led to the companionway of the lower deck.

"You will get your sea legs, soon. The cooler Atlantic breezes will make you feel better."

"With cooler breezes will come higher swells. I was sick on the voyage over and I fear that I will suffer for the entire return. After this, I will be content to spend the rest of my days with my feet planted firmly on the earth."

A day later, the *Madelaine* had made its way through the Strait of Gibraltar and entered the Atlantic. The horizon was obscured by a rolling swell of gray fog. The sea was almost calm but the dark water looked sinister. Christina wrapped her hooded cloak around her slender frame, but the fur-lined merino did nothing to alleviate the gripping cold dampness. She stood on deck, silently contemplating the sea.

"*Señorita?*" Christina jumped as a man tapped her arm. He was the first mate. She was alarmed by his familiarity until he gestured frantically to the sea and cried, "*Abajo! Abajo! Por favor. Pronto! Pronto!*"

Looming up out of the fog was a black apparition which grew larger and larger before her eyes. She gasped with shock as the oncoming vessel cut through the inky water on a direct collision course with the *Madelaine*. Where had it come from? The ship seemed to gain with every passing moment. The mate pried her away from the railing, but Christina didn't descend the companionway until she had witnessed the chilling sight which would remain with her forever.

Through the rolling mists, the gaping black mouths of cannon drew closer. The image of a skull and crossbones on a black field hung from the mainmast, a sign of destruction and death feared by all seagoing men. The poorly outfitted *Madelaine* was no match for the fast, fully armed corsair cutting in for the kill. Christina's face drained of all color. "Pirates!" Without another word she rushed below to her cabin and burst through the door. She ran to Annette, her green eyes wide with fear. "We are being attacked! Dear God, we are about to be attacked by pirates!"

"It can't be!" Annette sat up quickly, getting up from the berth to rush to the porthole. "I see nothing." The ominous roar of cannon nullified further denial. They gazed at each other in terror. Annette was the first to speak. "Promise me, child. If we are taken, you must not utter a word. Trust me in this." Before Christina could respond, a scream was torn from her lips as the ship lurched heavily to one side and she was thrown to the floor. The sound of a crashing mast rumbled overhead.

She scrambled back to her feet. "We have to get up on deck. I think we are going to sink!" The clash of fighting swords resounded. They could hear the screams of the Spanish crew as they were overwhelmed by their attackers. "Let's go! I'll not drown down here like some caged rat!"

"No!" Annette cried. "We must dress you in your finest gown. Hurry, before we are found!" She ran to the wardrobe and pulled out a deep blue silk gown. "Get into this quickly while I do up your hair."

Christina gaped, certain her elderly companion had completely lost her mind. "You can't be serious! Dress up to meet a crew of murdering scum?"

She soon discovered that Annette was deadly serious when the woman practically ripped Christina's clothes from her body. "Don't argue!" The order was delivered sharply in a tone meant to be obeyed. Christina attempted to question Annette further, but the hands pulling up her hair brought tears and had her quickly doing what she was told. "Wear this," Annette cried, taking a pale blue lace mantilla from among her own belongings and thrusting it into Christina's hands. "Keep your eyes downcast and your mouth shut at all costs. Do you hear?"

Wide-eyed, Christina obeyed, adjusted the lace over her head and caught a glimpse of herself in the mirror above the dressing table. Her regal image impelled her to speak. "I look like a Spanish *señorita* of high standing. I do not know what you are planning, Annette, but I fear we might drown before you accomplish it." She raced across the cabin, threw open the lid of her portmanteau and dug to the bottom. She triumphantly pulled out a rusty, pearl-handled pocket pistol from beneath the false bottom of the small leather case. "I was taught the use of this. Grandmother never traveled unprepared and this bag was hers. I hope this thing still fires. The powder is probably damp but if nothing else we can put up a show." She wielded the pistol clumsily, pointing it at the closed door.

"Put it down," Annette wailed. They both heard the sound of heavy boots tramping ominously along the passageway toward their cabin. They backed away from the door as the approaching tread halted outside their door.

"Stay behind me, Annette," Christina whispered as she steadied the gun with both hands.

The door burst open and two tall burly figures, brandishing gleaming cutlasses, advanced into the cabin. Annette shouted a warning in Spanish, reminding Christina to say nothing. Paralyzed with fear, she complied. One of the men, his eye covered by a black patch, openly leered at her. His bearded face sported a mocking grin. His tall form was dressed in tight black pantaloons and a billowing white shirt left open to the waist. The other man was shorter, older, and heavier. He wore a colorful bandana about his neck and billowing striped breeches. His bright red hair was in surprising contrast to his deeply tanned skin. His mouth showed several black spaces as he leered at the two women. "Blimey, cap'n! What's this?"

"Don't come any closer!" Annette shouted from behind Christina. "She will shoot if she has to."

Christina was acutely aware that she was too frightened to fire her dubious weapon. A creeping paralysis seemed to hold her in its grip as she tried to maintain an aggressive stance. The gun wavered in her grasp as she focused on her target. She hoped the vicious looking twosome who faced her would not see how her legs were shaking nor realize that her weapon was not properly primed.

"Two tasty morsels, mate." The tall figure bowed at the waist, showing no concern as he faced the gilded barrel of the pistol aimed at his heart. "Have no fear, ladies. Captain Nick Barker at your service." He sheathed his sword and held out his hand toward Christina. "May I have that, my lovely?" Christina took a step back and gestured with her insignificant weapon for them to get out.

"Careful, wench! I don't wish to get pricked by that trifling toy. You don't want to shoot, now do you? That trinket may explode in your pretty face." Captain Barker gave her a flashing white smile and continued to hold out his hand, confident that the small pistol would drop into his waiting palm. "You are completely outnumbered. The crew is held prisoner and if you shoot me, you'll be strung up by your fragile neck." His one good eye gleamed with amusement. "You can't hold us off long, my love. You have but one shot in that ancient piece and Jackson, here, will be upon you as soon as I fall."

The pale lace of the mantilla kept Christina's features in shadow so the pirate couldn't tell how desperately afraid she was. His voice grew more impatient as she hesitated. Annette spoke near her ear, begging her in Spanish to give up her weapon and do what the arrogant man commanded. Christina had lost her ability to move.

"Has she been struck dumb?" The pirate asked Annette, coming closer every second. His unpatched eye narrowed on Christina's face. He moved like a stalking panther, always aware of danger, but confident of its own superiority.

"She speaks no English!" Annette exclaimed as the pirate captain pounced upon the gun. He grasped the weapon by the barrel and jerked it away from Christina's bloodless fingers. As soon as his hand grabbed hold of her wrists, her paralysis fled. She was filled with pumping adrenalin. "No!" she screamed and brought her sharp teeth to the large hand which clamped her wrists. The pirate let out a startled oath and snatched his hand away. She used the opportunity to run behind the small round table anchored near the berth. She panted like a cornered animal as the pirate placed his wounded hand to his mouth and tried to soothe his injury. "Hellcat!" he proclaimed as Annette rushed to Christina and placed her body protectively in front of her.

"Small creatures who bite should be muzzled," he hissed between clenched teeth. He proceeded to pull the linen from the berth and viciously ripped off a long strip of material. He snapped it taut between his hands and rounded on Christina.

Annette clutched Christina to her breast, her words a false bravado. "If you harm one hair on this innocent's head," she shrilled, "you shall not live another year. She is Spanish nobility."

The black-haired pirate laughed, harshly. "The vixen used her teeth on me, madame. It shall not go unpunished, pedigree or no." He strode to Annette and firmly pulled Christina away from her protective embrace. No amount of struggling could prevent the strong man from overpowering her and using his greater strength to gain the desired end. The captain held Christina by both wrists, using his free hand to grip the fragile bones of her jaw, ordering his companion to slip the white material between her teeth. "My hand had better not fester, wench, or you'll get worse than this," he snarled as his mate held Annette away from her with an outstretched muscle-bound arm.

"She is a condessa, I tell you!" Annette screeched. "And barely out of the schoolroom!"

She finally got the pirate's attention after he finished binding his hand with another strip of linen from the sheet.

"Very well, madam. I will handle her gently." He scooped Christina off her feet and over his shoulder. "Bring the old shrew, Jackson."

"Hope you're worth all this trouble, lady," Jackson declared as he easily hoisted Annette into the same ignominious position Christina occupied on his captain's shoulder. "At least you don't weigh more than a sack of meal."

"Thistledown." Captain Barker laughed and patted Christina's bottom lightly. Outraged, she beat upon his back, kicking her legs as she screamed against the gag in her mouth. The soft pat became the sharp smack of a hard descending palm and she went instantly limp. "Stop hurting me, little cat," her captor remarked with another laugh. "I bruise easily." They proceeded swiftly up the companionway and through the open hatch. Christina's heart pounded against the pirate's hard shoulder. His corded arms about her legs held her securely and she could not focus as she swung crazily against his back. Her mantilla slipped away and she felt the pins that secured her amber hair fall one by one to the deck. By the time she was set abruptly back on her feet, her hair was totally loose and shimmering about her shoulders like a veil. She stared with revulsion at her assailant's scarred face.

"God's truth, you're a beauty!" He reached out and touched a strand of her hair, toying with it until she pulled away. His hair fell over his forehead in raven black curls. A puckered red scar marred his darkly tanned face from ear to chin. His good eye, a sparkling gray, insolently surveyed her heaving bosom exposed by the deep oval décolletage of her gown. He placed one finger under her chin and grinned at her. His open shirt showed a heavily muscled chest clouded by curling black hair. His hot gaze burned through her gown as his eye traveled up and down her quivering figure. She would rather die than let him touch her and she looked to the rail, contemplating whether or not she had the courage to jump.

He must have read her thoughts for his hand snapped around her wrist and he pulled her to his side the instant she moved. "Oh no, my pretty. You shall not be food for the sharks." He swiftly hoisted her over his shoulder again. "I'm across, Jackson. Don't forget to search the captain's cabin. I believe our treasure may be found in his strong box." He finished giving his orders and grabbed hold of a dangling line. He seemed not to feel the strain of the extra weight he carried as he swung them both across the treacherous span between the two ships. Christina squeezed her eyes shut, unable to look at the choppy gray water which swelled below them. It seemed an eternity before he dropped easily to the deck of the pirate vessel and lashed her wrist to the mast, using a silk scarf he had stolen from her belongings as a bond. "Can't mar this tender skin," he offered before shouting orders to the scurvy crew that had gathered around him. Christina quickly pulled the gag from her mouth and threw it over the side. She spat on the deck near his boots but he chose to ignore her small show of contempt.

"Gor, cap'n. What bounty is this?" A thin, young looking sailor with a smudged face spoke for the crew.

"Never mind, lads. Get back to your tasks. No one touches the girl, understood?"

Christina misunderstood the offended looks of the crew, assuming that they had thought that she would be fair game for them all. She was confused when she heard one sailor mutter, "As if I would," as he walked away.

She looked across to the *Madelaine* in time to see Annette being escorted over a wide plank anchored between ships. The pirates efficiently carried crate after crate onto their vessel and secured them to the deck. She started to cry out but remembered the warning for silence when Annette was allowed to come to her. They stood mutely watching, clinging to each other for strength as the Spanish sea captain and his crew were huddled together on the deck of the *Madelaine*. The Spaniards were bravely facing their fate and Christina hoped that the pirates would be merciful. She gave a grateful sigh when she saw Captain Barker signal to his men to return to their ship, leaving the merchantmen to go safely on their way.

Annette whispered, "Do as I say and all will be well, child," as Barker turned his attention back in their direction. "These scum are only con-

cerned with money and we will tell a story that
will have them slathering with greed."

"Well, woman," the pirate leader spoke to
Annette, but his eye remained on Christina.
"You will now explain exactly who you are."

"I am *dueña* to this innocent. She is la
condessa, Teresa San Lupéz, the betrothed of
Felipe, duque de Val Déz. We are on our way to
join Don Felipe who is on a diplomatic mission to
England. He will pay handsomely for her safe
arrival. Surely you realize what you will lose by
harming her. She is little more than a child, just
in her seventeenth year and untouched."

"So you say, madam. And who might you be,
the empress of France?" He questioned sarcastically, obviously disbelieving Annette's fantastic
story. "How is it that a Spanish aristocrat is
traveling on a second-rate merchant ship?"

"If you know the Val Déz family, then you
know the answer to that. Too many covet their
wealth. It was thought that if Doña Teresa
sailed to England aboard this nondescript ship,
none would accost us. We did not think that
pirates would taken any interest in such a poor
vessel as the *Madelaine*."

You were misinformed, madame. The *Madelaine* may have looked down on its fortunes but
we were told by our sources that she carried
great treasure. I think that I might be looking at
my prize right now. So far, our booty is worth-
less. If you speak true, I have the wealth of the
Val Déz family within my grasp. Proof of your
identity must wait until we reach the English
shore. Then I will find the scurvy sea rat who led

me to your ship and drag the truth out of him. We shall know, then, if this little red-headed princess is the *Madelaine*'s missing treasure."

His crew shouted angrily over each box they had brought to their decks. As each wooden crate was ripped open, their annoyance increased. "I must think on this later. Jackson! Install this woman below." He frowned at Annette as Jackson came to take her arm and warned, "You are certain this princess speaks no English? I do not deal lightly with those who would deceive me."

"She can tell you nothing, *señor*. Everything you say to her must be interpreted by me. We cannot be separated."

"For what I have in mind, no interpreter will be necessary," he vowed with a mocking grin. Unable to protest without revealing their deception, Christina watched helplessly while Annette was dragged below.

"So, little one. Let us become better acquainted. I have heard that some of the Spanish have your fiery coloring and fair skin. Felipe Val Déz is a lucky man." His voice was curiously cultured as he spoke his thoughts aloud. "I did not expect my plunder to take the form of a beautiful woman." He untied her wrist and before she could turn to run away, he forced her hand behind her back and drew her to his chest. "You have nothing to fear from me. I shall not hurt you." He drew her closer and watched curiously as green rage sparkled in her eyes. He was much too strong for her to fend off very long, but Christina made a valiant effort to arch away from the smiling lips which hovered close to her throat. Finally, when she realized that there would be no escape, she used the defense she had been taught as a child in her grandfather's stable. She brought up one knee and sharply struck him in the groin with all of her might.

She was released instantly as the pirate grunted with pain and went down on his knees to the deck. She ran swiftly toward the open hatch where Annette had disappeared, but was stopped seconds before her feet landed on the first step. A man's tight hold on her waist dragged her back from the safety of the hatch. He brought her struggling form before his fallen leader. The captain was slowly getting to his feet, his face a gray mask of pain as he clutched his groin. The gathered crew shouted words of encouragement to him as he tried to stand upright. Their laughter was raucous and Christina began to tremble. What would he do to her for humiliating him in front of his crew? Would he kill her?

His face was twisted in a savage grimace which puckered the crimson scar on his cheek. His grotesque disfigurement looked even more sinister than when he had burst into her cabin. He was having difficulty regaining his breath, his chest heaving as he fought to control his rage. "You have maimed me once too often, you damned little hellion!" He reached for a coiled rope which was lying beside him on the deck, slowly gathering the thick hemp around his arm. Would she be hung from the yardarm for her crime? Trussed up and tossed into the sea?

Fear, greater than she had ever known, gripped every fiber of Christina's being. Her body grew cold as she faced what must be the last moments of her life.

The man who held her arms to her sides shouted close to her ear. "She fights like a street urchin, cap'n. I doubt if she learned that little trick in Ferdinand's court." Christina cowered against the firm wall of her captor's chest as the one-eyed pirate limped toward her with a menacingly grim expression on his face.

"Make sail, Smith. Give me the damned wench."

"Sure you can handle her this time, cap'n?" Smith laughed and pushed her toward his leader. Frantically, Christina looked around for some sort of weapon, some means of escape, but the crew formed a circle around her and she was held prey for the angry man who stalked her.

"You can do it, cap'n!"

"She ain't near as tough as she looks."

"Think she could be duped by a good right cross, cap'n!"

"Watch out, that red hair shows a sign of her temper. She's quick!"

The jeers and shouts came from every side, the circle tightened around her as they stepped closer, waiting to see what she meant to do next. Christina stared at the captain, her eyes like huge green mirrors reflecting both horror and dread. The deck began swirling around her as she swayed, terror-stricken alarm washing her face of all color. The sea of savage, jeering faces

that surrounded her blurred until she couldn't
see them at all. She fell, crumpling slowly
like a broken sapling. She felt two strong arms
slip beneath her and heard the captain's voice
come to her from a great distance.

"Fools! We may bloody well have frightened
her to death."

Chapter Two

CHRISTINA AWAKENED WITH A JERK, HER BODY tensed for action. It was dark and as her eyes adjusted to the dim light, she realized with growing dismay exactly where she was. She was lying on a narrow berth inside the pirate's cabin and her loathsome captor was standing across the compartment from her. He was bent over a wash basin. Silently, she watched him strip to the waist and lather his face, preparing to shave. The only light in the cabin came from the lantern gently swinging from a hook over his marble-topped washstand. She must have been sprawled across his bed for hours, oblivious to her surroundings while he prepared himself for the evening's pleasures. If he thought she would give herself to him, he was mistaken! She had to escape—escape or kill him! The thought of his

scarred face anywhere near her brought on
waves of nausea. Swallowing the bitter bile at
the back of her throat, she sat up in the shadows, hoping he was unaware of her return to
consciousness.

She kept one eye on him, watching him rinse
his face, while her fingers searched the alcove
for a weapon. She was appalled to see her silk
scarf dangling from his slim hips like a trophy.
When her fingers closed around a heavy pewter
candlestick which stood beside the berth, she let
out a soft gasp of relief. Cautiously, she slid to
the edge of the bed and dropped her feet to the
floor. She removed the taper from the weighty
holder and placed it on one pillow. Crouching
low, she left the berth and crept silently across
the room, each agonizing step making her heart
thump painfully against her chest. When she
was close enough to reach him, she lifted her
arm hoping the blow would knock him sense-
less. Before her arm lowered an inch, he was
upon her, twisting her wrist until the candlestick fell with a clatter to the floor and rolled
away out of reach.

She couldn't discern his features in the darkened room, but she could feel his warm breath
and sense the iron determination inside him as
she struggled futilely to escape from his steely
embrace.

"You wildcat! You would attack me again?
Since you do not speak my language, I'll teach
you a universal one."

She fought him as long as she could, but she
was soon crushed to his damp, bared chest and

pinned by strong arms encircling her squirming body. He used his superior height and weight to bend her slowly backwards until her legs gave way beneath her. His face, a threatening shadow, descended and his mouth claimed her quivering lips. She couldn't do anything but submit as his mouth plundered hers, not painfully brutal as she had expected but in a tantalizing way which brought tingles to the sensitive skin. He ran his tongue along the edges of her mouth until the sensation became unbearable and she parted her lips to cry out. She was shocked by her response to the sensual demand of his questing tongue and deeply ashamed when her easy compliance gained him access to the soft interior of her mouth where he explored at will. She did not faint, did not wretch, but trembled in his arms. He smelled of soap and a heady masculine spice that was very intoxicating. His cheeks were smoothly shaven and when his chin moved over the delicate skin of her cheek, it was a curiously pleasant sensation. She had to force herself to dredge up the terrifying picture of him she carried in her mind's eye. The image was completely at odds with the gentle seduction of his warm lips. When at last he let her go, she was shaking with reaction.

"Lesson number one, little one. I have excellent hearing. I suggest you do not strain my temper too far. Murder attempts make me angry."

He reached for the lantern and hung it from a hook on the ceiling above him, casting a soft glowing light on them both as they faced one another. Remembering her promise to be silent, Christina could not stifle the gasp which escaped her when she saw his face. She covered her mouth with one hand to prevent making another sound. Gone were the eye patch, the disfiguring scar and the dark beard. In their places were two sparkling gray-black eyes, alight with humor, smooth lean cheeks and a flashing white-toothed grin! Captain Nick Barker was an extremely handsome man! He laughed out loud when she turned swiftly to locate the makings of his disguise, discarded on the washstand. He folded his arms across his chest and leaned his tall frame negligently back against the paneled bulkhead of the cabin. Every line of his face, from the mocking charcoal eyes to the stubborn chin, declared him a man who made his own rules and expected others to follow, unquestioningly.

Christina's brain was swept blank by this transition from scarred pirate to—to what? Her eyes involuntarily shifted from his face to the strong column of his throat and down his naked chest. Soft black hair fanned across the broad expanse and tapered to a fine silky line which disappeared below the waistband of his tight black pantaloons. Her breasts had been pressed to that sun-bronzed skin, her hips clasped against those hard thighs. Her cheeks began to burn and she swallowed hard.

His laughter was all confident, unrestrained male. "So, you like me better this way, Teresa? I was sure that you would."

He raked her body with his eyes as he shoved

his shoulders away from the wall with a fluid
motion. His gaze lingered at the bodice of her
gown for many moments before he cleared his
throat and muttered something under his
breath. Clamoring to regain her scattered wits,
she jumped when he gestured roughly at a
chair. She was happy to oblige him by sitting
down, unsure how much longer her shaky legs
would hold her up. There was something about
him that was unnerving her, a strange awareness that she did not know how to handle. Her
mind constantly returned to the pleasure of his
kiss and her tingling lips still felt his touch upon
them. His silent regard did not help. Her color
mounted and she began to squirm in the chair,
feeling heat and cold follow each other through
her body. She was ready to run, bolt like a
frightened doe when he pulled up a chair, straddling it as he sat down to face her, resting his
arms on the back. "Since you can not speak
English, let me hear you say something in Spanish," he began, conversationally.

She started to say the first Spanish phrase that
entered her mind, but then, his treachery became clear. She took a death grip on the edges of
her chair and forced herself to remain silent, not
giving him proof that she was not whom she
claimed to be by falling for his trick. Nick Barker was dangerously clever and she had best be
constantly on guard if she hoped to outwit him.

He reached out and touched her cheek with
one finger, frowning when she flinched and
attempted to move her chair across the floor
away from him.

"No!" he ordered. "Do not move away." The negative was the same in most languages and she lifted her eyes warily to his face.

"Damn! I wish you could understand," he growled. "Maybe that tigress who protects you told me lies. You don't act like a condessa. Twice you have used the tactics of a street fighter to attack me."

Christina clenched her hands upon the frame of the chair, staring into her lap so he could not see the betraying light in her eyes. She had never forgotten the lessons taught to her by men who felt she might someday need to know how to protect herself from an attacker. Right now, those lessons were no use to her. She had to survive this attack by using her wits. She tried to ignore the masculine timbre of the captain's low voice as he scraped his chair closer.

"I would love to fondle those luscious round breasts I felt when I kissed you," he stated matter-of-factly, waiting for the betraying color to invade her cheeks. She dropped her hand to the protruding nail she had found beneath the seat of her chair and deliberately pierced her palm.

"Oh!" she cried. His triumphant expression erased the pain she felt from the puncture.

"I knew it!" He grabbed for her wrist, preparing to twist her up out of the chair. She began a mournful string of Spanish to draw his attention to her injury. Finally, the thin, red trickle of blood reached his fingers and he looked taken aback by the sight of it. "What have you done?" His eyes narrowed speculatively on her face but

she kept hers wide and guileless, her lashes
flickering with pain as she tugged on her injured
palm. Instantly he dropped her wrist, savagely
scraping back his chair as he got up from the
table to stride to the washstand. Seconds later,
he was back with a moist cloth to treat her
wound, but she was not about to let him off the
hook so easily. She shot an accusing look in his
direction and snapped angrily, *"Pirato Bruto!
Mi mano! Mi mano!"* She cradled her injured
palm until he looked suitably chastened before
offering it to him.

His large hand seemed to dwarf her small one
as he gently dabbed at her injury. He wrapped
her palm with a strip of white linen and apologized for his misjudgment. When he was finished he held up his own bandaged hand and
held hers next to it. "At last," he grinned,
"something we have in common."

She could not stop the tentative smile that
came to her lips as he cocked his head to one
side. Laughter threatened to overtake her but
she managed to control her inner hilarity. His
sense of humor was as highly developed as his
intelligence but so far, she was a match for him.
A victorious sense of pleasure bubbled up inside
her. She was growing increasingly confident
that she could keep up the act she was playing.
She would have to use all of her powers of
concentration but she was positive she could be
as cunning as he. He probably still doubted
Annette's tale and was not finished with his
attempts to trip her but she would be ready for

him. She surveyed the room for a focal point, something to hold her thoughts while he drilled her. Her eyes lit on the book-lined shelf on the wall behind the table. She tried to make out the titles. She was aware that he had left her side to return the cloth to the washstand but she denied herself the opportunity of watching him. Why did he have to have this peculiar effect on her? Why did she have the desire to stare at the naked burnished skin of his chest and imagine running her fingers through the haze of curling black hair that scattered across the hard muscles? This must be what Sor Margareta had meant when she lectured on the "sins of the flesh." Christina knew that her greatest battle against this man would be fought within herself.

When he came back to her, he immediately took up the attack again. "Are you wondering if you will enjoy my lovemaking, Princess?" he goaded intimately.

She memorized the first six titles on the bookshelf.

"I loved how you opened your mouth to me when I kissed you. Will you spread your legs as easily?"

She tried to connect the authors with the titles. *Macbeth*—Shakespeare. *The Philosophy of Antonius*—Plato. His mocking voice faded away and didn't return until he tapped her rather rudely on the shoulder to gain her attention.

"You are the first woman to consider me a bore," he proclaimed, his dark eyes blazing with frustration. "If you don't look at me pretty soon, I may start begging for your attention and make more of a fool out of myself than I already have."

She had succeeded! The rush of relief was enormous but she dared not relax her guard. He might only have decided to take another tack. She kept her features blank as she looked at him. It was difficult not to laugh at his downcast expression but she managed it by pressing her injured palm against the table edge until tears shone in her eyes.

"For God's sake, don't cry!" He stood up and jammed his hands into the waistband of his pants, then began to pace back and forth. "Why I am feeling sorry for you, I do not know. Every time I look at you I feel the extent of the injury you caused with your well-aimed knee. Never have I come so close to striking a woman. So, why do I feel like I am the one who has done the kicking?" He scowled at her like a boy who had just lost a fight to a much smaller opponent and was railing at the whopping injustice of it.

She couldn't resist and scowled back at him. She lifted her hand and waved him away with a dismissing motion. "*Usted es loco,*" she declared.

At first he looked flummoxed, but then, her audacity made him laugh. The booming male sound echoed off the walls of the cabin and rumbled around her. "You beautiful little devil." He returned to his chair and stared at her as if he could not get his fill of the sight of her. "Your defiance is beyond my understanding. I may very well be crazy as you say, for if I did not need the money your ransom will bring, I would keep you for myself. If I had the time, I would change that haughty expression you wear to one of total adoration. You are unfamiliar with passion and I would come out the victor in bed, I assure you." His lips twisted wryly and he cleared his throat, edging himself away. "At least, I would when the damage you've done me has healed. Who would have thought a wisp of a girl could incapacitate me? It is damned humiliating!"

It took another firm jolt to her damaged hand to keep the gurgle of laughter in her throat. If he knew that she could understand every word of his impassioned speech, his humiliation would be complete and she would pay a very dear price for bringing it about. He had no idea that he was stripping himself of pride with every word. It was imperative that he never discover her duplicity. When he found out no ransom would be paid for her release, what would he do? It was too frightening to contemplate. For now, she had to keep up the pretext of being a Spanish condessa and pray that somehow she could escape Nick Barker before he discovered her ruse.

When he had stalked the room a few times, he came back to her and reached for her hand. Melting under the heated appreciation in his eyes, she made no attempt to snatch it away from him. A tiny spasm of pleasure shot through her when he lifted her hand to his lips and placed a delicate kiss in the center of her palm. "Perhaps royal blood really tells," he murmured, strangely. A knock came at the door and he reluctantly dropped her hand.

"Who is it?" he barked out. The door opened and a cleanly shaven red-haired man walked into the cabin. He, like Nick Barker, without his disguise, looked far less loathsome, but Christina recognized the red-haired man who had forced his way into her cabin on board the *Madelaine*.

"I see you have shown the girl your good-looking face, Nick. Does she approve?"

"Who the hell knows," Nick grimaced. "You look better as a cutthroat, Jackson. Right now you wouldn't scare an old lady."

How could two such evil-looking pirates be so transformed? Why had they done it? Christina prayed that she might learn more as she heard Jackson tease his captain.

"What about this princess?" Jackson pointed to Christina. "Does she quake in her slippers at the sight of you? Practically a smooth-faced kid without that ridiculous getup you wear. Your women would swoon dead away if they ever saw that ugly scar you insist on pasting on your face."

"I think it is a most authentic touch," Nick shrugged and put his hands behind his neck. He brought his booted legs to the top of the table, leaning far back in the wooden chair. "She is exactly what her *dueña* claims. If not, she does not blush like any young woman would who has had all of her attributes described very bluntly."

Christina forced herself to look bland while the curiosity gnawed at her insides. Who on earth were these men? Pirates? Profiteers? How long could she count on them to leave her un-harmed?

Jackson threw her a suspicious look. "Don't be fooled by her, Nick. She could be anything. This whole mess seems kind of murky to me. Why would a simple merchant ship carry a passenger the likes 'o her? She'd be guarded to the hilt. I don't like this, I tell ya'."

Jackson poured himself some brandy from a bottle he took out of a low cabinet built into the wall. At Nick's nod, he poured a second glass and set it down in front of Nick. "We raided the *Madelaine* on old Barney's word and came up with nothing but this girl and her harpy protec-tor. That barnacle brain is a crafty sort and I tol' you he was up to no good. It ain't wise to mess with the nobility, son. I say we drop her back in Spain with none the wiser."

"Not on your life," Nick declared loudly. "This girl may provide us with enough funds to pur-chase more men than we could ordinarily in a year. Besides," he grinned suggestively. "I want to enjoy her company for a short while before I let her go."

"Best think on that, Nick. The old woman don't speak about nothin' but this girl's reputa-tion. Been schooled in some convent and pro-tected most of her life. Them Spaniards set great store by a girl's virginity and that chaperone of hers sure talks about nothin' but her honor and her innocence. I swear I'm sick o' hearin' it. She's puttin' up such a fuss, I'm 'bout ready to gag her. As soon as she saw me without my pirate getup, she started in even worse than before. She ain't scared of me, that's for sure."

"We don't frighten either of them," Nick agreed. "Look at this." He bent down to retrieve the candlestick from the floor. "She tried to bash my head in with it. I am deemed unworthy of her highness and because of that blow she landed, I can't prove otherwise—at least for a while." He saluted Jackson with his glass and both men started laughing. When they finished their brandies, Nick became serious. "Was anyone, besides me, injured during the raid?" he asked with concern.

"Nary a one, Nick," Jackson smiled. "We scared them Spaniards so bad, they might reach port before they notice not one of them was harmed."

Christina's curiosity grew and grew, the longer they talked. A pirate attacking but leaving no injured in his wake? A sea raider concerned for the safety of the enemy crew as well as his own men? He said he purchased men, but could a man who tried not to cause injury be a slaver? She willed him to explain and wanted to offer her thanks when the conversation finally gave her the answers she was seeking.

"Every time I purchase another bond and free one more innocent man from a life of slavery, I feel good about the tricks we play to make it possible. This royal lady will suffer no real loss by giving up ransom, but several men will live out their lives in the freedom they deserve."

Nick Barker was not a pirate at all! He was a man who delivered the innocent from the cruel-

ty of transport to foreign soil where they would
live out their lives bonded to wealthy landown-
ers. She remembered her grandfather denouncing the injustice of a practice that often meant
transport for a man guilty of no crime or one so
slight as stealing a loaf of bread to feed his
starving family. Worse were the stories of honest
men guilty of nothing save being alone in the
wrong place and being seized by "spirit gangs."
Falsified papers were obtained and someone
operating under the guise of a legal bondsman
would transport the victims to New South Wales
and sell the men at a considerable profit. Once
the men were transported, it was difficult to
prove any illegality. Frequently, their relatives
never knew what had happened to them. An
honest yeoman had merely disappeared without
a trace.

Christina took courage in the knowledge that
her captor was apparently a liberator of innocent men and risked his life to save others. She
relaxed for the first time in hours until another
thought crossed her mind. What would he do
when he found out he would get no funds for
her? The risks he had taken to overcome the
Madelaine were for nothing.

"I can't think how those bonds disappeared. I
had the papers for every member of this crew.
Who would take them?" Nick asked his first
mate, scowling into his empty glass.

"No matter. They are safe from transport now.
Our crew won't be taken again. Only chance of
that would be if somebody used the papers to
prove to the authorities that they ain't freemen.

You paid for 'em and they probably got dumped somewhere without anyone realizing what they were."

"It's been a month or more," Nick said and then dropped the subject with a grin. "I'd rather think about the time when I discover if condessas make love like other women."

Jackson knew it was time to leave. "At least her companion ain't tried to murder me with anything but her sharp tongue." He shut the door behind him and once again, Christina was alone with Nick Barker.

"Teresa?" Nick's voice came close to her ear and she started like a frightened rabbit. His voice was deceptively soft and gentle as he reached down and drew her to her feet. She did not like this at all.

He gazed down into her face and watched her reaction as he placed her hand over his heart. "I am Nick. You are Teresa." His words were deliberately slow and carefully enunciated, meant to be repeated. "I am Nick Barker."

He was actually giving her a language lesson! It was easy to give him this small satisfaction and she nodded, "Nick?"

"Yes!" He smiled widely, boyishly pleased. "That's it. You shall call me Nick." His fingers curled over her hand, pressing it to his chest so she could feel his steady heartbeat. He urged her to repeat his name again and she complied. He credited her with the intelligence of a goat, she decided, as he patted the top of her head affectionately. "Nick," she repeated dutifully as if she were pleased with her own progress. How she would love to recite a Shakespearean sonnet beneath his outraged nose. If he wanted to think her a trifling piece of fluff, let him. She gazed at him with an expression as innocent as a lamb's.

"Lord! If you only knew what you do to a man with those eyes," he said and began rubbing the inside of her wrist with warm fingers, circling the soft skin with a delicate pattern that sent shivers of delight up her spine. This would not do at all, she realized. She waited for his next move in this gentle seduction. She should stop him, but found that she was enjoying not only his soothing touch but his increasingly meaningful compliments. He told her she was beautiful and every word committed him further to appearing foolish if her deception was discovered. She doubted her pleasure would mean very much to him when he discovered that she was no more a Spanish condessa than he was an ugly pirate.

"I have never desired a woman as much as I do you at this moment, Teresa. Can you feel it?" He spoke absently, almost to himself as he drew her closer to him. "Tonight and every night until I release you to your betrothed, I would enjoy teaching you about love." His hand moved to the back of her head and brought it to rest against his shoulder while his fingers moved languorously through her hair. "So very innocent and beautiful," he breathed into the flaming curls atop her head. "I am glad you don't understand when I tell you things I dare not say to other women. With you, I can say anything and you will not hold me to a word of it. All I want is for you to desire me as much as I desire you. You could easily wrap me around your little finger if you but knew it." His voice was coaxing, soothing. His embrace light and easy. His hand began a gentle stroking of her hair as if she were a wild thing to be gentled. She was trembling, for she did indeed desire him. Afraid of her feelings, she stiffened her spine.

She didn't know how much longer she could stand this enticing game, one she had never played or even imagined. When he abruptly broke off his embrace and turned his back on her, she did not know if she was relieved or disappointed. She loved the pleasurable feel of his stroking hands, enjoyed the deep baritone of his voice, was drawn to the lithe masculine body which ignited to flame some basic need inside her. She watched the play of muscles along his shoulder blades as he bent to his sea chest and pulled out a clean white shirt. She couldn't drag her eyes away when he pulled the linen over his head and tucked the ends into his pants. She was still staring when he finished his task and stood with his legs planted wide apart. One hand splayed across each hip as he looked at her. His aggressive stance jerked her out of her unconscious preoccupation with his body.

"Stop doing that, my pretty, or I will begin to think you do it deliberately. If I find that you have misled me, you will suffer the aftereffects for the rest of your life."

She didn't show by the slightest blink of an eye that she understood the soft threat he issued. She slowly brought her gaze to his face, making her expression cooly aloof. He looked pained and swore savagely under his breath. Immediately thereafter, he strode out through the door, slamming it behind him with so much force it vibrated on its hinges. She ran to it at once but it was already locked. His consternation had not stretched to the point where he had forgotten she was his prisoner.

She was given the better part of an hour to contemplate her plight. She spent the time searching his well-appointed cabin for a means of escape or a likely weapon she could hide on her person. She found a large cutlass hanging above the cabinet but knew that he would disarm her of it as easily as he had taken away her pistol and the heavy pewter candlestick. She stared at her image in the mirror over the washstand and marveled that she didn't look as exhausted and subdued as she felt.

Her eyes were sparkling with nervous tension, glittering like twin gems in her stormy features. Nick Barker affected her strangely, heightened every emotion and nerve. He was her adversary, considered her a means to gain funds, yet she was tempted to let him teach her the things she should someday learn from her husband. She felt no revulsion in his arms and almost wanted him to take her so she would no longer be the highly prized virgin bride bought for the Benton heir. The trend of her thoughts was disgraceful! She picked up a comb from the washstand and toyed with it for a few moments. It was made of silver and ivory. The matching brush lay nearby, its back elaborately engraved with a large "B." The worn surface revealed some sort of crest but she was unable to identify it. Puzzled by Nick's possession of such an elegant grooming set, Christina wondered about the kind of man he was.

His speech, the well-worn copies of books on the shelf and the expensive and tasteful appointments of his cabin indicated a man of breeding and learning. His masquerading as a pirate was for an admirable cause and she found herself feeling drawn more and more to him. He had given her her first kiss and awakened emotions she didn't know existed. It would never do to allow him to know how attracted she was to him. She knew that she would be completely overcome by Nick if he ever sensed her feelings toward him. She would have to continue her masquerade until they reached England and then find some means of escape.

She picked up the comb again and pulled it through her tumbled length of hair. She coiled the fiery curls into a tight knot at the top of her head and used her remaining pins to secure it. When he returned, he would find her looking like the noble personage she was reputed to be. She no longer possessed the mantilla which perpetuated the image but she adjusted her mussed skirts and smoothed the bodice of her blue silk gown until she was confident that she looked like a genteel lady. She had no idea that the upswept hair only served to expose the graceful slenderness of her throat and neck to make her appear enticingly vulnerable.

When Nick returned to the cabin he was greeted with a sight which took his breath away and renewed the swollen ache in his loins. She was standing in the golden glow of the lantern, her figure highlighted for his eyes. Her shy gaze in his direction made him want to scoop her up and carry her to the berth where he would bring about the inevitable result of the desire which held him in a painful stranglehold. His voice, when he was finally able to speak, was gruff. "I have brought our dinner." He set the large metal tray he carried down on the table and looked to her to arrange their plates for a meal. An irritated furrow deepened across his forehead when she made no move to assist in the preparations. "I suppose you are used to being waited on, aren't you, Princess?"

She bent her head to one side and gave him an innocent look. *"Cena? Gracias."*

"Bloody hell! I'm reduced to a servant on my own ship." Dark color invaded his cheeks as he strode to her and dragged her unceremoniously to the table. "Your chair awaits, milady." He waited, impatiently, for her to be seated, then uncovered their meal and passed the plates with undisguised disgust. "Must I feed you, too?" he growled ungraciously, but nevertheless picked up his fork and gestured for her to begin eating.

Struck by the unleashed power in him and the inherent arrogance, she was thrilled by her ability to disgruntle him and keep him off balance. She dropped thick lashes over twinkling eyes and kept them there until she was able to look up and speak to him in a normal tone of voice. Her Spanish fell on deaf ears, but she saw his lips twitch as she continued to speak, and his irritated frown turn to a smile of incredulous amazement.

She named each separate food she placed on her fork, mimicking the teaching tone he had used with her before. Her eyes told him she thought him a particularily dense language student but she was prepared to be magnanimous. When she picked up a savory morsel of meat and finished chewing it, she proclaimed, *"Delicioso, capitán. Gracias."*

"Delicioso, Teresa," he repeated spitefully. "Compliment me on the damned food would you? I will show you what else is good, my haughty minx, if it is the last thing I do."

She almost dropped her fork but caught it in time. She would be far wiser not to provoke him further. She was growing overconfident, aware he was not a pirate, not a murderer. Her position was still precarious. She gulped when her eyes strayed to the cabin's only accommodation for sleep. Was he expecting to share the berth with her?

"Ahhh," he followed her gaze. "I can see that at last you have begun wondering where I intend for you to sleep. I will enjoy having you beside me tonight, even if I do not make love to you. Tomorrow you can start worrying about your virtue for I intend to be fully recovered by then. Tonight, we will conquer your modesty, take you down a royal peg and believe me, I intend to relish every minute of it."

How foolish she had been to think for one minute that she had any control over this man!

He might not be able to complete her ravishment but she was sure he would show her other things equally intimate. She immediately lost her appetite but knew he would be suspicious if she didn't complete the meal she had declared delicious. She felt she might choke as she forced down the last of her stew. When he stood up to clear away the plates, she clung to her chair as if her life depended upon it. He placed the tray outside the door and reclosed it. He walked slowly back to her, his gray-black eyes alight with enjoyment of the situation. "Bedtime, my sweet," he said, flashing her a grin and nodding to the berth. He took no notice of her quickened breathing as he carefully pried her fingers loose from the seat so she could stand. The frantic shaking of her head brought no response as he firmly led her weighted feet toward the mahogany alcove which contained the berth. Finally, she began denying him with a repetition of panicky negatives. "No . . . no, *capitán* . . . No!"

"Not so sure of yourself now, are you?" he asked. "I only plan to get a little of my own back. If I tried to do what I would really like, I would only trample my already bruised pride beneath your dainty feet. I have suffered quite enough of that, my sweet."

Her relief was so great that she almost forgot that she was not supposed to understand him. She kept up the resistance on her wrists as he relentlessly pulled her along. When they reached the berth he pushed her shoulders down until she sat on the edge of the bed.

"Let's get those clothes off, little one. Very slowly so as not to frighten you completely. Virgins are a troublesome lot. I don't want you fainting to escape something that should hold no fear. When I am able to make love to you, I will send you back to that Spanish nobleman without the one thing that would make you only his. I will come between you at night but that is small satisfaction for the knowledge that you cannot be mine forever. I will be jealous of him for a very long time." His dark eyes burned with desire and Christina melted beneath the on-slaught of his warm gaze. The shock of his declaration held her motionless while his hand felt for the small fastenings at the back of her gown. He sat down beside her on the mattress and moved his head behind her in order to press feather-light kisses along the tender nape of her neck. Desperately, she clung to the knowledge that she was safe from him tonight. She closed her eyes. He pushed her gown off her shoulders and down her arms and she did not protest. His hands ran down the smooth skin of her bare arms and she felt weak. His lips on the sensitive cord of her neck shredded her concentration and she was lost. He turned her to face him and she couldn't find the strength to cover the provoca-tive curves of her breasts where they showed above the lace of her silk chemise. She was held by his mesmerizing dark silver gaze while his hands slid over the curve of her hips and came to rest beneath her breasts.

"I've got to have you," he groaned and lifted

her across him to lay her head on the pillows of the berth. He fitted his palms over her thinly clad breasts and she felt the weight of his body as he came down upon her. His thumbs began circling the silk-covered points his fingers cupped, and her nipples tingled with feeling. She weakly attempted to move away when his lips came down on her parted mouth but his urgent seeking tongue triggered explosions of heat through her entire body and she could not deny the pleasure of it. All thought of fending him off dissipated as his tongue darted inside her and her hands came up to cling around his neck.

The exquisite fervor of touch was brought to an abrupt end—not by her but by Nick. Her instinctive moan when his fingers slid beneath the lace of her chemise and tugged gently on the already hardened peaks of her breasts brought a harsh shudder down the entire length of his body. He recoiled from her and left the bed before she could assimilate his rejection. His face looked harsh in the moonlight, cut in deep lines of strain and his breath came in ragged gulps.

"Enjoy your virginal rest, Teresa." He spoke to her as if she were his enemy. "It will be short lived."

He was gone from the cabin before she understood that he had been floundering in the grips of a passion as great as that which he had awakened in her. She had been so enthralled by his tender caresses that she had not thought of his reaction. She closed her eyes, trying to fight off the tears which gathered behind her lids. She had not wanted him to leave her. Her strong reaction to him plagued her for hours and when she eventually fell asleep she could still see him glaring at her as if he hated her for what she could do to him.

Chapter Three

A TURBULENT SEA TOSSED CHRISTINA VIOLENTLY against the wall of the alcove. She scrambled up on her knees to the porthole where a battering wash of water crashed against the thick pane. The dismal gray light that shrouded the interior of the cabin indicated that it was early morning. She was alone, for Nick had not returned to take up residence in the bed and she must have slept through the night. She looked down at her scantily clad body, quickly surveyed the room for her gown, but it was nowhere to be seen. She shivered as the creaking timbers howled eerily. A damp blast of cold air filled the room when Nick rushed in. He was covered with dripping oilskins and his black hair was plastered to his head. He shrugged off the sodden covering and stripped out of his clothes, leaving them one by one on the damp floor as he toweled

himself dry. His naked body was beautiful, as
blatantly masculine as his face and the low
growl of his voice. His taut hips and tight buttocks were pale beneath the coppery shade of his
broad smooth back. A rush of heat flooded over
her face and spread throughout her body as her
eyes drank their fill of his male perfection. She
had never seen a man totally naked, and knew it
was shameful to stare at that part of him which
proclaimed his virility, but she was transfixed.
She could feel a frantic pulse beating in her
cheeks, a strange excitement building in the pit
of her stomach, and she forced herself to raise
her gaze. Her eyes shifted to his face and she
was relieved that he seemed to have forgotten
her existence as he wrapped a towel around his
slim hips and crossed quickly to the closed sea
chest standing at one side of the berth. He
continued to ignore her as he jerked on the brass
catch until he got the chest open. He cursed as
he began throwing things rapidly onto the berth,
one soft missile after another landing near or
upon her as he searched for what he wanted.
She tried to fend off the barrage of garments,
finally managing to come up from beneath the
mound of clothing he had thrown on top of her to
see him pulling on a woolen shirt and heavy
pants. He threw a thick leather tunic over his
head and plopped down on the bed to pull on dry
boots. He accomplished the complete change of
clothes in a matter of minutes, finally replacing
the shiny wet oilskins and marching back to the
door. "Stay put. Get some clothes on and pray I
can get us clear of this storm." Her wide-eyed

stare brought a look of total impatience to his face as he strode back into the cabin and reached for her arm. "First thing I do is teach you some English," he said as he pulled a coarse shirt over her shaking limbs and followed it with a thick jacket which totally swallowed up her body. By the time she got her eyes past the collar of the suffocating garment, he was out of the cabin. She could hear his boots racing up the companionway as he went back on deck to do battle with the elements.

She felt just like she had been victimized by a whirlwind. Her mouth had hung open with stunned reaction which he had mistaken for an inability to understand his terse commands. The pounding race of her heartbeats was not caused by the storm which raged against the hull of the ship. Nick was a far more potent force than the shrieking wind and foaming sea.

She huddled like a terrified castaway in the center of the berth, concerned not by the danger from the surging swells which lurched the ship from one side to the other, but by the image of Nick's naked perfection etched forever in her mind. She remained hugging her knees and rocking back and forth wondering when he would return from his battle with the sea. Eventually, the cabin stopped dipping and the savage motion no longer dashed the ship from one gigantic wave to the next.

Nick returned, his movements this time were slow and unhurried. Fatigue was as much a part of him as the rivulets of water that ran down his face and outer clothing to form puddles on the floor. Lines of tension had formed beside his molded lips and black shadows darkened his eyes to the color of ink. He struggled out of the heavy oilskins and let them drop to the floor. He saw that she had not picked up a single article of the things he had heaped upon the berth. At the sight of the mound of garments coupled with the disarray of the loose pieces of furniture that the storm had tossed about the cabin, his shoulders drooped with resignation. "As a housekeeper, you are pretty much useless," he proclaimed as he stripped down to the skin and once again wiped off the moisture with a towel. He came to the berth and brushed the pile of clothing onto the floor with one swift motion of his arm, then slid under the blankets, pulling the covering over his bare shoulders as his head came down on the pillow. She scurried back to the far wall but she need not have feared, for he was instantly asleep.

It took several moments for her to realize that the man in the berth beside her offered no threat. The steady rise and fall of his chest was clearly discernible as she reached a shaky hand and nudged him gently. He made a conciliatory move, rolling over on his back to leave space for her which she had no intention of filling. She tentatively stretched one foot over his reclining form and finally took a deep breath and jumped over him to the floor. When her feet landed, the thud didn't cause even a flicker of reaction from him. She stood staring at him, her lips curving into a smile when he burrowed his chin into the pillow and sighed like a small child in his sleep.

The image of his naked body flashed in her brain. She didn't understand her own thoughts. She should be afraid of him, consumed by virginal shock, but instead, she was awed by the wondrous differences that existed between a man's body and her own. Supremely aware of his nakedness beneath the sheets, she fought the insistent urge to touch him. She wanted to brush a stray lock of black hair from his brow, run her hand along the strong line of his jaw. He had kidnapped her, considered her a prize, part of the booty he had stolen from the *Madelaine*. She was but an attractive hostage who could satisfy his baser instincts before he ransomed her.

He freed men, why couldn't he free her? Her betrothal to a man she did not know was as much a form of involuntary bondage as the innocent men pressed into slavery. Why couldn't he be made to see that? His imprisonment of her and his intentions to make love to her were not so different from the men who spirited others into a lifetime of forced servitude. She would have to find a way to make him see the similarity, but how? At present, she was helpless, he was sound asleep and she would have to wait until he awakened to do anything about her present plight.

She replaced her gown, which she had discovered in a heap under the berth, and wondered how Annette was faring. The violent pitching of the ship during the storm must have renewed

Annette's seasickness. She had given her companion little thought since their separation. From the conversation she had heard between Nick and Jackson, she gathered that the very vocal Mistress Harcourt was being held prisoner in another cabin but that she was otherwise unharmed.

She took the liberty of cutting the thick shirt Nick had pulled over her head into a wide swathe which she used as a shawl to stay warm in the cool cabin. After that, she tidied the cabin. First, righting the furnishings, then replacing Nick's clothes in his trunk and finally draping his wet garments over the furniture to dry. The light became brighter and the cabin warmed as their ship sailed out of the storm front. She was able to discard the makeshift shawl by early afternoon. She grew increasingly restless as the day passed, and idly browsed through the books which lined the shelves, trying to keep her thoughts from the man who slept on and on as if he had no cares in the world. When the shadows lengthened once more, she was beside herself with nerves and temper. How dare he sleep through the entire day and leave her to torment herself with her own thoughts! The continual growling of her empty stomach added to her discomfort and anger.

She became increasingly restless from being penned up in the confines of the small cabin. She tried the door and found it unlocked and knew by the quiet of the rest of the ship that the major portion of the crew were sleeping soundly in their berths after the exertions of the long stormy night. It would be easy to escape her small prison, but where would she go? The ship was still in the middle of the ocean and he would easily find her anywhere she might be on board. Besides, though she knew it was not a pirate band, the faces that had surrounded her yesterday when she had wounded their leader had frightened her and she shivered at the memory. No, it was better to stay where she was. Nick, at least, was a known entity.

Angrily, she picked up a candlestick and waited for Nick to wake up. When she heard him stirring on the berth, she gleefully brandished her weapon and marched to the bed, waiting for him to open his mocking charcoal eyes. She had no intention of actually striking him but she did want his first sight to be unnerving. He deserved at least that much for letting her simmer in silence all day. She was beginning to feel as if she was well on her way to starvation. Nick Barker had shown no concern for her welfare. She could have been a stray dog for all the care he had taken of her. Nothing to eat and only the stale water in the pitcher to quench her thirst. Her black thoughts brought green sparks to her eyes and when Nick eventually opened his spiky dark lashes, she looked like she was preparing to murder him in his sleep. He shot up in the bed and ducked away from the threatening club in her hand. She glared as he jumped away from the fate he thought she had planned for him.

An irritated furrow developed between his brows. "You succeeded in frightening me out of my skin and I assume that was your intention." He pushed off the blanket and stood up from the berth, grinning knowingly at her swiftly averted face and startled jump backwards. "All I have to do to defend myself from you is take off my clothes. If you could only see your face, my innocent little princess, you would realize I have nothing to fear from you, but that you have one hell of a lot to fear from me."

As soon as he had pulled on his pants, she turned on him like a banshee. She wailed her complaints in rapid Spanish, pointing to her mouth and empty stomach to make it clear to him that she was weak from lack of food and drink. She wanted to hit him and almost did, but stopped herself just in time. What genteel aristocrat schooled in a convent would behave like she was behaving? A refined gentlewoman would probably order herself a meal in an imperious voice and show her displeasure by the haughty tilt of her noble chin.

Nick raised both palms in a defensive gesture. "I understand. I'm sorry, your highness, but at the time I forgot all about you. We almost lost out to the sea last night, sweetheart." Then, he seemed to remember who he was dealing with and shrugged his shoulders. "What am I explaining for? You can't understand a word. I'll get us something to eat." He pointed to the table, patted his stomach and gestured to the door. She nodded to him, sniffing disdainfully as she swept past him and took her place at the table. He laughed at her arrogant pose then shouted out the door. Within seconds, a young boy appeared and Nick told him to prepare some food for them. While the cabin boy went to comply with the order, Nick shaved and finished dressing. She ignored his activities and sat silently waiting. They didn't have to wait long for their meal to arrive. Nick responded to the knock on the door and the cabin boy re-appeared with a large tray laden with covered dishes. The dishes were quickly transferred to the table and the youth went about his duties serving the food, all the while stealing glances at Christina. She became more and more uncomfortable under his scrutiny but her hunger overshadowed all other feelings as the smell of the simple fare spread before them assailed her nostrils. She concentrated on the fish and potatoes heaped on her plate, attacking the food with gusto. Finally, her hunger assuaged, she leaned against the wooden back of her chair and blushed when she saw the open admiration on the youth's smiling face. When Nick finished eating, he leaned indolently back in his chair across the table. "That will be all, Aaron. Thank you."

"She sure is a beauty, cap'n." The boy continued to smile broadly as he gathered their dishes onto the tray and then walked out of the cabin.

Christina's discomfort grew as she realized what the boy Aaron, had been thinking. She got up from the table and clasped and unclasped her hands in front of her, her agitated fingers showing the strain she was feeling.

"Sit down, Teresa," Nick ordered and pointed her back to her seat. He cleared his throat and his lips twisted as she complied, looking as if he wanted to explain something to her. They stared across the table at one another. His face thoughtful and slightly mocking, hers pale and showing signs of panic.

She forced herself not to bolt when he moved his arm across the table and visibly relaxed when his hand grasped the crystal carafe of wine left by the cabin boy. He grinned at her while he refilled their goblets. "It was thoughtless of me to sleep all day and let you work yourself into a state of hysteria. You have nothing to fear from me, I won't hurt you," he began, accompanying his statements with vague hand signals that no one who hadn't heard his explanation could possibly interpret. He must have realized that, for he stood up and scooped her into his arms. He sat down on the berth and held her on his lap, stroking her hair back from her face with gentle fingers. His words were low and delivered in a calm soothing voice but she understood every single word.

"I'm going to make love to you until you will never be able to accept any other man." He slowly pulled the pins from her hair and tenderly ran his hands through her silky curls. "You will be more mine than the man who marries you, more mine than a wife whose main concern is for family and society and not her husband's desire for her body." Christina squirmed away from his touch, wildly trying to stem the tide of feelings that flowed through her in reaction to his words.

When his hand stroked up her spine and began unfastening her gown, she panicked completely.

Her breath came in tortured gulps as she jumped off his lap and began backing away.

Nick's scowled reaction to her abrupt departure softened as he gazed across the expanse of the cabin, seeing her white face and green eyes widened in frenzied alarm. "Teresa? You'll like this," he coaxed gently. He stood up slowly, hesitating before taking a step toward her as if any sudden movement on his part would panic her further. "I need you," he continued huskily, in the same gentle tones. He started to close the distance between them, pausing after each step, while Christina cowered against the far wall. With every step he took, her breathing became more rapid until he could hardly keep his eyes from the agitated movement of her breasts.

"You are the first woman I've ever had to coax into my bed, little one." Each word he uttered was like a caress as he continued his advance, setting a trap with the liquified silver of his entrancing eyes.

Christina could feel herself being drawn to him, wanting to respond to the tender words he spoke. She was immobilized by the fervid intensity of his gaze and her breath caught in her throat when he stood inches away from her, adoring her features. She stood frozen while his fingers cupped her chin and cradled her face between his large palms. For a long moment, they stared into each other's eyes, until Nick slowly lowered his face and lightly brushed her lips with his. No more than the faintest caress, nevertheless, the contact sent a shudder throughout her entire body and Christina's knees went weak. His thumbs began a gentle circular stroking along her cheekbones, a soothing motion enhanced by his lips which continued to move lightly over hers. His fingers threaded through her hair, sliding through the silken strands at her nape, easing her inner tension but inciting her senses with erotic delight. When Christina moaned softly and swayed toward him, Nick immediately swept her into a possessive embrace and took fierce ownership of her lips. The tip of his searching tongue probed the inner edges of her soft mouth seeking entry and with a low cry, she opened to him, moving her small hands up his chest and around his neck. Needing to touch him, mindlessly responding to the pleasure of his kiss, she surrendered to the instinctive call he was issuing with every part of his body. His tongue plunged inside her mouth, muffling his groan of desire that erupted from somewhere deep inside, a primitive sound that increased her excitement and fired her body to comply with his hungry need for all that was hers to give. His hands splayed across her back to press her closer to his chest. Deft fingers unfastened her gown and slid the silk down her shoulders to fall in a crumpled heap at her feet.

"Oh Teresa, tonight I will savor every inch of your delectable body," Nick's voice was so soft and low, Christina could barely distinguish the words, her eagerness matching his frenzy. She closed her eyes, trembling with both excitement and fear. She was unable to do anything but feel—react—bestow. She did not protest when he lifted her into his arms and carried her to the berth. She could not speak when he blew out the lamp and she knew he was disrobing, and made no sound when he came to her, but her lashes fluttered open, her eyes filled with awe at the sight of him wanting her. His smoothly muscled body glistened like silver in the shafted light from the full moon and she couldn't swallow, couldn't think.

He came down beside her, resuming their kiss like one who was starved, while he swiftly stripped off the gauzy undergarments which had kept her full beauty from his sight. He raised his head and his eyes went dark as his pupils widened at the vision of perfection beneath him. "Such flawless splendor," he complimented huskily, drinking in the sight of her pearly translucent flesh, the full round breasts gone heavy with desire, the delicate line of her hips and the shapely curves of her long legs. He stared at the tender flower of her mouth, reddened by his possession and with a soft intake of breath, he lowered his head.

His tongue flicked along the curves of her lips, tantalizing their soft contours until she avidly responded to his search by opening her mouth. She was about to lose her innocence to this man, but never in her wildest dreams had she imagined anything like this. She was frightened of the flaming soul-stirring sensations he was capable of inspiring in her untried body. She had never known a man's touch, never knew her body could dominate her will. But Nick was tender as he soothed her inhibitions away with warm, discovering hands. She enjoyed the feel of his lean strength against her softness, the magic fervor of his touch upon her sensitized skin. Would it be like this when she was in the arms of her husband? Or, would she always remember Nick as he had claimed she would? She was trembling with a strange tension that began deep in her belly and enveloped her whole being. Her breasts swelled in the stroking hands of the man who was intent on taking her, possessing her until she wanted no other. Her body was burning, tingling with longing as he lifted his head to look at her. "You are even more beautiful than I thought possible," he murmured thickly, as his hands ran over her skin, delicately smoothing her nakedness as his eyes drank their fill of her beauty, feasted on her body's quivering delight from his caresses. "My woman," he whispered, thinking she did not understand.

He dropped his lips to her breasts, placing moist kisses along the swell of each, then ran his tongue in searing circles around her nipples. A shuddering warmth surged through her body as she succumbed to the rampaging desire overtaking her. Her breath came rapidly, frantically, as his lips sucked fleeting tucks of pleasure along her fevered flesh. His hands, warm and caressing, traveled slowly down her belly and across her thighs until they gently parted her legs, running along the sensitive insides.

She could not bear the total intimacy he was taking but no longer had a will of her own. His fingers stroked and caressed, butterfly soft and erotically exciting, exploring the delicate folds of her womanhood. Her inexperienced body reacted with a tortured rush of feeling. "Oh—oh—" she moaned as her body arched against him. She betrayed herself completely when his fingers tantalized the heart of her womanhood and gave her a hint of completeness. The instantaneous pleasure drove her insane with need. "I—I," she cried as he positioned himself above her, his face reflecting the hunger she felt inside herself.

"Hush, little one," he breathed, flushed with the fever of a desire so strong it consumed him. "There is more, so much more, let me show you."

He entered her slowly, his agonizing delay only increasing their passion. She needed, wanted, had to have relief from the waves of mounting tension that gripped her. After one fleeting stab of pain, there was nothing but pleasure— soaring pleasure. Her cries of rapture when he surged inside her seemed to come from outside herself, yet she knew they were her own. He set a rhythm of thrusts which carried her higher and higher until with one wonderful, overwhelming moment of glorious release, she knew completely what it meant to be a woman.

In wonder, she gazed dreamily at the man who had caused this total havoc with her senses. He had one bronzed, muscular arm wrapped around her waist, his face was nestled between her breasts, his breath, hot on her flesh, the black hair of his head crisp against her skin. The beat of his heart mingled with

her own. It was as if they were united spirits,
one being. Spent by the turbulent completion of
their lovemaking, she closed her eyes as he
rolled to one side and gathered her close. Her
head rested upon the hollow between his neck
and shoulder and she slid one hand across the
smooth skin of his chest. "Oh Nick," she sighed,
drowsily. "I didn't know it would be like this for
us."

"Nor did I, princess," Nick whispered in a
dazed tone against the fragrant halo of her hair
spread across his shoulder. He smiled tenderly
when he realized that she was already asleep.

Recovering slowly, Nick recalled the over-
whelmingly passionate response of her beautiful body to his lovemaking. It was as if she had
been made for him, the perfect counterpart for
the needs of his body. He recalled her frantic
words uttered in the throes of passion, disbelieving phrases—love words. He stiffened. *English
words!* "My God!" His whole frame gave a con-
vulsive jerk but the shocked spasm of muscle
did not awaken her. Instead, she snuggled
closer, sliding one silken thigh across his belly.
Every pore in his body broke out in a cold sweat
and the blood boiled up in his face.

"Bloody hell!" he groaned, unable to quell his
instinctive reaction to the feel of her warm leg
resting upon his manhood. Rapidly, he took several gulps of air, desperately trying to think
coherently, fighting to dispel the rekindled desire that rushed through his loins.

Who the devil was she? She spoke English!
Understood English! She had made a fool of him

in front of his men—worse, he had made a fool of himself in front of her. She had understood every word he had ever spoken to her! A muscle twitched furiously along his jaw as his own words came back to haunt him. *Never* had he fallen so completely under a woman's spell. *Never* had he made such adoring admissions to one! He had only made them to this woman because he had believed she could not understand. The worst humiliation of all was knowing that every feeling he had admitted to her was true. How she must have laughed at his lovesick endearments. He had behaved no better than an adolescent worshiping at her feet. He clenched his fists to keep his fingers from her slender neck. Every muscle in his body was rigid but went limp when he heard her murmur his name in her sleep, softly, sweetly, His anger died as her hand moved, sliding up his neck. Her small tender palm came to rest slightly below his ear as if it belonged there.

Surprised by his own reaction, he brushed the hair away from her forehead, inspecting her face as if trying to find something that might tell him who she was. All he saw was her long lashes lying upon the creamy pearl skin of her cheeks, her soft mouth like a crushed rose. She looked so pure and innocent he knew his questions would wait until morning. No matter who she was, he could not bring himself to disturb her. He savored the feel of her warm body fitted so perfectly against him, and stared at the ceiling until, rocked by the rolling waves of the sea, he fell into a deep, troubled sleep.

Chapter Four

NICK TWISTED, THRASHING AND FIGHTING TO escape the hands that held him. He could hear Michael's terrified screams but there was nothing he could do but watch, his eyes glowing black with frustration and horrified dread. "He's only twelve! Twelve, you bastards!" he yelled over and over again, waiting, knowing he would soon meet the same fate as his young brother. "No! No! Please!" he begged, ashamed of the pathetic inflection in his cracking adolescent voice. His own desperate pleas woke him.

Sitting up in the berth, he shuddered in the darkness as the sweat poured from his body. The recurring nightmare washed over him, held him in its terrible grip, wouldn't let him go. "Michael," he whispered, hot tears rolling unheeded down his cheeks. He swung out of the berth and stumbled to the cabinet for brandy. He poured himself a stiff measure and gulped it down, waiting impatiently for the aftereffects of the nightmare to fade. His flesh was covered with perspiration. He shivered in the cool night air. Despondently, he pressed the empty glass to his forehead, trying not to think, ordering himself to do nothing but breathe, in and out, in and out. Finally when the chills became stronger than the memory of his dream, he returned to the berth.

His eyes opened wide at the sight which greeted him there. A small feminine form curled like a child in his bed. He had almost forgotten her! Teresa. No! Not Teresa, but who? He remembered her deception, but swallowed the surge of anger that rose swiftly within him. Here lay exactly what he needed. A beautiful, supine woman, waiting to warm him when he most needed warmth. Tomorrow would be soon enough to confront her. He slid beneath the blankets and brought his cold body into contact with hers, smiling spitefully when she muttered a soft protest in her sleep. He deliberately gathered her closer, curling his body around her smaller one until his face was buried in the flame of her hair, and he was breathing in the fresh sweet smell of her. His shivering flesh was soothed by her warm silken skin. His hands cupped the lush softness of her breasts, enjoying their incredible texture as he began to relax. For this short time, she belonged to him. He didn't need her calculating mind, only her body. As he held her, she snuggled closer to the hard length of his naked body and brought up one slender arm to rest over his chest. For the first time in his life, he fully appreciated the reassurance of a woman's touch, glad she was unaware of how vulnerable he was for the moment. Eventually the memory of his nightmare receded as he found solace again and again in the receptive flesh of the woman he held in his arms.

Christina opened her eyes when some object prodded her gently in the ribs, but she didn't want to wake up and her lashes drifted back down. Seconds later, she felt another irritating jab which brought her fully awake. "No!" she exclaimed, abruptly realizing where she was. The memory of what had transpired in the berth the night before returned with startling clarity. Nick Barker had made love to her over and over throughout the long night, teaching her the ways of love as he had promised and she had been a willing and eager pupil.

She scrambled to her knees, clutching the sheet around her nakedness, her wary blue-green eyes searching and finding Nick, the man who had initiated her into womanhood with devastating proficiency.

He was sitting near the berth, his chair balanced precariously on its back two legs, his booted feet propped up on the bed. His arms were folded across his chest. He was wearing a billowing white shirt, tight black breeches tucked neatly inside his shiny, black boots. It had been the toe of one of his boots which had

none too gently prodded her awake. Totally unprepared for his intent regard, she stalled for
time, rubbing the sleep from her eyes as she
tried to control her shattered composure and
strove to overcome the fiery blush that stained
her cheeks.

"Good morning, princess," he greeted her in a
sarcastic tone that made her instantly alert to
some impending danger. Her eyes flew to his
face to be met by a mocking grin, but there was
no hint of humor or warmth in the cold steel
gray eyes which riveted her to the berth. She
gained the impression that he was waiting for
something, biding his time until she did whatever it was he wanted. She knew she was still
blushing under his probing gaze, her skin heat-
ing feverishly as he laconically outlined her
curvaceous figure barely camouflaged beneath
the thin sheet. There was no sign of the passionate, tender lover he had been the night before.
She was both hurt and frightened by his lazily
intent scrutiny. There was an insolent twist to
his sensual lips and flickering danger in his
scorching dark eyes. Not wanting him to guess
the extent of her discomfort, she gave him a
tentative, shy smile. "Nick?" she questioned
warily, *"Hay problema?"*

"Problema?" he shouted, his reaction both
immediate and violent. The legs of his chair
thudded loudly to the floor as he jerked his feet
off the berth and stood up. He towered over her,
his hands planted on his hips, rage apparent in
every rigid line of his threatening tall frame.

"Indeed! There is a problem, wench!" he sneered. "But, it is all yours. Your pretty blush tells me that you remember what went on between us last night, but you seem to have forgotten some of the more memorable details." His voice rose an octave and he mimicked, in a sarcastic duplication of her soft voice. "Oh Nick, I didn't know it would be like this for us."

She flinched, all color draining from her face as her body went cold. She realized why he was angry with her, comprehended the full magnitude of what he had discovered about her the previous night. She had spoken to him in English, forgetting everything but her overwhelming response to his ardent lovemaking! In the game of wits they had played, she had outwitted herself. She bit her lip, frantically searching her brain for the means to appease him but unable to form one coherent thought with his probing dark-lashed eyes flickering over her pale face.

"You have reason to be afraid," he finally ground out, satisfied that he had made her supremely aware of her precarious position. "Perhaps your plan included my making love to you. That is what your words last night implied. You said that you didn't think it would be like that between us. So tell me, how did you imagine it would be? Did you hope that I might feel obligated to marry you since you were supposedly a highborn Spanish virgin? Is that why you pretended to be something you are not?" He cursed himself for not being able to control the desire he still felt whenever he looked at her but his face did not reflect his feelings. He was not going to let her beauty and innocent expression forestall his getting the full truth from her.

For the better part of an hour this morning he had waited for this confrontation. From the very beginning he had been suspicious, his involvement with the *Madelaine* seeming more and more like some kind of trap. Was she part of some conspiracy against him? His gaze swung back to her accusingly.

Christina had scurried across the bed out of his reach, pressing herself against the cool mahogany panels at the far corner of the alcove. Cowering like a cornered animal, appalled at the erroneous trend of his thoughts, she cried, "I—I only did what I had to do."

"To accomplish what?" He didn't move but she had never felt more threatened. "To secure some poor English sea captain for a husband? Somehow I doubt that. Perhaps you know more about me than you dare admit."

Her blank gaze seemed to dispel some of his anger. "I had no knowledge of you before you attacked the *Madelaine*," she insisted.

He didn't think she could feign the total lack of comprehension on her face and he expelled his breath in relief. Pinning her against the bulkhead with the strength of his gaze, he sat down on the berth, trapping her. "You will tell me who you are, madam, and you will also pay for making a fool of me." He moved swiftly and she had no chance to slip out of his grasp as he neatly captured both of her arms and roughly dragged her across the mattress. Her limbs became uselessly tangled in the sheets, her breasts bared as the linen slipped, exposing her to his scornful gaze. He held her at arm's length in front of him.

Nick's fingers dug into the soft flesh above Christina's elbows, shaking her until her utterly terrified expression registered and he found himself strangely affected by her fear. Why should he care if he frightened her, had she not done far worse to him? He berated her harshly, "You deserve one hell of a lot more than a shaking, woman. I should beat the truth out of you and if I don't get it this time, I shall do just that." He loosened his painful grip on her arms, amazed that his fingers had left a visible impression on her fragile skin. Her eyes were like the blue-green waters of a misty sea, full of mute appeal as she soundlessly begged for his understanding.

"Answer me," he demanded, refusing to be swayed by her piteous look. "There is little you can hide from me now."

"You—you kidnapped me," she accused, knowing there would be no escape from him this time. "Annette thought that if we could make you believe I was of the Spanish aristocracy and that a handsome ransom would be paid for my safe return, you would spare us our lives."

"You are no more Spanish than I am," he spat, a nerve jumping along the line of his jaw as he recalled how thoroughly he had been duped. "Where did you learn to speak the language like that?"

"The convent," she gasped.

"So that part of your story was not a lie?" His

eyes dropped to her bare breasts. "A most unlikely candidate." His eyes were dancing with amusement as twin flags of offended color rose in her cheeks. She began struggling in earnest.

"Let go of me," she demanded furiously, trying to claw at his face, but he easily trapped her fingers in one hand and pulled her onto his lap with the other.

"Before I allow your more than considerable charms to deter me, we shall continue. Upon landing in London, I would have quickly discovered that there was no missing Spanish royalty. What did you plan to do then?" He centered his concentration on her outraged face not bothering to hide his pleasure at her discomfiture. He kept hold of her wrists and adjusted her squirming body on his legs, wrapping his other arm around her to keep her still.

"I planned to escape." She lifted her chin in a small show of defiance, her eyes, more green than blue, glittered with fury. "It was you who attacked our ship, Nick Barker. This entire affair is your fault!"

His hearty laughter rang out, the flashing grin on his face reminding her of the moments after their first kiss when she had discovered that he was not the vicious pirate he had pretended to be. "Point taken," he admitted, still chuckling. "But, I insist that you tell me all about yourself, beginning with your name." He tightened his grasp until she was firmly cradled against his chest, one of her breasts pressed so tightly against him that she could feel his thundering heartbeat through her own flesh. Her mind raced. Was it still too risky to reveal the whole truth about herself?

"My name is—Anne—Anne Harris," she lied, combining her middle name with her grandparents' surname as she groped for a believable story.

He raised a quizzical brow at her hesitation and she knew that she had to allay his suspicion. "There is no one who will ransom me now," she cried, forcing a self-pitying tear from beneath her lids. She was relieved when his expression immediately softened. He believed the newest lie she was forced to tell to protect herself. She lowered her lashes, her expression downcast. "You have ruined me."

He pushed her off his lap and stood up, his expression savage. She quickly grabbed for the sheet and covered herself, pulling the linen up to her chin. "What I did to you cannot compare to what you have done to me. You didn't sound like you minded being ruined, madam. Since you were the only thing of value we discovered aboard the *Madelaine*, I wonder who has ruined whom? However, I am willing to prove that I heartily enjoy you in bed."

He gave a swift tug on the sheet but she held firm, shouting, "Touch me again, you bloom'n hulk and I'll kick you as I did once before! You are nothing but a great bloody sea snake with the brains of a flea!"

"And you are no innocent virgin!" he shouted back. But, she had been innocent, he alone knew that. He was completely mystified. She was an accomplished actress, could fight like a street urchin, curse like a sailor, yet her body had never known a man's until last night.

Crossing the breadth of the cabin, he poured himself a full glass of brandy and drank it down. "Perhaps I shall make you my mistress after I get the truth out of you."

"You have kidnapped me, forced your attentions on me and I shall tell you nothing!" she cried, pulling the sheet tightly around her.

Nick's jaw tightened, then he shrugged his shoulders and strode back to the berth. "If you want my protection, you will tell me everything, is that understood?"

Ignoring the determined gleam in his eyes, Christina blurted, "I don't need your protection. I am betrothed to a fine man who will kill you when he discovers what you have done to me."

"Can you never say anything that is the truth?" he growled. "You have already stated that you have no one to ransom you." He recalled the fine laces, satins, and silks he had discovered in her trunks. Did she belong to some other man? The thought made him seethe. "Will this fiancé of yours be content with my leavings?"

The fire died in her eyes and a shamed glow took its place. The Bentons would never accept her if they knew she had been bedded by another man. What would happen to her grandparents if the Bentons refused to admit her into their family? The full consequences of her actions hit her with a terrible force and her fear changed to rage at the man who had ruined any chance she had to secure her grandparents' safety.

"All is not lost," Nick's voice, full of arrogance, broke into her thoughts. "I will make you a very wealthy woman, set you up in a house in London, buy you jewels and fine clothes. You will lose nothing by becoming my mistress, I promise you."

He sat down, preparing to take her into his arms. Incensed with his presumptuous conceit, she lashed out with her elbow and caught him in the stomach. She had the great satisfaction of hearing his harsh grunt. While he strove to regain the breath she had knocked out of him, she snatched up the sheet and scurried out of the berth, trying to reach the door before he came after her. Just as she pulled back the latch, the door opened. She squealed and backed away, clutching the sheet to her bosom as Jackson entered the cabin.

"Three ships, Cap'n! Approaching from all sides," Jackson announced without preamble. "I can't tell for sure but I think they are the Earl's. What do you want to do?" Jackson tried not to show that he had noticed his leader was bent double on the bed clutching his belly and glaring ominously at the frightened woman who cowered near the door.

When the first mate's lips involuntarily twitched, Nick gasped through his clenched teeth. "I thought I explained my position to that man very well the last time we met." His angry voice was breathless as he rose from the berth. "Dammit! Get Topside!" He stomped across the cabin and took his cutlass down from the wall. "Wait for me here, you little hellcat," he snarled at Christina. "I can't spare the time for you now." He buckled on his sword and followed Jackson to the door, vowing, "You are my woman and we both know it. Think about that while you are waiting."

Up on deck, Nick squinted through the spy glass. Spectral sails cut through the rolling swells. Under full sail, three armed vessels were closing in fast. There was not enough time to come about and outrun them, nor space to sail safely between them. The *Libertine Lady* was trapped, outmanuevered and outnumbered. "They are his, alright. What the hell is he planning? Damn the man!" He handed the glass back to Jackson.

"Looks like they're intendin' to fire on us, Nick. Do we just stand here and let them?" Jackson looked to the younger man and saw the indecision across his hardened features. "Maybe they'll back off if we send off a few rounds."

"Fire close to midships," Nick ordered, stoically. "At least we can show we intend to offer resistance."

The first ball landed harmlessly in the sea alongside the closest vessel veering in on them. Nick could make out the captain, standing on the quarterdeck ordering a crewman to signal the other vessels into position. He grimaced angrily as the *Libertine Lady* was swiftly surrounded on all sides. Smoke billowed around him as he ordered his men to continue firing, directing them to defend themselves in this grossly uneven battle. "Dammit, Carstairs, I can see your hand in this," Nick growled as the hostile vessels manuevered his ship expertly into their trap. There would be no escape.

The nearest ship, *The Monique*, an East Indianman, ranged alongside, its crew immediately preparing to lay aboard. Nick pulled his sword from its sheath, cursing emphatically as he jumped down on the quarterdeck to greet the first boarders. He heard the crashing sound of wood being ripped from its moorings and turned to catch a glancing blow to the head from a falling spar. He staggered back and fell to his knees, a flashing light exploding inside his head. Fighting off the dizziness, he groped back to his feet, pulling himself up by a line which dangled from the crippled foremast. "Blast you, Carstairs, you'll pay me for this one." He wiped the blood from his forehead with his sleeve and charged toward the rail, ordering his crew to stand fast.

Minutes later, with the sound of clanging weapons resounding around him, he stood sword to sword with the captain of the *Monique*.

"You know I can't kill you, Tony. What the devil is this in aid of?" Nick challenged the sandy-haired man who faced him. Anthony Carstairs, his light-blue eyes darkened with sympathetic shadows, parried Nick's half-hearted thrust. "By the saints!" Nick growled at his opponent's continued silence. "He's gone too far this time!"

"I must ask for your sword," Carstairs stated quietly, keeping a close watch on Nick's offensive stance and menacing weapon. They had faced off before, but then it had always been in a sporting match. This time, more was at stake than victory points.

"I have my orders, Nick," Tony offered apologetically, a set look upon his reddened face. Blue eyes clashed with gray. Aware of Nick's fierce pride, Tony was sickened by his own part in his employer's scheme. "Surrender. You are surrounded, outmanned, and wounded," he said grimly. "By God, I'm sorry." Nick was bleeding profusely and swaying on his feet—his injury had certainly not been part of the plan.

"My men won't give up until I give the sign," Nick declared.

"Don't be a fool, man," Tony pleaded. "Your position is untenable!" A tense silence followed this statement while he watched the conflicting emotions war on Nick's face. Finally, Nick dropped his weapon to the deck in contemptuous resignation. Instantly the fighting around them stopped. All hands stood to watch what would happen next between the two young captains.

Nick went rigid when Tony asked him to turn around so he could bind his wrists. He hesitated a fraction of a second, then turned his back and stood stiffly as his hands were firmly bound behind him. A growl of offended rage echoed from his crew, but Nick's glare silenced them.

"Now what, Tony? Does he plan to sink my ship? To what lengths is he prepared to go to stop me?" The blood from his head wound dribbled into his eyes and he squeezed them shut to stop the stinging pain.

Tony nodded to one of his men to wipe the blood away from Nick's eyes. "The Earl will explain. He is waiting for you on board the *Monique*." He resolutely edged Nick toward the plank spanning the space between the two ships but Nick halted after a few steps.

"Let me see to my men, Tony. I want to give them a few instructions."

A nod from Tony brought two sailors to grip Nick's arms and insure his crossing to the waiting *Monique*. "No, Nick. I'm under orders. Talking to your crew would serve no purpose. The Earl wants this accomplished quickly. Jackson Fry can take over." He ordered the sailors to proceed as Nick began struggling in earnest. Eventually, reinforcements were called to carry him off the ship.

Tony turned away from the rail, disgust raging inside him. He had been given no choice. All of the proceedings had been watched from beginning to end by the man who had ordered it all. "Jackson?" Tony shouted. "Where are you?"

"It ain't right, Tony." Jackson came up beside him, his eyes accusing. "The Earl's timing couldn't be worse."

"Nick will take off again, first chance he gets," Tony predicted. "You know nothing will keep him from the path he's chosen. I suggest you make repairs as quickly as possible and wait for Nick. I swear, Jackson, I'll not be a part of anything like this again."

He nodded below decks. "I want the women, too. Word of their abduction was given us by a distraught merchant captain who had been set upon by pirates." His expression lightened and he winked at his burly companion. "Think of it!

Murderous felons are loose somewhere in these waters. Those poor Spanish sailors are lucky to have escaped alive!"

The two laughed together and went below, their arms linked companionably about each other's shoulders. "Come join us, Tony," Jackson suggested. "You could make a mean looking blackguard if you practised up some."

"Believe me," Tony frowned seriously. "When I've finished with this business, I'll give it serious thought."

Chapter Five

A TALL, MIDDLE-AGED GENTLEMAN, HIS HAIR A startling shade of silver, stood to greet Christina as she was escorted inside a well appointed cabin on board the *Monique*. Gray eyes that seemed somehow familiar held hers for a moment before his lean face broke into a welcoming smile. His clothing and demeanor bespoke a noble dignity and wealthy position. She tentatively returned his polite greeting, but the small smile that had formed on her lips died when she saw the others present in the room. Nick Barker was slumped between two burly seamen, who gripped him by the arms. He glared at her and ineffectually tried to break the hold of the men who restrained him. Fresh blood showed through a white bandage wrapped around his head, his clothes were torn and stained.

Stunned, Christina returned the accusatory stare from his gunmetal eyes and took a deep, calming breath. The gentleman took her hand and drew her to a chair, ignoring the two crewmen and Nick until Christina had been seated.

"You are quite safe," he assured, then gestured for the men to propel Nick toward a large chair placed a few feet away from Christina's. It was difficult for her to believe that Nick Barker, the strong masculine animal, so inexorably arrogant, looked almost too weak to stand. She was further amazed when, after being pushed down on the chair, he remained silent, staring at the man who had casually ordered him there. She grew more confused with every passing second, nervously pleating the azure silk of her frock.

"I realize that this affair has been terribly trying for you," the gentleman began gently in a deep resonant voice. "A horrible ordeal but it is all over now."

"I—I don't understand," Christina stammered, feeling Nick's eyes boring into her face as she spoke to this man who had ordered her rescue from the *Libertine Lady*, provided her with her own trunks and had installed both her and Annette in the comfortably large compartment in the stern.

"As Captain Carstairs has explained," he continued in a sympathetic tone, "we are proceeding to London with all due haste. Let me assure you that you shall suffer no further harm." He came to stand before her, taking both of her hands in his and brushing his lips across her knuckles affectionately. "You truly are a most beautiful young woman, Christina. I approve most heartily and have only one thing to ask before telling you what has brought about this precipitous meeting at sea."

"For God's sake!" Nick's voice cut into the man's smooth speech. "If you are playing out this farce for my benefit, don't bother!"

"Silence!" the gentleman commanded, his voice as harsh as Nick's and backed up by the crewman who immediately stepped forward to insure that Nick would obey the terse interjection.

The tension in the room was a tangible thing, the battle of wills between the two men gathering strength. Christina's heart began pounding, her brow furrowing with astonishment as Nick clamped his mouth shut, clenched his hands into fists and lowered his gaze. Nick Barker bowing to the will of another? She was shocked, curiosity consuming her. Who was this man that he could exert such control over Nick?

"Do you have a grievance against Captain Barker?" The question was asked quietly, but the tone was not casual. "Was he cruel to you in any way?"

Christina swallowed nervously, afraid to look at Nick and terrified that her answer might mean life or death for him. He was a prisoner, that was certain, and being taken to London to face—to face what? Was the intent to gather incriminating evidence to be used against Nick in an English court? Was he being brought to justice for his crimes? The *Monique* was not one of His Majesty's ships of the line and there were no Royal Navy uniformed men on board, but Nick was a prisoner and this gentleman seemed intent on accumulating evidence against him. The thought of Nick languishing in prison or worse, being hanged, was too hideous to contemplate. He should be free—free to go on saving innocent men bound for servitude in New South Wales, free to sail the sea as master of his own fate. She would not be the one to force his incarceration. She knew what it was like to be imprisoned. Hadn't she been a prisoner since the day her father had taken her away from Briar Park, torturing her with the knowledge that her grandparents' safety depended on her behavior and how well she followed his orders? The convent walls had been a physical prison, its strict rules of conduct another kind of prison, but neither imprisoned her as much as the fear for the well being of the two people she loved most in the world.

"I have no grievance against Captain Barker," she declared bravely, meeting the man's gaze levelly. At once, she could tell that it was not the answer he had been hoping for. She dared a glance at Nick. He was grinning, but the sardonic smile did not reach his eyes.

"Might I suggest she is holding out for a loftier sum?" Nick asked. "I have dealt with this woman for days and I can tell you that she has a keen mind. I have probably offered her a more lucrative proposition than you first proposed."

"Be silent!" the man commanded again, but

this time Nick looked smug as he reclined back in the chair, crossing his booted legs before him as he moved his gaze from Christina to the man seated before her, then back again.

"I do not wish to embarrass you, Christina," the older man said gruffly. "You were discovered in a most revealing state of undress inside Captain Barker's cabin. You must tell me the truth, child. Have you been compromised?"

Christina heard the ruthless determination in his voice, but his expression was kind, his gray eyes pleading with her to confide in him. She didn't know what to do. It was apparent that he already suspected the truth and was merely waiting for her to confirm it, but why did the humiliating admittance have to be spoken aloud? Why must she be the one to determine Nick's fate? Wasn't it enough that he had been found out as her kidnapper? That the goods aboard his ship were stolen from a Spanish vessel? Why must there be another serious crime to place on his head? She didn't know what compelled her to spare Nick any blame concerning her, his contempt for her was so readily apparent she could almost taste it.

"He did not force me," she murmured, shame burning in her cheeks. "I—I was willing."

"You have nothing to be ashamed of, child," the man declared firmly, triumphantly. "I am well aware of my son's powers of seduction. Counted on them, in fact."

Christina blanched, her eyes dilating wide with shock. Had she heard correctly? "Your son?" Her shaky question was edged with a mounting hysteria.

"That is correct," he smiled gently. "I am Sir Albert Benton, earl of Larleigh and Captain Nick Barker is my son Nicholas—your betrothed. His full name is Nicholas Alexander Benton, viscount of Larleigh."

The name she had first heard months before, the man she had dismissively labeled a simpleton, the aristocratic family she had feared would condemn her—she was face to face with them now. The room receded in a gray mist as Lord Benton's shocking disclosure began to echo and re-echo inside her head, louder and louder. "Nicholas Benton—my son—Nick Barker is your betrothed."

"Drink this, my dear," Lord Benton was pressing a glass of amber liquid into her hands. Still unable to form words, Christina accepted the glass, gulped the burning brandy and gasped for breath as she tried to digest what she had just learned. "How—why?" she mouthed stupidly, unable to assemble what had just been disclosed.

"I fear you will not understand the lengths I have had to go in order to insure the continuation of my family," Sir Albert explained, his lips twisted in self-derision. "This was arranged between your father and myself. Do you understand what that means?"

An icy hand gripped Christina's heart. Was Sir Albert yet another man who planned to use her for his own selfish goals? She lifted her chin, trying to decipher the meaning behind his statement, her heart sinking when he leaned forward and whispered so that Nick would not overhear him. "I promise you that as soon as you marry my son, your grandparents will be safe from Bristol's threats. Will you accept him?"

She shook her head, totally rejecting his words but knew she had no choice but to give him the answer he sought. "I—I will marry him."

"Nicholas, Miss Bristol has consented to marry you," Sir Albert said smoothly, turning to face his son.

"I'm sure that she has but I have no intention of marrying her." Nick tried to sit straighter in the chair, every muscle rejecting her presence, every feature in his face coldly rigid. He wiped a trickle of blood from his brow with the back of his hand then scornfully brushed the new stain across his already soiled shirt.

"I have arranged for the ceremony to take place soon after we land in London. Hopefully, you will have resigned yourself by then," Sir Albert continued, ignoring Nick's comment. "After the ceremony we shall proceed to Larkhollow."

"I repeat—" Nick interjected loudly, pain creasing his brow. "I'll not marry that bastard's —Damnation! Father! Find some whore on the street, I'd be much better off."

"Enough!" Sir Albert shouted thunderously. "You will not speak so in front of your intended ever again. Not in my presence! You forget that you are in no position to argue."

In appalled silence, Christina studied the two

men. Why hadn't she immediately noticed the resemblance between them? It was there, in their arrogant expressions, the stubborn set of chins, the challenging lift of brows. The same silver-gray eyes. Sir Albert was only an older and more refined version of his son, but he was easily as ruthless and perhaps even more autocratic.

Christina had never endured a more uncomfortable silence, watching the tide of red that ascended Nick's face. The thought of being married to him, bound to him for life overwhelmed her, made her tremble like a willow reed lambasted by the wind. She only half heard Sir Albert as his commentary went on as if Nick had never spoken.

"Today marks the end of Nick Barker's privateering and the resumption of your duties as the Benton heir," he addressed his son. "It was a simple matter to bring the two of you together and since you could not resist Christina's beauty and compromised her, you shall marry her." The earl's hardened expression softened as he turned slightly to speak to Christina. "My dear, you shall have my unceasing gratitude if you marry my son. However, in the event that you fail to deal well with each other, I have determined an option which should suit us all."

"An option?" Christina asked fearfully, positive she would not like this forthcoming answer any more than what she had heard from him thus far.

"On the day that you produce the Benton heir, Nicholas will be free to return to his ship if he so wishes. I can only hope that my grandson will take better care of his inheritance than his father." Sir Albert relayed the next installment of his plan in a coolly disdainful voice.

"Oh my God," Christina breathed and clutched the arms of her chair for support. On the day she gave birth! It sounded so cold, so lacking in human regard. Their marriage would be nothing but a formal breeding. "Oh please, my lord, you cannot mean that?"

"Oh, he means it all right," Nick intoned sharply, finally meeting her gaze. With difficulty he pulled himself up in the chair, his face ashen with a mixture of strained anger and pain. He glared at Sir Albert, "Tell me father, will you also order when I am to perform, send spies to make sure we are mating regularly?"

Sir Albert visibly flinched at Nick's crudity but was quick to offer a rejoinder. "Your reputation has precluded any doubt I might have. Now, I will leave the two of you alone to adjust to this situation." Sir Albert turned and walked to the door, gesturing for the two guards to precede him out of the cabin. "I trust you to remember that Christina has as little choice in this as you, Nicholas. I will not have her punished for schemes which are mine alone." He left the room, casting one more sympathetic but unyielding glance at Christina. She felt as if she had been physically beaten and doubted that Nick could damage her more than his father had already done.

Silence descended, the only sound in the cabin from two sets of lungs gathering air for recovery from severe shock. Nick was the first to speak.

"Well, do you want to spend the next few months flat on your back beneath me?" he asked harshly.

"I hate this—" Christina snapped. "At least as much as you. If you never come to me it will be too soon."

"That's too bad, for you will have me coming inside you day and night until your belly grows unless we find a way out of this."

"There is nothing we can do." Her words came out in a whisper, devastated by his coarse threat.

"So!" he lashed out. "You were in on this whole scheme, weren't you? He knew if I saw you, I'd take you. I'm sure you have been paid well but tell me, how did he arrange for the Spanish ship as bait? Seems a trifle drastic to gain you my bed." The cold contempt in his accusation took her breath away. How dare he think she was part of his father's mad plot.

"You—you are solely responsible for this!" she cried, furiously. "How dare you say I planned it."

"You flaunted your sweet body until I took you. You knew as soon as I slipped between your legs that you had won, didn't you? To think I offered to make you my mistress. You already knew that you would gain much more from me. Well, you shall pay for this, madam. My father can't protect you forever. Someday I'll get my hands around your lovely neck and break you in two."

"The thought of being married to you sickens me!" Christina shot back. He had no threat hanging over his head as she had. "If you do not wish to marry, refuse to sign the marriage certificate."

Nick laughed, a strident, flat sound, totally without humor. "You know damned well what will happen if I do that, don't you?"

"I have no idea what you are talking about," she shouted shrilly. "My honor need not concern you. I shall be grateful if I never have to see you again."

"It's a damned sight more than your honor that is at stake here." Nick tried to stand up but the pain in his head made the room lurch and he had to lean his head back against the chair. "Those bondpapers my father has waved in front of my nose since he dragged me aboard this ship will not be returned until my signature is on that marriage certificate and my seed grows in your belly. I hope you think of my crew each time I do my marital duty for I'll only take you to keep those good men from being transported as slaves."

"What papers?" Christina didn't comprehend.

"God knows why I'm explaining anything to you," Nick raked one hand through his hair.

"Each member of my crew was ready for transport before I purchased their bonds, each one innocent of any wrong doing, other than being the victim of spiriters. My father confiscated those papers, stole them from me and is prepared to sell my men back to the lousy scum who would have sent them to their doom, making a sizable profit for himself. Your father, I believe, Miss Bristol. Every fine thread on your back has been purchased with funds tainted by the blood and agony of innocent men. Knowing I have touched Bristol's filthy spawn turns my stomach."

Christina swayed in her seat, sickened by the images Nick's words inspired, the hatred in his eyes. Her father would indeed sell men with no thought to their fate. Hadn't he sold his own daughter to the highest bidder? No wonder Nick despised her. She had to do something, but what? Nick was a victim of the same kind of blackmail as she. "Where are the papers?" she demanded, desperately trying to think of some way of preventing Sir Albert from forcing their marriage.

"My father carries them on his person. He wouldn't trust anyone but himself to keep them safe." Nick fought against the dizziness that blurred his vision. "What are you thinking?" he asked, both surprised and suspicious of her reaction to his commentary. He almost believed she really had no prior knowledge of the papers when she suggested that they should steal them back. Thinking he had little choice but to grasp the tiny straw she offered, wanting to believe that she was innocent of the loathsome plot, even when he knew who she was, he began outlining a plan he had conceived to retrieve the papers. His astonishment grew as he got her swift compliance and he advised, "If my father's hands are otherwise occupied, I should be able to get the papers away from him before he knows what is happening. I'll throw them out the porthole before he has the chance to grab them back." His pain-filled eyes darkened as his hand went to his forehead. "I'll only have the strength for one try, so play your part well!" He got up from the chair slowly, propping himself up against the wall as he edged along to a place behind the cabin door. Christina called to the guard outside.

A bearded sailor opened the door, allowing her to leave. she stepped into the passage, smiled at the guard, then closed her eyes when he crumpled to the deck after Nick hit him. "Help me drag him in here," Nick gasped, his breath coming far too fast to be normal. His shirt was saturated with sweat by the time they had pulled the unconscious man into the room. Nick's features were twisted with strain and his hands shook.

"You haven't the strength," Christina began, but he didn't allow her to continue.

"My father is probably in the cabin up ahead. You go in and ask to talk to him, than faint in his arms. I'll do the rest," he whispered, ushering her swiftly down the passageway, not giving her the chance to question the wisdom of his hasty plan.

"You can hardly walk, let alone come crashing through the cabin door," she insisted, fearing their scheme was doomed to failure.

"Just make sure you land in his arms when you swoon." His charcoal-gray eyes burned into hers and she was forced to nod her agreement. The flicker of admiration she saw in his eyes gave her the courage to continue with this desperate gamble.

"Sir Albert? May I speak with you. It's Christina," she knocked twice before the door was opened.

"Of course, my dear," Sir Albert escorted her into the room, leaving the door to the cabin ajar. It seemed almost too easy and seconds later, when a hand was placed over her mouth from behind she knew that she was right.

"Oh my child, you look faint," Sir Albert exclaimed loudly, then scraped a chair across the floor as if he had swiftly come to her assistance. Two men waited on either side of the door. When Nick ducked inside, he was pinned between them. They held his arms behind his back and dragged him before the earl. Christina was lowered to a sofa by Tony Carstairs who had held her quiet and motionless since her entrance. She looked to Nick. The anger was so strong on his face that she shivered with dread. He looked murderous and when he spied her, she became the victim of his black scowl.

"You double-crossing spawn of the devil!" he ground out. "I fell for your treachery yet again!"

"Don't blame Christina for the failure of your ill-conceived plan. This rash action proves that you are not to be trusted. We will not put your marriage off another moment," Sir Albert exclaimed angrily. He moved behind his desk and ruffled through a drawer to extract a large piece of ornately trimmed parchment. Christina did not have to be told that it was a marriage certificate.

The two men forced Nick before the desk, his

handsome features were a mask of pain and frustration. "I'd rather marry a—" his voice trailed off and he closed his eyes, then opened them again. "Father—you can't," his muscles sagged and he went limp, his head lolling to the side and down upon his chest.

"He's fainted!" Christina jumped up to go to him but Captain Carstairs took hold of her arm.

"I'm sorry, Miss Bristol." The pained tone of his voice was proof of his sincerity.

"Get on with it, Tony," Sir Albert addressed Carstairs. "It's probably better this way. I don't think I can stand those condemning eyes much longer." There was a pinched look about Sir Albert's mouth and his complexion was tinged with gray. Christina would have felt sorry for him if she didn't despise the ludicrous plan he had concocted.

"Miss Bristol?" Tony Carstairs, his wide mouth clamped in a thin line of disapproval, helped Christina the distance to Nick's side. Moments later, he began reading the wedding ceremony in a monotone. He didn't look at either Christina or Nick. It was Sir Albert who placed the heavy sapphire-studded band on her bloodless hand and Sir Albert who held out the pen for her signature on the parchment. He nodded to the crewmen and they half carried, half dragged Nick behind the desk and slumped him into the chair. Sir Albert placed a pen in his son's hand.

"Nicholas," the earl held up Nick's chin and lightly tapped his cheek. "Wake up, son, and sign one more paper, then you'll have all the men you need for your crew." He directed his son's actions in a gently reassuring voice that broke with emotion. Christina saw Nick's eyes open, his pupils dilated. He was barely conscious yet his hand moved across the paper, then fell away.

"It is done," Sir Albert proclaimed, solemnly. "Get him to bed." His eyes were moist as he stroked the black hair from Nick's temple, revealing the fresh blood showing through the stark white bandage. "No!" he declared sharply when the men came behind the desk to assist Nick. More softly, "I'll do it." He lifted Nick into his arms as if he were a child and carried him across the room, his features twisted in agony. Christina couldn't speak as she watched their departure from the cabin, tears coursing down her face. Her shoulders began to shake and she felt herself drawn against a firm masculine chest. It was Anthony Carstairs. It didn't matter who it was for the sobs that wracked her didn't allow her the strength to move away. She needed to lean against someone, anyone, and let it all come out. She heard Annette's voice coming to her from across the room. The older woman cut the space between them and began patting Christina's shoulder. "It will be fine, darling! Everything will be fine," she crooned and with Tony assisted her back to her cabin in the stern.

"Lady Benton," Carstairs said gently before leaving. "Please don't blame yourself. You did what you had to do as I did and as Nick did. It's over now and nothing can be done."

Christina shuddered, her eyes brimming with misery. It was not over but only beginning. She was Lady Christina Benton, married to a man who despised her. "He wasn't even aware of what he was doing," she exclaimed in a tortured voice. "He was unconscious."

Chapter Six

A SHAFT OF GOLDEN SUNLIGHT BEAMING through the porthole warmed Nick's face. Squeezing his eyes tightly shut against the bright light, he took a deep breath of the tangy sea air as he struggled to wake up. A haze of confusing images began dispersing inside his head as he sought the strength to open his eyes. He tried to sit up, but the throbbing pain was intense. Groaning, he sank back on the pillows when the room began to pitch and swirl. Recognizing his surroundings, he kept his eyes shut. He was on board his father's ship. Resentfully, he relived every moment of time from the attack on the *Libertine Lady* to being delivered like a trussed parcel into his father's hands. A huge hammer still pounded inside his skull but he gingerly turned his head to one side searching for a guard. Instead, he found his father, asleep in a nearby chair. The earl's usual impeccable appearance was marred by his crumpled and creased clothing, his pale haggard looking face showed at least a full day's growth of beard.

Convinced that if nothing else he had managed to postpone his father's plan for him to marry Christina, Nick tried to think of another way out. Christina Bristol, the thought of her increased the pain in his head. How many times would he have to readjust his thinking concerning that woman? She answered to several names but at least Lady Benton was not yet one of them. He mentally pictured her sitting so demurely in his father's cabin, looking so innocent when he had come charging in to steal back his crew's papers. That image would remain with him forever. He thought of Tony Carstairs, who had ordered him off his own ship, abiding by Sir Albert's instructions without hesitation and betraying his supposed best friend. He could not trust any of them, certainly not Tony or the beautiful little redhead who had been planted as the perfect bait to trap him. Well, so far he had eluded her trap, had not yet been forced to swallow the bait and didn't plan to, if he could help it.

He glanced over at his father, wishing for a brief moment that he could be what the earl wanted but knew it was not yet possible. He would force himself to remain unmoved by the emotional pleas his father would inevitably make to convince him to marry.

His mind wandered backward in time, fixing

on the day of his young brother's funeral. That bitter gray day when he had stood before Michael's freshly dug grave and vowed to avenge his brother's death. He could not explain to his father what had driven him away from his duty to family, could never tell him that Michael— No! He would not put his father through the hellish torment he himself had suffered all these years.

It had taken him the last three of those years, but at last he was close to confronting his enemy, having slowly gained the power to destroy him. His mouth twisted in an ugly grimace and he opened his eyes. His father was standing over the bed watching him.

"How are you feeling, Nicholas?" Sir Albert asked, his voice gruff with concern.

"Do you care?" Nick returned grimly, knowing he could not let his father sway him from the path he had chosen. Not yet, he was too close, too close to a final victory!

"It's over Nicky," the earl said, using the old childhood name Nick had not heard in years.

"Thank God!" Nick sighed in relief. The man has come to his senses at last. As for Christina Bristol—he was not finished with her yet. He would find a way to punish her for her part in his father's plan and rid himself of the lust he still felt for her, even if it took months. He thought of her curvaceous body twisting seductively under his, burning with a sweet passion he had not felt from a woman before. She had satisfied him totally, but he now knew what she was like—but he was not yet willing to give her up. When he had satiated himself with her, he would send her back to her father, used and worth nothing on the marriage market. That would be a fitting end to his relationship with the Bristols. The vengeful glimmer in his eyes died when he looked at his father. Something was wrong! Alarm registered throughout his body when he saw the sudden sag to his father's shoulders.

"You married Christina yesterday," Sir Albert said quietly.

"The hell I did!" Nick sat up, then slumped back as an explosion of pain went off in his head. His eyes burned, growing dark with disbelief. He must have misunderstood. Then, comprehension dawned—they had not waited for him to recover consciousness! "It's not legal. Even you must know that." His mouth twisted bitterly. "I didn't sign anything."

The earl reached into his coat and pulled out the certificate. Nick's shaky scrawl loomed out to condemn him, not his usual bold hand, but his signature all the same. It no longer mattered how they had accomplished it, they had.

"I'll never forgive you for this. Your precious family name means one hell of a lot more to you than I do, doesn't it?" Nick jabbed spitefully. "Do I receive my crew's papers now?" he asked in an icily controlled voice, the voice he reserved for his adversaries.

"I promised they would be returned when you present me with a grandson and they shall. I wish you would—"

"What I wish doesn't come into it, does it?" Nick spat. "You've made me into as much a whore as the woman you've shackled me to, but don't worry," he jeered. "I'll take her three times a day in front of you if I have to in order to get away from you both!"

Sir Albert was unable to hide the pain in his voice. "Nicholas—please—try to understand. If I can't have you—I will have another—your son. Your wife is a sweet and beautiful woman who should make you happy."

"My wife is a bloodthirsty little slut who saw a chance to become a countess and took it," Nick forced out. "She'll live to regret it, I promise you."

"She's entirely innocent," the earl insisted.

"You expect me to believe that?" Nick demanded, a furious pulse beating in his temple. "She has pulled the wool over my eyes for the last time. You have tied me to a conniving little liar. I hope you can rationalize that to yourself, Lord Benton, for you will never convince me."

"Won't you make the best of it?" Sir Albert entreated, looking deeply into Nick's eyes. "I know you too well, Nicholas. You are my son and you want that girl as much as I want grandchildren."

"You have no son!" Nick's voice rose but his head was aching so badly he could hardly see. His father's stricken face swam before his eyes. "You now command Bristol's valuable breeder and a prime stud. Why don't you bring her in? Let me give the bitch what you want." He pressed the heels of his hands to his temples, unable to focus, and gave a low moan before gratefully sinking into oblivion.

Sir Albert remained where he was for a long time, staring at Nick, consumed by guilt for what he had felt forced to do to his son. He'd been so sure that when Nick saw Christina, the idea of marriage would no longer be so repugnant. There was no doubt in his mind that Nick was attracted to her before he knew her identity and still was. Months ago they had argued bitterly about the marriage agreement Sir Albert had made with Nick storming out of Larleigh House before even learning the identity of the intended bride. Sir Albert had been so sure that Nick would finally agree, though he expected him to put up some initial resistance, the older Benton had never expected the vehemence Nick had displayed upon learning Christina's surname. There was more than reluctance to marry, it had something to do with Christina's father. He was at a loss to even begin to understand Nick's obvious hatred of Benjamin Bristol. It went deeper than a dislike of the man's nefarious business practices.

Though he was concerned for Nick's condition brought on by the injury to his head, he was almost grateful that he had slipped back into unconsciousness. Sleep was what the younger man needed now. He looked down at his son whose face was peaceful while he slept. He could almost see the young, carefree youth he had been. The young boy who had laughed easily, who had been quick to anger but just as quick to forgive and forget. The little boy who had followed his father about the estate, doggedly mimicking his every action. Nicholas was no longer that boy. He was making this hard, perhaps unbearable for both of them. Yet, hadn't he lost Nicholas long ago? Wounded by his son's condemnation, hating the methods he had been forced to use to insure the continuation of the family, Sir Albert knew he must live with the consequences of his actions. He bent and brushed his lips across Nick's forehead and felt the burning skin sear his lips.

"Forgive me, Nicky, for wanting another like you by my side." He got up and found himself face to face with Christina. Dressed in a simple pale green muslin day dress, the soft fabric gently clinging to her young curves, and her hair streaming down her back, held away from her face by a matching green ribbon, she looked so very young. What had he condemned this child-woman to? When he had pursued the alliance, he had believed it to benefit both Christina and Nicholas—but now? Her wide blue-green eyes fixed upon his face so intently, an inner illumination emanating from their depths, and the earl knew that whatever the future might bring between these two young people, he would make sure that this lovely young woman was protected. He looked back to his son, lying unconscious and feverish from an injury that he was as much responsible for as if he had struck him with his own hands. The earl's gray eyes clouded with pain from his own inner anguish and the pain he wished he could take away from his son.

"You do love him, then, don't you?" Christina's voice was gentle and soft. The earl shook his head gravely.

"Very much, though it must not appear so to you." He took a deep audible breath, blinking his eyes to ward off the gathering moisture at their corners. "All my hopes center on Nicholas, my dear. I know I seem a selfish old man and perhaps I am, but I do not want you to hate me. Our family dates back to William, and with the death of my youngest son Michael, the only Benton male left other than myself is Nicholas." The earl's face twisted at some agonizing memory and Christina took a step forward, instinctively wanting to comfort him. Her sympathetic expression encouraged him to continue his narrative and he sat down on the chair by Nick's berth, reaching for his son's hand.

"Nicholas blamed himself for the accident which killed his brother. He and Michael had entered their sloop in a regatta on the Thames, but I denied them my permission to attend so they bribed our old coachman, Cyrus, to take them. Only Nicholas was thrown clear when the carriage went over a cliff on the road to London.

"After Michael's death, Nicholas grew away from me. We could not talk of Michael, still can't, and later, he renounced his responsibilities to the estate and title and went to sea. He served valiantly in the Royal Navy, but when hostilities ended and I thought it time he marry and return to Larkhollow, he flatly refused, telling me he was married to the sea. You may not understand what has driven me to go to these lengths to insure the continuation of my family, but I was desperate. Nicholas and I have become strangers, but in the time left to me, I had hoped—" his voice trailed off, his throat closed by emotion.

Christina knew that he could not bring himself to say more. She stepped closer and placed her hand on his arm. He covered her hand, accepting the warm-hearted gesture he knew he didn't deserve.

"I will stay with him, my lord. Perhaps you should rest. You have been up with him for over twenty-four hours."

The earl seemed not to hear her suggestion and spoke as much to himself as to Christina. "I should have known he would react like this. You are everything my son could want if only his pride would allow him to relinquish the stand he has taken." Abruptly, he stood up and left the cabin without looking back.

Christina stood silently, staring at the closed door. He new father-in-law was a difficult man to understand, as difficult as his son. She turned to look at her husband. Husband! The thought made her stomach muscles bunch into knots. She belonged to this pantherish male who had inducted her into a world of passion and pleasure that was far beyond her wildest imagination. Even in sleep, Nick could send her pulses racing. Dark, untamed, he ignited her senses to flame. Unable to stop herself, she reached out and touched his cheek, startled by the burning heat that seared her fingertips.

Deciding she must do something to relieve his fever, she splashed fresh water from the pitcher into a basin, dampened a cloth and sat down upon the berth beside him. Throughout the long afternoon, she changed one cool cloth after another until moisture beaded on his chest. His fever had broken.

She stood up, arching her back muscles to relieve the strain and stiffness. She replaced the basin on the washstand and reached for a towel. Nick's body was bathed in sweat, his dark hair clinging to his forehead, his shoulders damply gleaming as he shivered. Afraid he might take a chill, she went to work again, wiping his skin, quickly and efficiently, keeping as much of his body covered as she could while drying him.

He moaned softly when she toweled his chest and she dropped the cloth with a startled gasp. He moved restlessly and the sheet fell away, exposing his flat belly, his loins, his rock-hard thighs. Her breath caught in her throat and she averted her eyes until his even breathing reassured her that he was oblivious to her presence. She placed her palm upon his chest and whispered, "Nick?" There was no response. She let out her pent-up breath. What would she have done if he had answered her? Her eyes ran down the length of his naked body and with her senses out of control, her fingers followed their path, crossing the breadth of his shoulders, moving tentatively down the wide and powerful chest until a muscle involuntarily leaped below her hand. She threw the sheet over him quickly and stepped back, panting open-mouthed until he mumbled something unintelligible under his breath and rolled onto his side with his back to her.

It took several minutes before she had enough courage to replace the sodden sheets wih fresh linen and was completely out of breath by the time she had completed her task. Drawing a fresh sheet up to his chest, she discovered that his eyes were open and he was staring at her. She gave a soft cry and jumped back, hotly blushing. She tried not to look at his face, knowing that she would see nothing but contempt and naked hatred for her written in the steely gray depths of his eyes. Taking another step back from the berth, she jumped again when he spoke.

"You have a gentle touch, milady." The soft almost tender sound of his voice quickly drew her eyes to his face. There was not a trace of the hard, reckless adventurer about him. His gray eyes were soft and luminous, slightly bewildered. He smiled weakly, a lopsided endearing smile that was totally out of character. He reached out for her hand and caught it tightly within his large palm, as if he were unsure of himself and of her. "Should I know you?" he asked. "I—I'm sorry, but I don't seem to know where I am or why." He tried to sit up and the sheet slid below his waist. He made a grab for it, seemingly embarrassed. Chagrined eyes searched for Christina's, reflecting a boyish innocence.

Christina was astonished and a bit unnerved. He touched the bandage on his head and winced. "What happened to me? Have I been in an accident?"

Alarmed by the question, Christina stared at him, a bubble of panic welling in her throat as she choked out warily, "Don't you remember?"

He smiled, weakly. "If—you could tell me who I am, I would greatly appreciate it. I can't seem to recall."

Was it really possible that Nick had lost his memory? What should she do? She had to say something, could not ignore the imploring look on Nick's face or the insistent pull on her fingers. "Eh—" she groped frantically. "Someone else will be better able to answer your questions. I—I'll fetch him." She jerked her hand free and in a flurry of rustling skirts and lace-edged petticoats ran to the door, not giving him a chance to detain her.

Minutes later, Christina burst back into Nick's cabin, quickly followed by Annette and a white-faced Sir Albert. Sir Albert brushed past her as he crossed the cabin and went to his knee beside the bed. "Nicholas? Nicholas?" He touched Nick's shoulder and gently shook him. Christina stood at Sir Albert's side as Nick's dark lashes lifted, dropped down, then lifted again and his eyes focused on their faces. She heard the earl's sigh of relief and felt the same as he when they saw that Nick's eyes were clear and bright in his tanned face. "Nicholas, you frightened Christina," Sir Albert admonished, gently. "How do you feel?"

"I'm sorry if I frightened anyone, sir." He spoke in a strangely formal voice.

"Oh my God, Nicholas. I am still your father," Sir Albert intoned, believing that Nick was deliberately negating their relationship. "Don't keep punishing me. You will only hurt us both."

Nick's eyes registered no recognition as he stared up at his father. Sir Albert backed away in torment, but Christina reached for his hand to keep him from leaving. She was positive that the earl's estimation of the situation was incorrect. Nick had been behaving unnaturally since regaining consciousness and seemed genuinely confused. She took a step toward the berth.

"Nick?" Her voice was soft. "Do you recall how ill you have been?" His bewildered expression had not changed since she had run from the room in panic.

"Are you my nurse, pretty girl?" He smiled weakly, his dark eyes soft with entreaty.

"Sir Albert," Christina implored, not taking her eyes from Nick's face. "He doesn't know, he really doesn't know any of us." Her voice quivered until she saw anxiety invade the gray eyes of her husband and she quickly reassured him with an encouraging smile.

"Nicholas?" The earl queried, hesitantly. "Are you saying that you really can't remember who you are?"

Nick struggled to sit up. "I—I'm sorry. Should I know you?"

"I am your father, Albert Benton, and this is your wife, Christina."

Christina blushed, taken aback, when Nick's

eyes lit up with pleasure upon learning her identity. He gave her a charming smile before returning his attention to his father. "You called me Nick and I seem to remember that. Nick or Nicky." He hesitantly touched the bandage on his head, his expression quizzical. "I remember someone calling me Nicky."

Unshed tears glistened in the earl's eyes. "I call you Nicky, sometimes. I always called you Nicky when you were a boy. You are my son, Nicholas Alexander Benton."

"What happened to me?"

Christina and Sir Albert exchanged worried glances. What could they say? Annette was the only one who seemed to have gathered her scattered wits. She stepped into the circle of Nick's vision, shooing everyone away. "Enough excitement for now, my lord. You have indeed had an accident but you shall soon be quite well. We are on board your father's ship and are proceeding home to England. We had a storm some days past and you were hit by a flying piece of wood. Your dear wife has been sick with worry along with your father, but you are on the mend." Annette sounded like a starchy nanny, calmly ordering her charge to relax which he did almost at once. She plumped his pillow and ordered him to lie flat as she smoothed the sheets and firmly tucked them around him. "Do not worry about what you cannot remember. It is a perfectly normal reaction to a good blow to the head." She bustled about in her self-appointed role as nurse, smiling encouragingly, and Nick smiled back. "I am Annette Harcourt, Lady Benton's maid. Together, she and I will care for you until you are completely recovered."

Nick bestowed a charming smile on both of the women standing by his bedside. "Then, I shall surely recover quickly."

Chapter Seven

HESITANTLY, NICK TOOK CHRISTINA'S HAND AND led her to the sofa in his cabin. She took her seat and he lowered himself beside her, swinging his long booted legs up and over the cushions, dropping his head onto her lap. A tight feeling boiled up inside her and she swallowed the sudden obstruction in her throat. She looked down, unable to rebuff the boyish pleading in his eyes, the vulnerable expression of his face as his thick lashes closed against the pain in his head. "It is worst at the temples, Christina," he implored, nestling his dark head more comfortably in her lap.

Brushing away a rebellious black curl, she began a gentle stroking at his hairline. "Are you certain this will help, Nicholas?"

"Mmmm," his voice was a low sigh of gratification that ignited a responding chord of pleasure in her lower limbs. She delicately massaged his temples, her fingers trembling as her eyes traveled down his long muscled frame, taking in the width of his shoulders showing clearly through his thin white linen shirt, the narrow waist and the powerful thighs beneath his fawn colored breeches. His arms were folded across his chest, the cuffs of his shirt rolled back to reveal the bronzed forearms sheened with dark hair. His long tapered fingers were at rest, but not many days ago they had touched her, explored every inch of her body, and she yearned to feel them caress her once more, ached for the pleasure she had enjoyed in his arms.

Nick had readily accepted that they were a happily married couple, accepted her presence at his bedside and constantly requested her ministrations. How long would it be before he remembered that he hated her and would want nothing more to do with her? She concentrated on her task, gently kneading the firm skin above his cheekbones. She could not tell him, could not explain why she feared him, yet desired him at the same time. Could not admit to him that they were living a lie.

"I am the most fortunate of men to have you, Tina," he whispered faintly. "The others seem so strange to me, but you—it's as if I've known you forever. I can't ask these personal favors of the others without feeling as if I were imposing on a stranger."

Since he had lost his memory, he had made it clear to everyone that he only felt comfortable with his wife. He barely tolerated Annette's hovering and was formally polite with the earl, but always, he welcomed Christina. She seemed to be the only one who was able to soothe the recurring headaches and dizziness he suffered. Nick called on her often and her guilt made it impossible for her to refuse his requests, even though his nearness caused her great inner turmoil. She was very glad that they were arriving in London tomorrow, anxious to escape the close confines aboard the *Monique*.

She took a deep breath, trying not to squirm as he readjusted his shoulders upon her thighs and began toying with the fragile white braid that underlined the bodice of her gown. As his fingers absently outlined the interlacing, his knuckles brushed the full undersides of her breasts and immediately her nipples throbbed to life. She fidgeted uneasily. "I—I should think that your headaches would be subsiding." She needed to say something to break the sensual awareness that was rapidly accelerating inside her. "I am anxious for further explanation of these spells from the physician in London."

"*I* am anxious to return to our country estate, Larkhollow. The earl tells me that he shall not accompany us from London when it comes time for us to go." He grasped one of her hands, pulling her fingers away from his brow and bringing them to his warm mouth. He began nibbling her fingertips, one by one, the soft bites sending tingles of pleasure up her arms. "I cannot say that I will be sorry to be rid of the man. I find we have little in common. He assures me that I shall have little trouble dealing with our country estate, but I don't know. It all seems quite alien to me."

"I—I thought you wanted me to ease your headache," she stammered, disengaging her fingers from his and returning them to his temples. The thought of living alone with him at Larkhollow, beginning their married life together and continuing to field his increasingly pointed probing, filled her with dread. "Perhaps your father's physician will think it wiser for you to remain in London. Larkhollow is a full day's ride from town. What if you become ill there, with no physician at hand? I think it best if we stay with your father for a few weeks at Larleigh House until we are sure you are completely recovered."

"You aren't putting off being alone with me, are you?" Nick lifted his head off her lap, his warm breath caressing the bare skin above her bodice. "You did say we were happy in our marriage, didn't you?" His voice was a deep low caress as his eyes searched hers for an answer.

"Of course we were," she lied, breaking their gaze and assisting him to sit up on the sofa, then immediately lowering her hands into her lap to avoid further contact. How could she admit that they had had one night of delirious pleasure before their marriage? That as soon as he knew her identity, he had denounced her as "the spawn of the devil?" "I am merely concerned for your health. I think you ask far too much of yourself, too soon."

"Nonsense. Sir Albert insists that our estate

manager is a competent man and all I have to do at Larkhollow is recuperate, refamiliarize myself with my surroundings and try to convince my shy wife that even without my memory I greatly admire her."

Christina bit her lip and averted her eyes. She wanted to cry out, "For how long, Nick? How long before you turn against me?" She pushed away the thought and blurted, "I—I admire you too, Nicholas, but I feel we must be careful—go slowly."

"I suppose," he agreed reluctantly, his lower lip drooping petulantly. "It is so frustrating. Have some sympathy, Christina. I woke up and was told that I am married to a beautiful woman, that I am lord of a fine manor, but I can remember nothing." He reached out with one finger and lifted her chin, frowning when she attempted to turn her head away. "You see!" he pronounced. "Sometimes I feel as if you are actually frightened of me. Have I given you reason to fear me?"

Christina licked her suddenly dry lips, ensnared by the dark gray smoke of his eyes. "Of course not," she reassured. "Why would I fear my own husband?" She hoped he misread the panicky tremor in her voice. She bravely held his gaze, trying to withstand the inner knowledge that somewhere within her husband's body a tiger lay waiting to pounce. A man who had threatened to "break her in two" when he had the chance.

"I don't know." His voice was a husky low drawl. "Your husband, yet somehow, a stranger.

I don't even know how long we have been married. You are so very young that it can't have been long."

Panic rapidly escalated to hysteria. "No, not long," she forced out, gearing her body to jump up from the sofa if he delved any further. Unwittingly, he prevented her from leaving his side by taking hold of one amber strand of her hair and curling it around his finger.

"Such beautiful hair." He smiled a dazzling white-toothed grin of pure enjoyment, distracting her long enough to ask another question. "You are absolutely irresistible, so how could I have forgotten making love to you?"

"Nicholas!" Her embarrassed exclamation made him laugh. "At the convent, I was taught never to speak of such things."

"You have a most becoming blush, milady," he complimented, releasing her hair. "It is difficult to picture you within the confines of a nunnery. Tell me true, did you really think to take the veil?"

His seemingly innocent query was so much like the similar conversation aboard the *Libertine Lady* when he had gazed his fill of her naked breasts and his mocking eyes had sarcastically dismissed the possibility that she would enter religious life. Could he be remembering? She had to get away from him, at least for a little while. "It is time for tea, Nicholas. If your headache is better, which it must be since you are doing entirely too much talking, you must feel strong enough to join us in the forward cabin." She stood up and resolutely walked to the door, without daring to look back. "And I never thought to become a nun," she stated firmly as she opened the door, unnerved by the sound of his wholly male chuckle as she passed through the doorway.

Three days later they were on their way to Larkhollow. Nicholas had easily convinced Sir Albert that he was fit enough for the day-long carriage ride after the physician who had examined him had declared Nick physically well, but in need of fresh air and sunshine. Deciding that he and Christina should take up residence at Larkhollow without delay, Nick listened to none of Christina's pleas to stay longer in London, declaring that her concern for his health would be far better met in the Kentish countryside. She dreaded being alone with him, already parted from her companion, she felt defenseless. Annette had left Larleigh House to join her invalid sister in Chelsea for a short time before seeking another position as chaperone for a young lady.

Dressed in a fashionable, deep-russet satin traveling dress with a black braid-trimmed spencer and a silk-lined straw bonnet, Christina felt none of the confidence that the stylish ensemble should have given her. Though she presented the picture of a sophisticated young woman, she warily faced her husband across the closed carriage, feeling trapped by his overwhelming presence in the small enclosure. The landau was to be kept closed during their travel for there was a sharp chill in the spring breezes and the skies were gray, heavy clouds threatened rain. She threw a suspicious glance at the smug smile which curved up the corners of her husband's strongly carved lips. "You seem highly pleased about something, Nicholas," she said thinly.

"Shouldn't I be pleased, Lady Benton?" He grinned, a devilish twinkle in his eye that made her shiver with apprehension. He wasn't remembering was he? He hadn't arranged for them to be alone in order to punish her for what he believed was her part in his father's plot? Her face paled with the thought, recalling vividly the black rage that had emanated from his powerful body before he had lost his memory. A shiver ran through her body.

"My dear wife, you are ill? Are you cold? Would you like a rug across your legs—or I could sit beside you and possibly keep you warm?" The mischievous twinkle in his eyes was swiftly replaced by a concerned expression that she interpreted as sincere.

"No, I'm fine." She searched his face but saw no more of the audacious pirate captain who lurked in Nick's soul. "Why are you so pleased to be leaving London and why did we have to so soon?"

"It is as if I have been released from prison," he stated without remorse. "Everyone was constantly hovering. My father was forever filling my already over-taxed brain with instructions concerning the estate and you were happily avoiding me whenever you could. Now, we can begin anew." He gave her a lustful once over with his eyes, chuckling at her reddened cheeks. "I'm sorry, Tina. It is just that you are exceedingly fun to tease. I am sure I spent the majority of our courtship attempting to make you blush."

She quickly changed the subject, wanting to test him further and becoming more and more adept at steering their conversations away from the personal or the past. "I understand that there is a great deal of debate going on in the House of Lords over the transportation of prisoners to New South Wales as well as an investigation into the unlawful indenturement of men. What do you think of spiriting, Nicholas?" Would he pass her test? She reached for the papers lying on the seat beside her and handed him the latest edition of *The Times,* pointing to an article concerning the illegal capture of bonded labor. Her eyes searched his face, missing nothing, but his expression remained disinterested as he read the article.

"I think that you will have a great deal to do in order to bring me up to date on the latest issues." He waved the paper in the air, then hurled it across the seat where it landed on her lap. "I can't be concerned with the affairs of state when my own affairs are still a mystery to me."

He stared out the carriage window, his eyes darkening to fathomless gray pools. "I see nothing out there that strikes a responsive chord inside me, Tina. This countryside could be anywhere as far as I am concerned." He turned back to her. "Do you know that I have begun having the most unusual dreams? I am staring out across a stormy sea, standing on the deck of some ship and I feel—at home. Isn't that odd? We docked in London a few days ago and I was extremely happy to be put ashore. Why do you suppose I constantly dream of the sea?"

"Didn't your father tell you that you served in the Royal Navy?" Christina offered quickly, hiding the sick feeling that churned in her stomach. "I'm sure you will remember it all one day, Nicholas. I dream strange things too and I have not lost my memory. Everyone does."

"What do you dream, Tina?" The soft question was posed in a curiously gentle tone of voice.

"I dream of riding a strong-blooded horse across the moors. Riding and riding until my hair blows away from my face and my skirts go flying. It's a nice dream. It makes me feel free, free like the wind." She could not relate her other dreams. The fantasy of lying naked in his arms, being stroked to a mindless fervor of passion until her body soared.

He gave her a strange look then returned his regard to the passing countryside. A long silence fell between them which Christina did not fully understand. Had she said something to offend him? Did he remember something? He looked so handsome in his claret-colored, superfine coat, and buff-colored trousers. His cravat was intricately tied and its snowy crispness contrasted sharply with his bronzed square chin. She lowered her eyes to prevent herself from staring.

During the many long talks she had had with Sir Albert while on board the *Monique* and then during the short days in London, he had advised her to put aside her fears and give in to her

admitted affectionate feelings for Nicholas. He
believed that if Nick's memory returned, he
would already be so much in love with her that
he wouldn't blame her any longer. Sir Albert had
told her to show Nicholas what she was truly
like while she had the chance. Show him her
interests and share her philosophies with him so
that he would come to know her. He had made
no further mention of his desire for an heir, but
she could see that he had not stopped hoping.
Why else would he encourage her to make her
marriage a real one? She resented his ulterior
motives for encouraging intimacy with her husband almost as much as she resented the treacherous longings of her body which desired the
same. Although Nick was unaware of the condi-
tions under which they had wed, she thought of
them constantly. Sir Albert expected her to produce the Benton heir. Perhaps it would be best if
she did conceive Nicholas's child quickly, then
if he regained his memory and became Nick
Barker again, his obligation would be already
fulfilled and he could return to the life at sea.

The inner battle she fought with herself
waged on and on, until exhausted by her conflicting emotions, she rested her head against
the wall of the coach and drifted to sleep.

"We have arrived at the inn," Nick announced
sleepily, having awakened only minutes before
his wife. "We shall have a chance to stretch our
legs and enjoy a meal before continuing our
journey. The sun has come out and I thought
you might enjoy a short walk. There's a pretty
little brook just beyond the tavern's courtyard."

She would enjoy relieving the cramps in her legs and Christina accepted Nick's assistance out of the carriage and his hand at her elbow as they walked toward the brook. Their conversation was pleasantly light and they laughed together at the antics of the ducks swimming in the small stream and bobbing for food. They lingered over the tasty fare the innkeeper provided for passing travelers until their driver came to say that the fresh team had been harnessed and all was in readiness to continue. They were back on the road again a short while later and their impersonal conversation continued sporadically as they each pointed out interesting aspects of the countryside and small villages they passed through. Finally, they lapsed into silence until as the sun slipped lower in the spring sky, the coachman called attention to the towering gates of Larkhollow. Christina sat up straight, peering out of the carriage for her first glimpse of her new home. A sprawling brick structure rose majestically at the end of the long tree-lined drive. The twilight sun bathed the pink bricks with a soft glow, turning the myriad of glistening mullioned windows golden as they reflected the dying rays. Her eyes grew wide with awe. She was the new mistress of this gracious manor.

More than a dozen chimneys stood out atop the gabled roof. The imposing brick facade stretched endlessly across a manicured green lawn. The surrounding parkland was equally as well kept with spring blossoming bushes studding the grassy land. "It—it is," she breathed.

"Yes, it is." Nick's tone was as awestruck as hers. She watched his face, wondering if he would now remember everything upon seeing his family home. His gaze swung back to her. "Will you enjoy being mistress of this grand house?" he asked, a certain grimness to his voice that he quickly banished with a smile. "Are you prepared to assume control of this household?"

"Sir Albert has assured me that there is an abundance of well-trained servants, Nicholas. You and I shall not have overmuch to do." She didn't want him to feel as if the entire weight of running the estate rested on his shoulders.

"I'm sure my father made that clear to you," he commented sardonically.

Startled by the derision in his voice, Christina wanted an explanation but before she could ask him what he had meant, the carriage door was opened by a liveried footman. Nick helped her alight and together they walked up the wide marble steps where the majordomo welcomed them inside. The tall, distinguished, gray-haired gentleman introduced himself as Chevingson and allowed the faintest of smiles to cross his dignified face as he greeted Nick. The man had served Sir Albert for many years and though Nick might not remember him, Chevingson obviously remembered Nick—and with some affection.

They were ushered into the great hall where the staff had been hastily assembled as soon as their arrival was announced. Chevingson introduced each member of the staff as they stood in

a long line as if on review for inspection. As soon
as the introductions had been completed, all
were dismissed except the housekeeper, Mrs.
Fargate, and one maid and a young footman who
had been assigned to the personal needs of the
young master and his new bride. Chevingson
disappeared, leaving them in the housekeeper's
care.

As soon as the authoritative butler had disappeared, Mrs. Fargate, a tall woman with a long
angular face and snapping blue eyes, welcomed
them a bit more effusively. She, like Chevingson, looked upon Nick with affection as she
bustled them up the grand staircase and showed
them to the master suite of rooms. She announced that a light repast would be waiting for
them as soon as they had refreshed themselves
from their journey. Christina's new maid, a
smiling young girl named Elise helped her new
mistress change while the young footman,
newly elevated to the position of valet, did like-
wise for Nick in the adjoining room.

Nick and Christina were guided to a small
salon off of the large formal dining room where a
meal was waiting for them. They were unnaturally quiet as they ate and Nick made no
comment when Christina excused herself
promptly thereafter, saying she was exhausted
from the journey.

Once in her room, Christina ordered a tub
brought to her and soaked for over an hour in the
warm, sweet-scented water, then allowed Elise
to help her don a thin blue night dress before she
crawled into the large four-postered, cano-

pied bed, but sleep would not come. Was Nick
having as difficult a time as she? Was he lying
abed, wondering if she were on the opposite side
of the connecting door of their suite waiting for
him? She heard him enter his room, talk quietly
with his valet, and could hear water being
brought for a bath. Finally, all was quiet.

She grew restless in the silence and finally got
up from her bed and walked across her silver-
shadowed room to the window, unlatching the
leaded casement to push it open. Staring across
the moonlit park surrounding Larkhollow, she
scanned the night-mantled hedges and trees,
taking comfort from the shrouded serenity of the
scene below her. The piercing screech of an owl
set her overwrought nerves farther on edge and
she wrapped her arms around herself to ward off
her anxiety. The garden below was tranquil, but
for Christina there was little peace. She was
living under a cloud of deceit, drawn to a man
who at any moment might recall that he hated
her, that he had described the purpose for their
marriage in the crudest of terms.

How much longer could she go on? She was
beginning to feel like a suitable candidate for
Bedlam, needing answers to questions she dared
not ask. Why did Nick hate her father so intense-
ly? And—why was he so ready to believe that she
was a willing participant in *his* father's plot?

She leaned her cheek against the cool window
pane and let the fresh spring breeze wafting up
from the garden soothe her senses. Sitting down
on the window seat, she brought her knees to
her chin, gazing outside at the carefully kept

lawns of her new home. How long would it be
before she would share her husband's bed?

It would be so easy to love Nicholas, perhaps
she already did. Since losing his memory, he had
treated her like an equal, not a beautiful play-
thing provided to satisfy his prurient interests.
His gentle demeanor was highly appealing. He
stimulated her intelligence, heightened her
senses, but she had to remember that under-
neath his presently easygoing and gentle exteri-
or was a man who had turned against her in a
raging fury and might do so again.

Chapter Eight

"CHRISTINA?" NICK'S VOICE WAS SENSUALLY low, cutting into her thoughts as she swung around on the window seat and saw him coming through the connecting door of their chambers. "May we talk for a few minutes?"

"Of—of course, Nicholas," she stammered. She got up from her seat and walked shakily across the room in order to retrieve her dressing gown from the bed. She was barely given enough time to slip her arms into the lace-edged garment and tie the satin ribbons at her throat before Nick lit a small lamp and gestured for her to be seated upon a floral chintz-cushioned chaise. She nervously fingered the smooth, cool fabric of her peignoir as Nick lowered his tall frame onto the delicate Queen Anne chair a few feet from where she was sitting.

"You can't sleep either?" He smiled gently, exuding his heady charm. "It's a damnable situation we have here, at best."

"Yes," she quickly agreed, trying not to show her awareness of his state of undress. She was positive he wore nothing beneath his black robe, loosely tied at the waist. She moistened her suddenly dry lips with the tip of her tongue as he leaned back in the small chair and stretched out his long legs before him. The edges of his dressing gown gaped open to reveal the crisp curling dark hairs of his chest, and the brocade material slipped off his knees exposing his bare calves. Caught off guard, she couldn't hide her reaction to the sight of his bare legs. Remembered passion smoldered in her eyes as she looked at him.

"Peculiar that we are a married couple and I can't recall kissing you, holding you, or sharing your bed." Although his tone was not threatening, the sudden move he made startled her. He was on his knees in front of her before she knew what he was about. He took both of her palms within his hands and placed a delicate kiss in the center of each. Her eyes grew wide, appearing like glittering emeralds as the tingling pleasure of contact with his warm mouth shot through her. The touch evoked vivid memories and she could not resist the invisible pull he had on her senses. She swayed toward him, but he released her hands and stood up, looked down at her for a few moments then said, in a soft voice, "I'm sorry to have disturbed you, Christina. I'm sure you must be exhausted from our journey from town. I should leave you alone, but I—I had hoped."

What had he hoped? She needed to know and stood up quickly. "Nicholas?" She posed the soft question, longing to feel his arms around her. "Would you like to kiss me good night?" she asked, desire running like wildfire through her veins. All fear of him fled and she took a hesitant step toward him, closing the scant feet between them.

Gently, he reached out for her hand and pulled her closer to him. Her lashes closed, she leaned against him, her lips parted to accept his kiss. When she felt the brief touch of his lips against her burning forehead and the immediate hesitation that followed, her eyes flew open with question. Where was the demanding lover who had mastered her body? Why hadn't he crushed her against him and accepted what she was offering? When he lost his memory, had Nick also changed so much that he was fearful of instigating their lovemaking? She sensed an awkwardness in him, a timidity that was in direct contrast with the brash male who had seduced her. Perhaps he was waiting for more encouragement.

"You aren't going are you?" Her voice was a low seductive purr, more invitation than question.

He put a hand to his brow and turned away from her. "My thoughts for you are unseemly. You are so young, so sweet. I can hardly credit that you are my wife." His voice was strangled.

"Oh Nicholas." The dejected slump of his broad shoulders tore at her heart. "I *am* your wife and want you to stay," she whispered and reached out to him, lightly touching his arm. At first, he didn't move, only stiffened in response to the slight grazing of her fingertips.

Taking a deep audible breath, he turned back toward her. "Are you sure I would not frighten you with my carnal needs? You are a genteel lady," he said wistfully. "I realize that you would only endure my advances to produce children as is proper and it is entirely too soon to think of an heir." His voice was apologetic and once again he turned to go. He tightened the sash of his robe with a dismissing gesture of self-contempt. The fabric stretched across his loins and his desire for her was readily apparent.

She stepped forward, refusing to let him go, knowing that she would have to make a stronger overture and prove to him that she would not be insulted by his lovemaking. "Nicholas, I want you to stay."

By sheer willpower, Christina banished the last remnants of her memories of a raging Nick Barker. Nicholas Benton stood before her and he was her husband. She was alone with him, wanted him and knew he wanted her. There was no sound in the room besides the whisper of a soft breeze that caressed her shivering flesh beneath her silk garments. She stood seductively in the halo of moonlight which silvered the room. Her eyes shone sea green with longing but Nicholas waited. "You are my husband, Nicholas," she murmured, swaying toward him, drawn to the magnetic force that radiated from him, the invisible, irresistible field of virility that surrounded him. "You do have rights," she whispered, the words pulled from her lips by the same irrevocable force that had made her call him back to her, the catalyst that prompted her to act.

Still, he did nothing, hesitating in a manner that irritated her. What was the matter with him? Did she have to beg him to take her? Wasn't she being obvious enough? No, he was looking at her with a mute question. How much further must she commit herself? She felt like a wanton as it was, yet he still seemed unsure of her wishes. Flushing with the heated fervor of desire that enveloped her, she could not look at his face.

"Tina, I do not want to repel you," Nick said. "I must have behaved as an animal on our wedding night for I often see the fear in your eyes."

Detecting agonized remorse in his tone, Christina walked to him, took his arms and placed them around her, then stood on tiptoe, shamelessly pressing herself against him, revelling in his quickened breathing and the muffled groan that escaped his lips. Sure that the passion that had once flared between them would be renewed, she looked deeply into his dove-gray eyes. "I want you, Nicholas." She offered him her lips and when he still hesitated, she reached up and pulled his head down to her. Sipping

delicately of the firm contours of his wide
mouth, she attempted to prove that she was not
afraid. When she lifted her lips, he whispered,
"Are you sure?"

"Yes," she breathed and stepped back, holding
his eyes with her ardent gaze. She slipped out of
her robe, then slowly, enticingly loosened the
ribbons at her shoulders and let the fragile night
garment fall to the floor. Boldly, she reached for
the sash at his waist, untying it with trembling
fingers, then slipping her hands beneath the
satin lapels to push it off his shoulders until he
was as naked as she.

Entranced by the sight of his body, his wide
muscular shoulders gleaming in the moonlight,
she experienced a total recall of the first time
she had seen this man without clothing. The
sensations she had felt then returned a hundred
fold and she was lost in a passionate reverie of
need, swept away by his magnificent male beauty. She led him to the bed and pulled him down
beside her slim body. She turned eagerly into his
arms, expectantly waiting for his first exquisite
touch, wanting the rapture that he alone could
give her. Her eyes were starved for the sight of
him, her fingers lonely for the feel of his smooth
bronzed skin, her lips thirsty for the taste of
him.

"Show me what you want, Tina," he whispered, devouring the naked curves of her full
breasts with silvery hot eyes. "Rid yourself of
whatever ghosts that haunt you, so you need
never fear me again." His voice was controlled,

tense with the determination to keep his own need under firm command until she had allayed her fear. She felt a swift surge of pure joy. Nicholas cared about her feelings, wanted her to prove to herself that he did not consider her a possession but a woman with emotions, with needs that were hers alone, not dictated by some man.

Her desire for him was so strong, she couldn't wait a moment longer to touch him. She wanted to see his gray eyes on fire with passion, wanted her touch to drive him wild with longing. She ran her fingers across the curling dark hair on his chest, smiling as she felt the muscles quiver beneath the smooth surface. He was holding back but she held back nothing. She rubbed herself against him, drawing his hands to her breasts, her own exploring his body eagerly. It was almost as if she were the experienced lover and he the untried, as he let her initiate them every step into total intimacy. She would not settle for anything less than the first time they had been together and his passivity inflamed her to ever increasing excitement. All she wanted was the passion which would carry them both away. She didn't want to think, only to feel.

"Show me," he growled in a barely controlled low drawl that drove the last of her inhibitions away.

She did show him. She did everything she had ever done with him in her dreams. She brushed her hands across his chest; followed the silky line of hair down his body to his smooth flat stomach.

She raptured in the contraction of muscle as her hand brushed the taut skin of his belly and marveled at the tight play of virile nerves beneath his skin. Did she dare venture further? It was arousing, frustrating, exciting to be in control of their passion and she had long since lost her last tiny shred of restraint. His increasingly harsh breathing encouraged her to continue her exploration. Tentatively at first, her fingers touched him, felt him shudder in reaction. He groaned with pleasure and she grew braver, drawing one satiny smooth thigh over his outstretched legs, her fingers enclosing around the velvet sheath of his manhood.

"Yes," he breathed as she lifted herself on top of him and pressed against his length, undulating her hips. She loved the feel of his hard thighs beneath her, her breasts crushed to his hair-roughened chest as she brought her hands to his face, pressing her fingers to his lean cheeks as her soft mouth came down on his. Her tongue ran lightly along the inside of his mouth, exploring the warmth with unskilled delight. She heard an agonized moan well up in his throat and his hands moved along her sides to her breasts. She trailed her lips to his cheek and over the beard-roughened skin of his chin and jaw, her fingers running through his crisp hair as her excited journey to explore his body became a deep need commanded by her loins.

"Oh Nick. I feel—so—So—" she gasped, moving up and down his torso in the seductive female movements of pleasure.

Cradling her aching breasts in his palms, his fingers stroking the throbbing nipples, he demanded in a husky whisper, "Tell me."

"I need you to fill me," she moaned. "I am empty without you."

"Oh God!" he clasped her to him, his hands molding her buttocks.

"Love me," she cried exultantly, guiding his pulsing shaft between her thighs. She controlled their pleasure, desire firing her to a frenzied rhythm that transported them both. She clutched his shoulders with both hands as they shuddered to a perfect climax of movement, each in tune with the other. It was an explosion of soaring pleasure, hers to give and to receive as he shook with the wealth of her passion.

Nicholas would not remember all he had taught her of lovemaking as Nick Barker, but she had remembered and showed him what an apt pupil she had once been in his arms.

In the soft moments of recovery, she nestled her head in the hollow of his shoulder and burrowed close as his arms closed possessively around her. She had proved the extent of her desire for him and from this night forward he should feel free to do the same. Tonight, he had wanted her to exorcise all of her fears and she certainly had, and by his response he had thoroughly enjoyed her methods.

Not once had he tried to change their positions or take control. She rolled over to his side and propped herself up on one elbow. His eyes were closed, hiding his dark gaze and the love she hoped to see there. His tousled hair curled

damply about his ears and forehead and she
brushed it away from his brow in a tender
gesture of affection. She looked at his mouth,
startled to see his lips quirking in silent amusement. When she stiffened, he opened his eyes
and stared full into her face, a wide grin cutting
across his face.

"If I had known being a hired stud could be so
damned pleasurable, princess, I would have
taken it up years ago!"

Chapter Nine

"OH NO!" CHRISTINA BREATHED. IT WAS NICK Barker who was surveying her face and naked body with his all too familiar insolence. Her mind whirled in horrified shock. It couldn't be true. Not now! Not when she had been so sure that Nicholas cared for her as much as she cared for him. She was numb. When he chuckled the deep, throaty, mocking laugh she so remembered, her body's instinct for survival surfaced. She made a dive for the floor, but was pulled back immediately. He had known she would try to escape and had no intention of letting her go. She fought him with all of her strength, kicking, scratching, biting until to her horror she was flat on her back beneath his heavy body, her wrists pulled firmly above her head and his thighs clamped across her legs. "No! No! No!" She tossed her head from side to side, tears of humiliation and dread pouring down her face.

"Oh milady," Nick's voice challenged. "Surely you don't wish to leave the arms of the man you just seduced?"

How long? How long had he had his memory back? How long had she been making a fool of herself? She was consumed with rage. "How could you?"

"What a short memory you have, princess. Maybe it's contagious." His sarcasm was laced with barely controlled laughter. "As I recall I merely lay here and you couldn't keep your dainty little hands off of me. In fact, I would say you have used me, wouldn't you?"

"I hate you!" Christina panted, unable to twist away from his lazy regard. His laughter came from deep in his chest.

"Changeable, damned changeable. First, she seduces me, then she hates me." She was totally helpless to stop him as he began a slow steady exploration of her body with one hand, while the other kept firm hold of her wrists. "I hope you never learn to control that passionate nature of yours, my sweet. I suppose you are dying to know how long I've had my full senses." His fingers traced patterns across her quavering belly. "I never lost them."

Christina sucked in her breath, cringing away from him, her body rigid. "Why?" she gasped.

"I faked my malaise, sweet lady, for revenge and to escape my father's coercion. I began planning this while you were bathing my fevered brow. Even then, you were hard put to keep your hands off of me." He slipped his hand between her thighs and instantly her body responded to his touch. She tried to concentrate on what he was saying, but could not. The feelings he aroused within her tormented her, making her squirm.

"Tonight I succeeded in my revenge against the fiery vixen who made the whole thing possible," he declared triumphantly, his fingers sensually stroking. A fire exploded in her and she cried out, humiliated by the burning shudders of passion he inspired. She was unable to move away from his erotic touch.

"I allowed you to make as much of a fool of yourself as you once made of me," his voice was husky as she twisted beneath him.

"Don't," she begged, but it was as if she were molten clay in a sculptor's hands. She was going mad, driven insane by his stroking, and his head came down and his tongue danced inside her, exploring every soft recess. He waited until her kittenish moans became part of each breath, then moved his lips to her breasts. His tongue curled around one throbbing nipple, tugging it gently with his teeth until he decided the other deserved equal attention. His fingers continued to inflict exquisite torment, bringing her to the brink of release then retreating, steadily multiplying her need. "Males mark their territories, princess, and every delicious inch of you shall know my touch," he promised thickly as his mouth and hands explored her fully. He freed her wrists but instead of pushing him away, her hands moved across his shoulders and down his back.

She welcomed him as he brought her over the edge, his body pressing hers down upon the soft mattress. Her muscles contracted in involuntary spasms as he thrust inside her. She clung to him, responding to his possession and meeting it on equal terms. She heard him groan something unintelligible as she arched against him and her nails raked his shoulders as his fingers entwined in her hair.

They lay panting. She could feel his heart pounding as the rapture drained away and realization of his sensual power over her returned to taunt her. Dazed, she listened to the thundering beat of their hearts. Abruptly, he rolled away from her and off the bed, reaching for his banjan and jerking it on. Like a stalking lion he began to pace, darting looks at her, his expression mirroring disbelief.

"There were no losers here." He raked one hand through his unruly hair, fighting some inner battle that she didn't comprehend. His silver glance was accusatory, as if he thought her guilty of eluding some trap he had set. Was she supposed to have fought him? How could she not respond to a man who erotically aroused her body even as his mind condemned her?

Nick turned away from her, cursing himself for his feelings. He actually felt guilty for his vengeful attempt to humiliate. From the beginning, she had bested him at every turn and she had just unwittingly done it again.

He had intended to show her how completely he could dominate her, but he had not dominated her at all. It was he, who had become the willing supplicant in a primitive battle that produced only victors. She was the daughter of a man he despised with all of his being yet she flamed his senses like no other and held him captive with her almost child-like innocence and her uninhibited responses in bed. He had used his time to gain her confidence and trust, intending to use her own feelings against her, but it was he who suffered. It would kill him to let her go and never experience again what she had just given to him.

He walked back to the bed, his mouth set in grim lines as she cringed away from him, covering her nakedness with the sheets. "Do you think I am moved by that frightened act?" he gritted. "How quickly you forget that you are an untamed wildcat." Jerking away his robe, he pressed his fingers to the reddened scratches she had made on his shoulders. "Look at these, Lady Benton," he demanded. "I introduced your body to passion and it will always respond to me as it did tonight. You were crazed for my touch and it will always be so!" He watched her bite her lip in agitation, her eyes refused to meet his gaze, her fiery hair was a mass of long tangles which made her look like a tawny tigress. He felt a twinge of guilt that his angry words had hurt her and that he had not the courage to admit that he had been crazed to touch her and that she had introduced him to a passion he had never experienced with another woman. He almost shook his head to rid himself of the idea and plunged on further in demoralizing her. "No matter how we look at this situation. We are legally wed and will remain so. After tonight, I'm inclined to think it won't be so terrible to continue our relationship." Again the guilt returned when she did not speak and he lost his temper. "Do you think you have a choice?"

Christina raised her chin and condemned him with her green-blue eyes, glittering with a fiery light. "I will not be used by you or any other man," she said with a strong determination. "I will tell Sir Albert that I—"

"No you won't!" he raged, stunned that she would still try to defy him. "I'll double whatever my father paid you to go along with him in this farce." He strode across the room, disappearing for a few minutes into his bedroom but returning before Christina had gathered her wits enough to attempt an escape. He held out a soft doeskin bag. "Consider this the first installment, madam, and there is plenty more where that came from." He threw the bag onto the bed.

"I will leave you, Nick." She recoiled from the gold coins which fell from the bag and scattered across the bed. Would he pay her like some harlot? Insult her with gold for services rendered? He despised her, yet desired her as well. He intended to salve his own conscience by treating her like a tart because he could not suppress his own needs. Contempt shimmered in her eyes as she jerked on the sheets and swept the coins onto the floor. "You don't have enough gold to buy me."

His savage oath cut through the tension in the room. "By God, we shall see about that. My father is a rich man, Christina, but I have enough wealth to satisfy even a Bristol's needs!" He leaned across the bed and took both of her hands, gripping her fragile wrists while glaring at her with dark fathomless eyes. "You are bonded to me as legally as the men whose papers my father holds—though your servitude shall last for a lifetime. It is too late for this marriage to be annulled and too soon to know if you have conceived as my father decreed. But, we *will* fulfill our obligation," he threatened. "And I will enjoy every minute of the trying as shall you."

"No!" She tried to pull out of his grasp, appalled. "Why? Why don't you go back to your ship? There is nothing to hold you here."

"You highly underestimate yourself, Tina." He laughed down at her pale face. "Marriage to you shall not be the ordeal I first believed it would be. I shall not worry that you shall pine away for me while I am at sea or reject my lovemaking when I return. I will please my father by siring the Benton heir and I will even keep Larkhollow running smoothly. I have discovered that marriage to you agrees with me."

This last might have been pleasing had not his tone been so cold, his eyes so unfeeling. All breath left her body. "You are mad! You cannot keep me here against my will."

"Do you doubt it?" He came down on the mattress and pinned her beneath him.

"Leave me alone, you brute!" she cried, struggling ineffectually. "Why are you doing this to me?"

"Calm down, my love. Nothing has changed." He held her firmly but made no attempt to do anything but gain her full attention. "This is a perfectly suitable arrangement for us both. You have nothing to lose and everything to gain. A fine home, plenty of money, a respected title and a man who knows how to give you the pleasure you demand."

"You're insufferable! Everything has changed!" Angry tears rolled down her cheeks. "You are not the man I wanted. You are not my hus—" But he was her husband! The acknowledgment lodged like ice in her chest. Only a short time ago, *she* had seduced *him*. She had almost told him that she loved him. "I cannot believe this has happened. You were so polite, so charming, so kind. I actually liked you. Nicholas was—"

"I am Nicholas and Nicholas is me," he stated, wiping her tears with the back of his hands, but still not letting her go. "You made love to me tonight, Tina. Me with all of my faculties. You must see that it is me that you want," he reminded gently, not without some sarcasm. "As I recall you said that you wanted to belong to me, that you were empty without me."

She could not deny that she had said exactly that and more. She had to think. How could she live with a man whom she both loved and hated? "You still believe I was part of this marriage scheme from the beginning, don't you?"

"Does it matter?" The marauding eyes that were inches from her own became shuttered. "You did not escape my retribution and for me, it was enough."

"I will leave you as soon as I can, whenever I am free of the hold you have on me. I shall never belong to you, Nick! Your gold, your child, your family name, none of them will make me completely yours!"

His fingers bit into her shoulders as his mouth descended. "You are mine," he vowed against her lips, rolling to the side but clasping her to him with both arms wrapped around her. "My touch will always make you mine. I will operate from here from now on. It will comfort me to know that your sweet body will be waiting for me when my ship is moored in the cove."

Her surprise made him smile. "There is a perfect natural harbor nearby and my men have always known that they could meet up with me here if we became separated. Why do you think I wanted to leave London so soon?

"I have some unfinished business in the city, so you will have some time alone to resign yourself to this situation as my father so kindly advised *us* on board the *Monique*."

"You are despicable!" She struggled futilely against him but he held her tightly until she was exhausted. He wrapped his arms and legs around her, warming her cold flesh, cradling her stiff limbs until a long time later, they relaxed and she shifted pliantly to rest. "You are mine, my Tina, and I will prove it if it takes me a lifetime," he whispered into the silky scented flame of her hair, but her lashes had already fallen to her wet cheeks. She was asleep and did not hear his words spoken in a softer tone. The promise was lost in the veiled night, drifted away to dissipate in the gauzy mists of darkness.

Chapter Ten

"I COMMEND YOU, NICHOLAS," SIR ALBERT complimented, watching as Nick placed the leather-bound packet containing his crew's papers into the inside pocket of his coat. "Your loss of memory put me off guard—as was your plan?"

"It was," Nick agreed, intense gray eyes locking fiercely on his father's face. "You should have informed your servants to guard against my arrival." He gave his bulging pocket a triumphant pat. "If you were anyone else but my father—I'd—I'd—"

"I am aware of that." Sir Albert didn't need to hear the rest of the sentence. "Your wife? Did you inform Christina that you have been in full possession of your senses all along?"

"She knows," Nick gritted through clenched teeth. "Was there anything else, Lord Benton?"

"You haven't harmed her?" Sir Albert inquired in a tight voice. "She has not suffered for something which was not of her doing?"

Tension gathered force in the room, stretching tautly between the two men until finally, Nick expelled his breath. "As I recall, you stated the like once before," he acknowledged begrudgingly, striding to a chair and sitting down in a posture of frigid resignation. "Last time, I did not listen, but this time I'll hear it all from beginning to end. You needn't fear for Christina. She is well." The admission seemed to gall him.

Sir Albert nodded, hiding his relief by turning away and pouring them each a large glass of claret from the crystal decanter on his desk. He crossed the room, handed one glass to Nick, then took his seat in an opposite chair.

"How much?" Nick demanded. "How much did you give her? I plan to repay every pound, do you hear me? Every damned shilling!"

"I paid *her* nothing," Sir Albert said quietly. "Christina married you solely to keep her father from selling the roof from over her grandparents' heads. Upon your marriage, Benjamin Bristol released the deed of their estate to me in exchange for membership in my club and certain properties of mine that he coveted. You see, Christina's grandparents, George and Caroline Harris, are old friends of mine, or rather my father's. Bristol was planning an alliance between Christina and a known lecher, old enough to be her father. George had once done my father a great favor, saved him from a disastrous business venture, and I was only too happy to repay

the debt. George Harris is a proud man and
would never have asked for help for himself. He
was desperate when he came to me for assistance in preventing Christina's marriage to one
of society's worst. I saw it as a chance to solve
my problems with you and approached Bristol
with a better offer. He sold his daughter for a
solid position in society and a seafaring vessel
which he needs to resume trade with New South
Wales. You know what cargo he generally carries. I regret my part in assisting his sleazy
endeavors, but I will never regret saving a dear
girl like Christina from a terrible fate."

"Damn!" Nick shouted, slamming his glass
down on the table beside his chair and jumping
up to pace across the room. "You—" he clenched
his fists, his jaw working but emitting no words.
Sir Albert watched as Nick fought an inner
battle with his emotions and remained silent
until Nick's shoulders slumped and he moved to
the fireplace to stare into the empty grate. "I was
ready to destroy him before you—" He paused,
torn by conflicting thoughts. "Christina is another of his victims. All this time I thought I had
married a money grubbing little slut, the daughter of a man I despise." He turned stricken eyes
on his father. "When I think of that beautiful—
that tiny innocent—" The emotional impact of
his own feelings shocked him and it showed on
his face. Seeing the knowing gaze of the earl, an
unwilling smile slowly lifted the corners of his
mouth. "So, father, I admit that your choice of a
woman was good. I resent how you accomplished it, but I want my wife. Do you realize

what position that puts me in? What this does to my—" he stopped himself, then continued in another vein. "I thought to pay for whatever it cost you to gain her consent. I would not have a wife I had not purchased myself." He moved to the table and downed his drink in one gulp. "It turns out that I want a woman who has good reason to hate me. She probably hates all of us, you, me, and her father. We have all used her, manipulated her for our own purposes." He glared at his father and shook his head.

"What will you do?" Sir Albert asked.

"I don't know," Nick replied, staring into space, pulled apart by his plans for revenge and his feeling for Christina. "I have vowed to kill a man whose daughter shall wear my name to her grave." A long silence fell between them until Nick burst out, "I won't give her up, I can't, not after—" He paused again, staring at the ceiling before returning his gaze to Sir Albert. "From beginning to end this affair has brought nothing but grief. Father, you have no idea what you have done. If Michael hadn't— Perhaps, I could stomach— Of all women, why Christina Bristol?"

"Tell me, Nicky." Sir Albert was fast becoming as agitated as his son. There was far more going on here than the marriage he had arranged between Nick and Christina. He stood up and went to Nick, demanding, "Why do you speak of Michael now? His name has always been between us up until today, unspoken, but there—always there."

Nick did not respond to his father's questions,

too deep in his own thoughts to consider how much he was disclosing without realizing it.

"If only Michael had not died." Nick's voice was thick with torment, his face deeply grooved with strain. "Damn Bristol to hell!"

"Why, Nicholas? Why do you despise Bristol so much?" Sir Albert realized he was catching his son at a rare moment when all his defenses were down. He knew it might not come again and he needed to know what had driven Nick away from him and into the dangerous life at sea posing as Nick Barker. He reached out and touched his son's arm, gripping the hard muscle and repeating the question. "Why can't you explain yourself to me?" he pleaded. "Don't you know how I wish I could change what has happened between us? You are my son, Nicholas. My only remaining offspring and I—" He swallowed, then plunged on, "Michael had only been given a few months to live. When he died I was almost grateful the end had been swift. I never blamed you. You must believe me." He continued in a harsh broken voice. "I didn't want you to go to London that day because I had only learned two days before that Michael was going to die. I wanted him close in case the end came sooner than the physicians had predicted, but I lost both my sons that day. Won't you tell me what has driven you away?"

"Oh God," the tortured whisper rasped from between Nick's colorless lips. He swayed as if he had just received a mortal blow. He turned and took his father by the arms, his strong fingers gripping like iron. "He was ill? He was dying?"

Nick's nostrils flared wildly and his eyes became the hard color of tempered steel.

Sir Albert returned his haunted look, wishing he could take the suffering he saw into himself. "It was his heart, Nicky. He would have died from the excitement of a race. The doctors told me any undue excitement would bring on a fatal attack. I—I wish now that I had told him to go to that race or told you why he couldn't. He would have enjoyed being with you, working the sails as you taught him. I should have gone with you boys instead of trying to hold on to someone I could not have. He would not have wanted to die a gasping invalid. The accident only speeded the inevitable."

Sir Albert felt the shudders that coursed through his son's hard body. He looked up and saw that Nick was no longer standing in the study but was back in some other time and place, recalling something so terrible he had kept it inside himself for years. Nick didn't notice when his father guided him to a couch and sat down beside him, taking his hand and gripping it fiercely as the words started coming, the poison spilling out from the invisible wound Nick had carried for years.

"Michael and I were on our way to London when another carriage came up beside ours. The owner looked wealthy and the horses were magnificent. He called to our driver that he knew us and wanted to speak to us about something and Cyrus stopped. Before we knew what was happening, they—there were men in the coach and one of them fired a pistol at Cyrus, killing him instantly. Outriders appeared and one of them ripped open the door and grabbed Michael and began shaking him. I threw myself at him, but the others dragged me off and they all started laughing. The leader opened the door and got out of the carriage. I'll never forget his face, never—" His voice trailed off as memory took over and Nick returned completely to that long ago day of horror. He almost didn't feel his father touch him and beg him to continue to tell him everything.

Nick was *there*. Watching Michael being held before the huge beefy man in the garish brocade coat who stood outside the large carriage. The men began removing Michael's clothing as Nick struggled against the arms of the men who held him back. Tears streamed down his face as he saw his young brother faint from terror when the men lifted him into the coach. He screamed at them, but his frustrated rage swiftly turned to horror when the gaudily dressed leader followed Michael's unconscious body into the coach then quickly pushed it back out again. "The puny runt has expired from the excitement," he announced and his cold eyes came to rest on Nick, his disgusted expression turning to a meaningful leer.

Revulsion sickened in Nick as the men began pulling at his clothes as moments before they had pulled at Michael's. "Older than I like them, but a nice shape for all that," the gravelly voice of his tormentor decreed, and his lascivious smile became broad as Nick was dragged toward the coach. Before he could be forced inside a loud bellow erupted from the hillside and a shot rang out from behind the trees. Nick was pushed to the ground as the outriders mounted their horses and the driver sprang to the seat of the carriage to speed its pederastic occupant out of harm's way.

"It was Jackson," Nick said, remembering how the huge barrel-chested man had helped him dress, heard his tale of misery and much later took him home. "I just couldn't tell you what had happened to Michael. What they wanted to do to me. That man was Benjamin Bristol. Years later, I recognized him and knew that someday I would destroy him for killing my brother. I was too ashamed to say anything to anyone—Jackson agreed that it would do no good to tell you how Michael had died so we set up the accident. We rolled the carriage off a cliff and when Cyrus and Michael were found, no one questioned that it wasn't an accident.

"Every man, woman, or child I can buy away from Bristol or help escape from one of his slave ships is my way of avenging my brother. I would have brought Bristol to his financial knees, presented myself and let him know who it was that had destroyed him. I planned to kill him, but— how can I kill my wife's father?" The face which turned to the earl was full of torment, a son searching for answers from his father.

Sir Albert wrapped his arms around Nick, holding him tightly as they mourned together, bonded at last in their grief. When they finally recovered their control, they spent hours talking. It was a new beginning for them. "We brought a lot of pain to the other by withholding information, my son." Sir Albert moved away to pour more wine and Nick nodded as he waited for his father to rejoin him.

"What an atrocious mess." Nick placed his elbows on his knees, running one palm down his face as he stared sightlessly at the floor. "Each of us doing what we thought was best for the other and thereby creating a situation wounding us both. I could have killed you for forcing me into marriage with that degenerate's daughter. However, you were right in your estimation that I would want her. I did from the minute she took aim at my heart with an ancient pistol she had hoped would protect her from me. On board my ship, she was magnificent and since then, I've come to know her. She is everything you tried to tell me she was, but I've been too blinded by my own quest for revenge to allow myself to believe it. How Bristol could have fathered a woman like that is beyond me." He stood up and looked down at the earl with a querying look. "I would give her the deed to her grandparents' estate. Do you agree?"

"Completely." Sir Albert went to his desk and pulled out the document. "With my blessing, Nicholas."

"Hopefully, I can use this to gain her trust. She has good reason to hate me."

Sir Albert could well imagine what his son had done when confronting his wife with his faked amnesia. "But, if you treat her well from now on, I am sure she will not long resist you. I am quite proud of how well I have chosen. Dare I hope that your growing affection for your wife will result in an heir?"

"I would not pursue that issue if I were you." Nick gave his father a pointed look that would have withered a lesser man, but brought a surge of guilty color to Sir Albert's cheeks.

"My apologies to both you and Christina." Sir Albert cleared his throat and saluted Nick with his wine goblet. "I never really wanted to interfere. From now on, what you do with your wife is not my concern."

"A wise decision, father, but tell me," Nick replaced his empty glass on the table and walked across the room to retrieve his riding cape. "Out of curiosity, if you were me, what would you do?"

Sir Albert shook his head. "Haven't you noticed that I make it a point never to interfere in someone else's business?"

Nick looked astounded then burst out laughing. "How could I have thought otherwise?" He walked to the desk and picked up the Harris deed, inserting it in his coat with the bonds-papers. "I carry a wealth of proof on my person."

He patted his bulging pocket, grinning at the older man. "Since you do not interfere in the personal affairs of others, especially your son's, you won't be there to witness me on my knees in front of my wife, begging her to forgive me."

"Would it help if I joined you?"

"Only one of us Bentons need make a total fool of himself," Nick said. "But on second thought, if I do need you, I'll send word." They exchanged a look of mutual understanding, then walked across the room together, pausing at the door for a short embrace.

"Wish me luck," Nick muttered, wryly, "I'm going to need it."

Chapter Eleven

CHRISTINA HEARD HER HUSBAND'S FOOTSTEPS echoing in the Great Hall, coming closer to the salon with each long stride. When Nick inquired after her whereabouts from a footman, she hid her uneasiness by busying herself with the long-stemmed roses she had recently cut from the conservatory, arranging them decoratively in a tall crystal vase. The sound of his footsteps and voice made her shiver. Her short reprieve was over. His day in London had not provided her with enough time to sort out her feelings and resign herself to the bondage she had been forced into.

"Christina?" His soft pronouncement of her name as he entered the room brought up her head. Dressed in a pale ivory gauze gown embroidered at the neckline and hem with green silk that matched her eyes, she was unaware that she gave an appearance of such fragile femininity that he could barely control his reaction to her. She had the delicate beauty of the flowers she held in her hands and he wanted to fall at her feet and beg her forgiveness, then sweep her into his arms. Her apprehensive turquoise eyes tore at his heart.

"You have completed your business?" she asked in a calm voice that told him nothing of her feelings, hiding the resentment she had harbored against him since his imperious announcement that she had no choice but to remain with him as his wife. She wished he didn't look so exceptionally handsome in a gray whipcord jacket, cream colored doeskin breeches that outlined his muscular thighs, and shiny Hessian boots hugging his calves. His great coat of navy blue hung carelessly about his broad shoulders, adding to his overpowering masculine appearance.

"Yes," he said as he casually slid the coat from his shoulders and flung it over the back of a chair.

"Oh," she commented, hoping her tone conveyed a total lack of interest. She returned her attention to her flowers, carefully cutting a few leaves from the thorny stems, intending to ignore him, but Nick came to her and carefully removed the flowers from her hands. He drew her with him to a low chaise arranged before the fireplace.

"I must speak with you Tina and I—I don't quite know where to begin." He waited for her to sit down, then shocked her by going down on one knee in front of her, taking both of her small hands into his. Wasn't this what he had done last evening before making a fool of her? What did he want?

Looking into his face, she was confused by the beseeching soft glow she saw in his gray eyes. His expression was so different from the last time she had seen him. Her eyes, full of suspicion, darkened to the color of jade, her mouth went dry. "Is something wrong?"

"Yes, everything is wrong," was his reply as he continued to hold her fingers trapped between his palms, despite her efforts to remove them. A pained expression furrowed his brow. His enigmatic answer increased her confusion and she renewed her efforts to free her hands. "Please, Tina. Listen to me for a moment."

She sat very still. He seemed almost begging for her attention. Her curiosity grew with each passing second. "Certainly," she agreed, willing herself not to be affected by the feel of his large hands squeezing hers, his thumbs gently stroking across the tops.

"I went to London to confront my father," he began, then getting no reaction from her went on. "I misjudged you from the beginning. I did not know of your grandparents, nor that you were as much a victim as I in the arrangements for our marriage. I beg your forgiveness, Christina, for the way I have treated you and the cruel things I have said." Letting go of her hands, he reached into his coat and extracted a thick sheaf of parchment. "This is for you. It is the deed to

Briar Park, and the least I could do to make things up to you."

Incredulously, Christina read the document, not believing that Nick would give her the deed with no strings attached. He had to have some motive. "Of course," she stated bitterly when she finally realized what he must have set out to accomplish in London. "You bought this away from your father. Your pride dictates that your wife will not be bound to another in any way. Isn't that true?"

Stung by the malice in her tone, Nick shook his head. "No, I did not. It belongs to you, a gift from the Bentons. My father and I agreed that Briar Park should be yours. You can inform your grandparents that they need worry themselves no longer. I know you have reason not to trust me, Christina, but relegating me to the same low position as your father is unfair. I will not keep my wife by blackmail. My father was desperate and felt his actions were justified. We no longer have an estrangement between us, but have reached an accord."

"I am happy for you, Nicholas," she replied in an emotionless voice. He was right, she did not trust him. "Did you also manage to regain possession of your crew's bonds?"

"Yes," he replied, slightly smiling. "My father will no longer interfere in what is necessarily my personal business." The autocratic pronouncement grated on her, but she covered her reaction.

"Then we are both free to go our separate ways," Christina blithely decreed. "Since I hold

the deed to Briar Park and you have the papers,
neither of us need abide by the vows we took
aboard the *Monique*. Since you were not aware
of signing the marriage certificate, it will be a
simple matter for us to have this marriage dissolved."

The hopeful light died in his eyes. She envied
the firm control he had over his emotions for his
voice was infinitely patient as he continued.
"Our marriage was quite legal," he declared. "I
have accepted you as my wife and would be
grateful if you would accept that I am your
husband."

"Why?" She leaned back, not bothering to hide
her bitterness. Nick abruptly jumped back to his
feet. As she had suspected, he was not able to
keep up his solicitous posture very long.

"Why!" he expounded, a vein throbbing out of
control at his temple. "Because I want you,
damn it! Besides, you may have already conceived my child, Lady Benton. You had best
consider that!" Not giving her the chance to
consider anything, he rounded on her, "How can
you ask why? You know why!"

"Of course, the Benton heir," Christina retorted. "How could I have forgotten the purpose of
our marriage. So, nothing has truly changed,
has it Nicholas? All that has happened is that
you no longer consider me such a despicable
candidate for the motherhood of your child or the
viscountess of Larleigh." Ruthlessly, she went
on. "I was of the opinion that you detested the
thought of touching a Bristol. What happened,
Nick, can you accept me in your bed, since you

now have all control over me in your own hands?"

Nick looked as if he didn't know how to proceed and Christina didn't know whether she should be proud that she had so perplexed him or frightened about what he might do next. "Then I may leave you, Nick?" she prompted. "You shall not attempt to hold me to this marriage?"

His answer was exactly what she knew it would be. A loud, forceful, unequivocal negative. "Then I repeat," she declared sarcastically. "Nothing has changed. Instead of being under the dominion of my father or yours, I am now under my husband's. Was there anything else you wished to discuss?"

"You frustrating, little vixen!" Nick burst out, jamming his hands into the pockets of his trousers in order to keep from shaking her. "I told you I want you. I've gone down on my knees for no other woman save you, but if you were expecting more, you will be sadly disappointed. I won't castrate myself for you or any other woman."

"There is no need to be crude." She stood up from the chaise and smoothed her skirts over her hips. "I have asked nothing of you, Nick, but the same does not hold true of you. You have asked me to give up everything. Hand myself over to you, body and soul. You speak of nothing but your lust for my body. You admit that you want me as if you are offering me some lofty favor for which I should be eternally grateful.

"You may keep your fine words, Nicholas Alexander Benton and I shall keep what is mine." Pretending a nonchalance she was far from feeling, she walked away from him and began gathering the roses left on the table into a large basket. At the moment, arranging flowers was the farthest thing from her mind, but she needed something to do while she made her next request. "I would like to visit my grandparents. I was not allowed to visit or communicate with them in any way after my father sent me to that school in Spain. I thought I might do so while you join your crew on the *Libertine Lady*. I presume that is your plan."

When he didn't immediately answer, she glanced over her shoulder. He was staring at her as if she had gone mad, a diabolical gleam in his eyes and a determined expression etched on the rugged, granite features of his face. Initially confronted with Nicholas at his charming best, she was now faced with Nick Barker at his arrogant worst. Her fingers rushed to replace the flowers in the basket and she pricked her fingers on a protruding thorn. She let out a startled cry, then in a small whisper exclaimed, "I must see to having this bandaged." She was about to run from the room when her husband's steely arm caught her around her waist and she was swung off the floor. His other arm came beneath her knees and he carried her out of the room, striding purposefully toward the grand staircase, stifling the protesting words she meant to utter with the savage look on his face.

He bounded up the stairs with her in his arms and walked into his half of their suite, dumping her down in the center of his large brocade-covered bed before crossing to the washstand for a cloth. He came back swiftly, reached for her injured hand, and wiped away the small trickle of blood on her finger.

"Hardly worth calling for a physician." He threw the cloth back in the general direction of the washstand and his grip on her wrist became as hard as a metal manacle. "I recall an innocent Spanish princess putting me off the track by injuring herself on a nail. Was this another poor attempt to forestall me?"

Her eyes grew wide as he shrugged out of his coat and waistcoat and pulled his shirt from his pants. "This is one place we speak the same language. You might not believe my words, but my body doesn't lie and neither does yours." He laughed at her attempt to hit him with her free arm, trapping it and the other together in front of her while he joined her on the bed, straddling her with one knee on either side of her. He forced her arms to her sides and effectively held them between his thighs as he swiftly stripped to the waist.

Knowing her body would betray her, desperate to stop him, she made her voice coldly devoid of feeling. "Yes," she agreed. "I can not deny that I enjoy your lovemaking, but you have no more than my body. If you were honest, you would admit that lust is all you bring to this marriage or want from it!"

A long interval of silence followed her statement as they stared at one another, testing the resolve to be found in the other's eyes. "That's not true," Nick said in almost a whisper. He let her go, cursing softly under his breath as he swung his legs over her body and sat up on the edge of the bed, not looking at her. "What is it you want from me, Tina?" The question contained a wealth of anger, frustration, and something else—some emotion Christina could not define. Pain? Had her rejection hurt him? No, the only thing she had wounded was his colossal pride that demanded she be willing, that she surrender herself without holding back anything. How could she tell him that she wanted love? A return of the love she had felt for him before he humiliated her. Did she still love him? She desired him, but maybe that was all there was between them.

"I want my freedom," she stated firmly, afraid to move lest he touch her again and prove to them both that she could never be free of him. She saw the already tense muscles of his back stiffen and his hands clench into fists. Yet, he did not confront her with the anger she was sure was on his face. His response, when it came after a long silence, sounded like defeat.

"I will agree to your going to visit your grandparents, but I— You belong to me, Tina. Go to Briar Park and think about what you would be throwing away if you persist in this vein. Sometimes I forget how very young you are. I am a man, Tina, and last night you came to me as a woman, a woman who knew what she wanted and was honest enough to take it.

"I shall be returning to London in the morning. If you wish, we can travel part way together." He picked up his shirt and drew it on, not bothering to tuck it into his breeches as he strode toward the bedroom door. "If you decide that you can bear my company long enough for the journey to town, I shall be leaving early."

Christina did not move from her position on his bed. There had been a distressing bleakness in his voice that bewildered her. She had not thought he cared enough about her to be hurt by anything she said to him. Now, she was afraid that she might have misjudged him, as he had always misjudged her. He had come back to tell her that he realized she had been innocent all along, that he wanted her. What had she done, but throw his peace offering back in his face? When he had brought up her age and declared she was no longer behaving as a woman, it had hurt, hurt deeply. Perhaps he was right. Would a mature woman have thrown away her chance to be Nicholas Benton's lover? Would she have wounded his pride, scorned his apology, ridiculed him for wanting her?

Her limbs were stiff and numb as she got up from the bed and walked slowly across the room to the connecting door. She entered her half of the suite, closing the door behind her, knowing that she was also closing off one chapter of her life and beginning the next. What she did not know was whether or not she would be any happier than she had been before. In two days she would be in the welcoming arms of her grandparents, but the knowledge gave her far less pleasure than she would have thought. She already felt the loss of a pair of masculine arms which had given her more pleasure than she had ever known. It was too late to call him back and it was more than likely he would not come even if she did.

"Oh Nick," she sighed, tears rolling softly down her cheeks. "If only you had said that you loved me, loved me as I love you. I would adore bearing your son, but not if that is all that you want from me, an heir and a female body to warm your bed."

When the family-crested carriage rolled out of the gates early the next morning, both occupants were coldly distant, submerged in their own disconsolate thoughts. Christina stared out of the carriage window, aware with every nerve in her body of the silent man seated across from her. Minutes became hours and the uncomfortable silence became an increasingly insurmountable barrier between them until finally, at the outskirts of London, Nick cleared his throat and sat up straight in his seat. "I would like to think we could part without rancor, Tina."

"Are we parting?" Christina asked in a strangled voice. The lamenting green shimmer of her eyes was taken by Nick as despair that was caused by her forced involvement with him.

He clasped his hands together until the knuckles turned white. "Only for a short time." He looked uncomfortable, then blurted, "All the things I said to you when I thought you could not understand were true and when I found you had understood every word, I felt like a fool. I said a lot of things in anger, Tina. When I thought you were some scheming wench, bent on bleeding my family fortunes dry, it galled me even more to discover that I still wanted you in whatever way I could get you. You may think that you are the only one who has suffered through this affair, but I can assure you that you have inflicted wounds that will not heal for a very long time."

"I—I don't understand," she returned, feeling as if she had lost something infinitely precious without knowing it had been hers ever.

"I realize that," Nick said, a resigned finality in his tone that made Christina want to throw herself into his arms and beg him to tell her, explain what was making her feel as if a great chasm had opened between them and he would not be there to save her when she fell into it.

"You know what I do aboard the *Libertine Lady*, Tina. I must ask you to keep that knowledge to yourself. If anyone learns that Nick Barker and Nicholas Benton are the same man, you will be a widow far sooner than you might think. Perhaps that would suit you. I can only hope not."

"No," she answered quickly, appalled that he would think she might wish him dead. "I would never wish that, Nicholas. I promise to tell no one what I know about you. You must believe me. I admire your efforts to save those poor souls. I have nothing but contempt for men who would sell others for profit."

"Even when that man is your father?"

"I have far more reason to despise my father than you do, Nick. His immorality does not surprise me and I am ashamed that his blood runs in my veins. You recall the feelings you had when you discovered that I was a Bristol? I often feel that way about myself."

His sudden movement took her by surprise and in seconds he had joined her on her side of the coach. His fingers were gentle as he took hold of her chin. "I don't ever want to hear you say that again," he growled. "You are not like him. Promise me you won't denounce yourself because your name was Bristol. Promise me."

"Al—all right," she stammered, staring into the angry silver eyes probing her face. Before she could utter another word, his mouth was on hers, sealing the vow he had forced her to make with a soul-rendering possession that knocked all breath from her lungs. She was crushed to his chest, every hard muscle of his body proclaiming his maleness. He kissed her like a man who believed he might never do so again, drinking in the honeyed sweetness of her lips, giving back a tormented promise with every thrust of his demanding tongue. Her heart was pounding louder and louder, her soul soaring with the freedom that comes from fulfillment when he let her go.

The carriage had stopped and he opened the door and jumped to the ground below, leaving her alone. He stepped out of her sight, calling sharply to the coachman. "On to Yorkshire, Standish. See that the lady arrives safely."

Christina fell back on the seat as the carriage lurched ahead. She leaned her head out of the window but there was no sight of Nick. He had already stepped off the street and disappeared inside one of the soot-covered buildings of the waterfront. Tears pooled in her eyes and she saw nothing of London as the carriage drove swiftly onwards, north to the moors of her childhood. North to Briar Park and the people she loved and who loved her.

Chapter Twelve

IT WAS WELL AFTER MIDNIGHT WHEN CHRISTI-
na's carriage stopped before the gates to her
grandparents' estate in Yorkshire. The looming
black shadow of the house waited silently until
the gates were opened and the carriage rolled to
a halt on the damp stones of the cobbled drive.
Christina gazed eagerly out of the window, smiling as the thick mist wetted her face. She listened to the sounds of the Northlands, was
comforted by the wailing night wind that rushed
the moors surrounding Briar Park and felt at
peace for the first time since leaving Nick behind in London.

No light could be seen from within the half-
timbered Tudor house and she guessed that her
grandparents were already abed. She stepped

down from the carriage, not waiting for assistance from the footman, and ran lightly to the huge oak doors. She raised the heavy brass knocker and waited for old MacDougald to answer her summons. She couldn't wait to see his leathery Scots face crease into a smile of pleasure at the sight of her.

"Who goes?" She heard his irritated burr from behind the door.

"It's Miss Christina, MacDougald. I've come home," she shouted happily, making allowances for his one deaf ear. The doors swung open, creaking loudly on old hinges, and then she was standing in the dim halo of light from MacDougald's candle. With a gasp of welcome, the old man gave her a clumsy hug while tears of happiness streamed down her face. The elderly gentleman had been with the Harris family too long to observe the usual respectful distance between servant and mistress. Besides he had always held a great affection for Christina.

"Ach, lassie, how long hae it been? I thought I'd die of old age afore I beheld your bonnie face agae." He held her out at arm's length. "'Tis sad, indeed, that ye grandmam couldna' see what a proper lady ye hae become. She worried for ye in that Papist foreign land away from those who love ye." He seemed unaware of the effect his words were having on Christina.

"I don't understand, MacDougald. Is grandmama not here?"

"Ach, lassie, dinna the messenger tell ye why ye must come?" MacDougald eyed her strangely, a sympathetic frown between his bushy white brows. Christina felt a sudden fear, a deadly cold apprehension creeping up her spine.

"What messenger, MacDougald? Aren't my grandparents upstairs?" She started for the staircase, intending to assure herself that they were peacefully upstairs in their rooms. MacDougald took hold of her arm before she had placed one foot on the bottom step.

"Nae, child. The fever took ye grandmam yesterday morn and ye grandfather is haer gone. We sent the messenger yester eve and I was think'n ye came to his call. The squire's been askin' for ye, lassie. Every moment since ye grandmam passed on."

"Oh no." Christina swallowed the welling hysteria mounting inside her. "Grandmama can't be dead . . . and grandpapa! He is not going to die. Don't say he is going to die!"

MacDougald helped her into the drawing room and gently pushed her down on a chair, leaving her side only long enough to fetch her a glass of brandy. "Dinna fash yeself lassie," he said in a gruff voice. "They both lived long lives and without his lady, ye grandfather would only wither away. They were so happy when they heard that you were wed to a fine mon. It was a great comfort to them to know that the Bentons would be alookin' after ye proper. Ye hae a husband now, lassie, so don't be griev'n for the squire who needs to be wie his lady on the other side."

"The physician, MacDougald," she demanded after swallowing the burning spirits. "Is he attending my grandfather now?"

"N'ere he could do, lassie. If ye are ready, I'll be taking ye up now. We thought he would pass on before ye arrived. He keeps sayin' there is somethin' that needs tellin'. It's keepin' him here, lassie, so go to him and listen. It's time for the auld mon to let go of this life."

Fighting down her grief, Christina followed the elderly Scot up the stairs, grateful that the darkened corridors hid her tear-streaked cheeks and sorrowing eyes. She needed to be in control when she spoke with her grandfather. Wiping away the tears with the heel of her hand, she was determined to be strong for him.

A single candle flamed at his bedside as she entered his room and took a seat near his head. She could barely discern his features, his white hair and pale skin blended with the linen bedding. "Grandpapa?" she whispered, taking hold of one lifeless hand. "It's Christina. I'm here."

The weary lashes lifted and the burning blue eyes focused on her face. "No time, Tina—so much—you do not know—"

"Hush grandpapa. I know that you love me and that is all that need be said."

The harsh rasp of his uneven breathing had already told her that MacDougald was correct. Her grandfather was on his death bed and the end was coming soon. Her words seemed to anger him and he tried to pull his shoulders up on the pillows. "Listen to me, child. If I die before you know the truth, there is a letter in my desk which bears your name. Read it and do not judge me too harshly." He fell back on the pillows, breathing rapidly. His hands moved restlessly.

The agitation on his face frightened her and a deep foreboding crept into her heart. "I'm listening, grandpapa," she reassured, squeezing his cold fingers in encouragement.

"Elizabeth never knew child—nor my sweet Caroline," he bemoaned in an agonized voice. "It was my doing—all mine and that blackguard Bristol. The misfortunes of this family rest upon my shoulders and I shall pay for them soon." He closed his eyes, his breathing more rapid. Christina held his hand tightly as if she could transmit some of her young strength to her weakened grandfather. "Not you, Tina. No more will I let my own suffer—was my fear—my pride."

He stopped speaking and his breathing became so shallow that Christina was afraid that he had already taken his last breath. She leaned forward when his eyes fluttered open, his next words were a barely audible whisper though his grasp on her hand was so strong it was painful. "Forgive me, daughter. Please—forgive me, Elizabeth."

"I forgive you, papa," Christina said, quickly. He smiled weakly, then his grasp on her hand fell away and she knew he was gone. "I love you, papa," she choked out in a whisper, staring down at the beloved face. Tears dimmed her vision as MacDougald's strong, bony arms drew her away from the bed.

"Now, now, lassie. He's gone and will be happy and at rest now. Ye mustna grieve for him. We've a fire started in ye auld room and 'twill warm ye. I'll see to the squire now." He helped her down the hall and into her old bedroom. "The squire told me what to do and ye needna worry over it. I'll be sendin' one of the maids up to ye. Shall I send for ye husband? He should be wie ye."

"No!" Her tone was sharp and she softened it when she saw the startled expression on MacDougald's face. "He is out to sea. Thank you, MacDougald. If you will send for the vicar in the morning, he will help me make the necessary arrangements."

The funerals of Caroline and George Harris had been over for several days before Christina thought about her grandfather's last moments and the letter he had left for her. The day after his death she had sent word to Sir Albert and he had come to pay his respects at the funeral. Sadly, he informed her that he had been unable to locate his son and assumed that he had gone back to playing Nick Barker. She had assured Sir Albert that it did not matter and that he need not stay with her at Briar Park after the burials. She told him that she needed time alone and wanted to close the house herself.

When the solicitor had read the will and revealed that the Harris fortunes were meager, she was not surprised. Her father had obtained possession of all but the house and a few tenant farms. She arranged for the dismissal of most of the servants, leaving a skeleton staff to maintain the house and the immediate grounds. MacDougald promised to take charge, saying that he was too old to seek another position and too young to retire to a cottage. Christina had smiled slightly at his reference to being too young to retire, knowing that the gentleman was as old as her grandfather had been.

Sir Albert had returned to London but had contacted Annette, who had arrived by post chaise the next day. The formidable Mistress Harcourt had swept in and taken charge of the household, informing Christina that she was prepared to stay with her until she was ready to return to Larkhollow. Christina did not tell her that she had yet to decide if she wanted to return to her husband's home. She was unsure of her feelings toward him and needed time to make a decision about her future that could either bring her happiness or a sorrow even greater than that which she suffered over the loss of her grandparents. In three years time, she had lost every member of her family, lost her freedom and was afraid she might lose even more if she returned to Nick.

Her grandfather's study was oppressively dark, the thick velvet drapes keeping out the light, the heavy furniture of dark mahogany and somber oak. Christina breathed deeply of the familiar scents of leather and tobacco as she entered the room, closing the door behind her. She crossed to the desk and opened the middle drawer, immediately finding the letter her grandfather had left her atop a stack of papers. She lifted out the thick envelope and broke the seal with shaky fingers.

At first, she didn't understand the importance

of what she was reading, but when she finally understood what her grandfather had kept hidden for almost two decades, she knew why he had agonized with guilt before his death. The letter began with her name, a sentence requesting forgiveness although undeserved, then the words that seemed to leap off the page.

> . . . I did not approve of Elizabeth's alliance with Brian Tremayne, an American planter who would have taken my only child away from England to a place so far away that I feared I might never see her again. I schemed with my young new solicitor, Benjamin Bristol, to bring their relationship to an end.
>
> Young Tremayne was in England on business for his father and as soon as those matters were concluded he was bound to return to America. He wanted to marry Elizabeth immediately and take her back with him, but I persuaded them to wait a while longer since Elizabeth was but seventeen years old. Tremayne agreed to go home and get his affairs in order before returning months later to claim his bride.
>
> Not long after Tremayne sailed, Bristol brought the false news to Elizabeth that Tremayne's ship had gone down at sea. She was overcome with grief and revealed that she was carrying Tremayne's child. Bristol stepped forward with an offer of marriage. God forgive me that I did not reveal the truth to Elizabeth but encouraged her to

accept Bristol. Months later, Tremayne re-
turned as he had promised but I told him
that Elizabeth had no love for him and had
married Bristol. I said nothing about you
and implied that my daughter and her hus-
band were very happy. The haunted look of
betrayal on Brian Tremayne's face was a
picture I carried to my grave. For years I
feared he would contact Elizabeth for proof
of my explanation. As time passed and he
did nothing, my fear of discovery was di-
minished.

By the time you were born, Bristol had
begun to show his true colors, rejecting his
wife for the effete male lovers he preferred,
and staking claim on the funds I had en-
trusted to him as my financial advisor. If I
ever breathed a word of his treachery to
anyone he would have told Elizabeth and
Caroline how I had driven Brian away and I
could not live with their hatred—

The letter continued with further recrimina-
tions for the way he had betrayed both his
wife and daughter, plus the blackmail he had
endured for his involvement in the plot that
kept Elizabeth from her young lover Brian
Tremayne. He revealed the location of a sum of
money that he had saved for Christina's use in
case she wanted to locate her real father and
ended with Tremayne's location, Whispering
Willows Plantation near Richmond, Virginia.
The last words her grandfather had written
stayed in her mind long after she had finished

reading. "Go to Brian Tremayne, my dear Tina, tell him Elizabeth never stopped loving him and that you are the result of that love. My confession in this letter is proof that Benjamin Bristol has no further means to blackmail me or mine."

A day passed before Christina showed Annette the letter. After hours of impassioned pleading, Christina was able to convince Annette of the rightness of her trip to Virginia. Annette demanded that she be allowed to accompany Christina or she would notify Sir Albert and Nick and thus the trip might be prevented. "This is no mean voyage you are anticipating, my dear girl. You will not travel so far unescorted!" Christina had no choice, but was grateful that her friend and sometimes protector would be accompanying her.

Two weeks later, they were ready to depart for London on the first leg of their long journey to America. Their coachman was a new servant who had been hired by her grandfather shortly before his death and had offered to stay on until Christina returned to her own home. A spindly bearded man with emotionless muddy eyes, Christina was surprised at his courtesy. As Annette and she settled themselves in the opened landau, he turned on the driver's seat and kindly asked if he should start.

"Yes, Crandel, thank you," she nodded and they pulled out of Briar Park. Christina swallowed the ache in her throat as she left her childhood home. She knew that she would not return for a very long time, but would always remember the happy years spent here, her mother's smiling face, and finally the clouded memory of the unhappiness her grandfather had brought down upon them all. That last memory cast a heavy shadow upon the others. It would be a long time before she could bring herself to return to the heather-covered moors of Yorkshire.

"It is against my better judgment that you have not contacted your husband, Tina. He should be the one to accompany you to America." Annette interrupted Christina's morose thoughts as the iron gates closed behind them. "I am only agreeing with your plan for fear that you would go off alone. You must know how happy your husband will be to learn that you are not Bristol's daughter. As Nick Barker he has tried to ruin that vermin's immoral business, but with this new information he may no longer need to pose as a pirate. Surely, the blackmail Bristol has forced your grandfather to pay all these years is grounds for prosecution." The carriage made a sudden sharp turn which jostled both women. "Have a care, Crandel!" Annette intoned sharply when she had readjusted her bonnet. "Keep your thoughts on your driving."

"Certainly, madam," the coachman replied decorously, but both women missed the gleeful narrowing of his murky eyes. They made no comment when he flicked the whip to increase their speed, having no idea that he was far more anxious to reach London than they. The information he had just gained about the pirate, Nick Barker, would earn him a fine pouch of gold from his employer. Yes, Benjamin Bristol would pay highly to learn the identity of the man who plagued his ships.

"I fear that there would be little gained by telling the authorities how Bristol gleaned my family's fortune. Grandpapa freely gave him his power of attorney and with the marriage to my mother, her inheritance fell legally into his hands. Nick will not stop until Bristol is ruined," she reminded. "He has some personal vendetta, Annette. I think he planned to kill Bristol until his marriage to me. I will tell Nick that Bristol is not my father, but not until after I have met Brian Tremayne. Nick would not allow me to travel to America. He—he treats me like a child, a possession to be safely tucked away for him at Larkhollow."

"I am sure you are wrong," Annette argued, but Christina ignored her and continued.

"I am sure he is at sea by now. I shall book passage on a ship sailing for America and send word after my departure. Are you certain your Aunt Eloise will not mind having me for a guest until our ship departs?"

"Not in the least," Annette reassured. "She will be the envy of all of her friends when she tells them that the viscountess of Larleigh was a guest in her home."

After a few days in London, Nick proceeded to the secluded cove near Larkhollow to oversee the repairs of the *Libertine Lady*. After two weeks had passed and the ship was again seaworthy Nick returned to London and Larleigh

House. Christina had not yet returned from her visit to Yorkshire and Nick hoped his father might have received some word from her. Sir Albert had imparted the news of the Harrises' deaths and bluntly informed him that Christina did not want to see her husband yet and wanted more time to be alone to sort out her feelings. Nick waited a few more days then dispatched a man to Briar Park to check on Christina's welfare. The man returned with the information that the viscountess had left Yorkshire. Nick took a horse from his father's stable and rode to Larkhollow expecting to find her there, and needing to know how she fared, whether she was ready to see him or not. He had been stunned to learn that she had not returned to the estate. Changing horses, he immediately returned to London, but no one at Larleigh House had any new information about her whereabouts.

A week had passed and there was still no news of Christina. "Where the hell can she be?" Nick slammed his fist down on the rickety table inside his room at the "Dog and Bone," a waterfront boarding house.

"Your men will find her," Tony tried to sound reassuring. "It's only a matter of time."

"Ain't got time," Jackson growled with annoyance, taking a long swallow of ale, then brushing his sleeve over his mouth. "Not if we aim to catch ourselves another slaver. You said that your informant told you Bristol's ship was sailing with the tide."

Getting no response from his captain, Jackson

continued more forcefully. "Every day we're moored in London Harbor, we take the chance that the authorities will discover that our ship is the *Libertine Lady*. That drape of canvas would be easy to move from over her nameplate and the men are gettin' mighty edgy, I tell ya'."

"I'm not leaving London until I locate my wife," Nick glared at his mate, looking at Tony to find out if his new first officer felt the same way. Tony had volunteered to serve with them, tracking Nick to the "Dog and Bone." Proof of his friend's loyalty had come as a pleasant surprise after what had happened the last time they had encountered one another. It was true that his spies had told him that Bristol was about to move another cargo of "spirited" men, but he could not think of that now. Christina was all he thought about, all he cared about. Her disappearance had obliterated everything else and as the days passed with no further word, he was close to losing his mind. All he had learned was that she had been overheard to say she was going to London, but if she had, the city had swallowed her up without a trace. Not even the carriage or the driver who had served her could be found.

"Well, she's changed you, that's a fact!" Jackson decried sharply. "That woman has you so befuddled you've forgotten your oath to ruin Bristol. She's ruined you and all our plans as well."

"Watch what you say about my wife," Nick snapped angrily, clenching his fists. "None of what happened before was her doing. What am I

supposed to do? Leave her in God knows what
situation while I go off to sea?"

"It's better'n than rotting here!" Jackson un-
wisely continued his tirade, ignoring Tony's
frantic gestures for him to back off. "The
woman don't want you or she wouldn't have run
off. She's Bristol's brat and no mistake. Bet she's
told him who you are and they're laughing together over the trick she's pulled on you."

Nick leaped up from his chair, furiously
swinging his fist in a wide arc toward Jackson's
jaw. Tony moved just as quickly, grabbing hold
of Nick's arm and placing himself between the
two men, keeping Nick at bay with one stiff arm.
"Hold on!" he advised tersely. "This does no
good for any of us. Jackson, we've already
checked Bristol's place and Christina didn't go
there. Now, if you want to keep a tooth in your
mouth, quit talking jibberish."

Tony pushed Nick backward, steering him
back to his seat as he roughly gestured for
Jackson to sit down. "Let's keep our wits about
us," Tony instructed, ignoring the furious glare
between his two friends. "Here's how I see it.
Everything is being done that is humanly possible to find Lady Benton. Nick, your father
lives in London and can continue directing
the search. The agents will inform him as soon
as they have located her. We can't let a shipload
of men sail off to their doom without trying to
stop it. I say we go after the slaver, then come
back as swiftly as possible. By then, she will
probably have been found. I doubt anything
much has happened to her with that old woman

along as her chaperone. As I recall, that sharp-tongued lady would strike fear in the most stout-hearted of men."

Grudgingly, both Nick and Jackson had to admit the wisdom of Tony's words. "All right," Nick agreed after a long thoughtful pause. "Inform the crew that we sail in the morning. I'll just have to trust she's safe with Mistress Harcourt and hope my father can find her while we're gone."

"Agreed," Jackson acknowledged and stood up. "I'd best start spreadin' the word that the *Lady* will be sailing. Last I saw, half the crew was visiting Mol's place. Might take me most of the night to roll 'em away from the willing wenches."

Chapter Thirteen

NICK STOOD ON THE FORECASTLE OF THE *LIBERtine Lady* bellowing orders. With hands on hips, legs wide apart, he squinted into the morning sun and barked at the men scrambling up the rigging to unfurl the sails. "Hoist away, men!" He passed his arm over his face to wipe away the dampness. They had been working steadily since first light, loading supplies and making haste to weigh anchor on the tide. Nick was everywhere, not trusting that a job was complete until he had checked it himself. His nimble body had climbed the foremast, only recently repaired, to check the rigging, making sure that all was to his satisfaction. At last, convinced by his own eyes and the assurances of his first officer that all was in readiness, he let his attention drift.

191

His gaze followed a passing vessel whose distinctive lines declared it American made. Its billowing white sails were brushed gold by the morning sun and lifted by the wind. He scanned the deck of the ship admiring how its bow cut cleanly through the oily waters of the river Thames. Its passengers lined the rail taking their last view of London before the long voyage across the Atlantic.

A fluttering movement in the periphery of his vision caught his attention and he smiled as a black beribboned bonnet was captured by a sudden gust and swept over the side. The high feminine shout of annoyance struck a familiar chord in his mind and his eyes darted to find the owner of that voice. His gaze locked on a flame of amber hair, ivory skin and a profile that was forever etched in his mind. Christina! It couldn't be! Nick leaped down the companion ladder to the main deck and rushed to the rail. He barely had enough time to recognize his wife's companion as Annette Harcourt before the distance between the two ships became too great to discern anyone.

"Christina!" he shouted, running the entire length of the deck. "Damn you, Christina!" There was no indication that anyone aboard the rapidly departing vessel had heard his frantic call. He leaned far over the rail as if he could reach out and somehow haul back the other ship. Seconds later, his fist slammed down hard on the top of the bulwark and a string of enraged curses drifted on the Thames.

"I never believed I would ever see you more

angry than that day we crossed swords on this very deck." Tony came up beside him, signaling to the wide-eyed crew to go on with their tasks. "Your wife must intend a greater separation than you thought."

"You saw her too?" Nick demanded, wondering if he hadn't imagined Christina, her silken tresses blowing in the breeze, stretching a slim arm over the rail to catch her errant bonnet. Hope that he had been mistaken died swiftly upon hearing Tony's confirmation. He was desolated! What was that little vixen trying to prove? His reaction turned to anger as he realized the enormity of what her presence aboard an outgoing American vessel implied. She'd threatened to leave him and she was certainly making good on her threat! "She's not getting away with this," he growled from between clenched teeth.

Tony shrugged, slipping his hands into the pockets of his trousers and idly pacing back and forth while Nick struggled to control his rage. When Tony figured that his hot-tempered friend was once again capable of rational thought, he said, "I sent Aaron to the harbormaster to obtain a list of passengers and the *Annie Lynn*'s destination. I would wager that we can catch up with her in the channel and get you on board, then meet up again when Jackson and I have disposed of Bristol's slaver."

"What?" Nick looked to his friend in stupefied wonder. He ignored the grin which lifted the corners of Tony's mouth and concentrated, instead, on the determined intelligence in the twinkling blue eyes. "I like the first part of your plan, but you aren't going after Bristol's ship without me!"

"Would you rather *I* go after your beautiful wife? I assure you that I would be more than happy to spend several weeks crossing the ocean with her without you standing by her side," Tony teased, then hailed Jackson.

"Come below, mate. Our friend here is blowin' a gale so we've plans to make. Tell the rest of the crew to stand ready, for we shall weigh anchor as soon as Aaron returns from the harbormaster." He strode toward the open hatch with Nick following closely on his heels. "I can't say I think much of Lady Benton's timing but if we intend to catch up with her, we'd better get our planning done now. There won't be much time for talking once we set off to overtake that Baltimore clipper. When you reach your lady, my friend, you can give her a few chosen words for me."

"It's not words she'll be getting," growled Nick, then stopped in midstride. He exchanged a stunned glance with Tony, then clasped an arm over his friend's shoulder. "I wouldn't trust another man but you with this. Jackson can tell you how we regularly operate but it's not anything you didn't do a dozen times during the war. Bristol's ships are slow and heavy. Put him out of commission and follow me to wherever it is my dear wife has thought to go." They reached Nick's cabin and were quickly joined by Jackson. The plans were nearly formulated by the time the cabin boy returned with the information Tony had requested.

"Virginia!" Nick expounded. "Why in hell would she go there?" His gray eyes scanned the passenger list, stopping when he came to a familiar sounding name. His face grew dark with rage. "Mistress Christina Barker. At least she didn't disassociate herself from me entirely. I will teach that little madam to use her correct name if it's the last thing I ever do. When next you see my redheaded lady she shall be calling herself Lady Christina Benton and will continue to do so!"

"A good regular beating would keep the likes o' her in line. 'Tis what she deserves," said Jackson, a disgruntled frown marring his features. "You've been lax with her, Nick, and she's defied you time and time again. Let me tell you about their first meeting, Tony—"

Nick stood up from his chair. "Save your story for another time, Jackson," he ordered. "We have work to do if nothing is going to go wrong. I can't leave this ship until I know there will be no mistakes with Bristol's slaver." He started toward the passageway. "Let's go topside and get underway. It shouldn't take long to overtake that merchant vessel for all its new American trim. I want everything planned out by then." The authoritative command in his voice softened only long enough to utter his sincere thanks to Tony for volunteering to captain his ship on such a potentially dangerous mission. Seconds later, he was on the forecastle issuing orders, every inch the master of his ship—if not his wife!

All hands were fully cognizant of their orders when the *Libertine Lady* entered the English

Channel. Jackson, serving as boatswain, sent the hands to the riggings. "Crack on, mates! Bear up! We'll sail close to the wind and overtake that clipper!"

Nick was at the bow, spyglass in hand as he searched the edges of the horizon for his quarry. At long last the lookout called, "Sail ho!" and the *Annie Lynn* was sighted. After signals were exchanged, the *Libertine Lady* ranged alongside while Nick climbed the mast with his duffel thrown over one shoulder. "Luck to you, lads," he shouted, taking hold of a dangling line and swinging across the choppy gray water to the quarterdeck of the American ship where its captain and a curious ship's company stood waiting to greet him. Dressed in a well-tailored bottle green jacket, cream trousers, and impeccably tied cravat above a buff-colored waistcoat, Nick was an incongruous figure as he dropped to the deck of the *Annie Lynn*.

"An unorthodox way to secure passage, sir," proclaimed a uniformed man, smiling broadly through his well-trimmed beard. Nick landed beside him and dropped his duffel to the polished planking. "I am Thomas Muldane, the ship's master." He extended his large, calloused hand in welcome.

"Nicholas Benton, captain." Nick accepted the friendly gesture and returned the older man's greeting. "I shall pay handsomely for your trouble, sir," he said as he sized the other man up. Muldane looked to be about forty with the weather-beaten complexion of one who has spent his life at sea. His deep, gravelly voice was in marked contrast with the humor-filled hazel eyes that sparkled below his grizzled bushy eyebrows.

"Might I ask how you convinced that Englishman to overtake my ship?" asked Muldane with guileless curiosity, then returned Nick's assessment with a shrewd gaze. "Looked like a privateer's schooner."

"Gold carries weight in any discussion and with almost anyone," Nick shrugged, not disclosing that he was the Englishman in question. Until he knew what Christina was up to, he didn't intend to disclose anything about himself. "It was urgent that I reach Richmond and yours was the only vessel embarking for that port in weeks. I made the necessary arrangements and here I am." He pulled out a small leather pouch and handed it to Muldane. "I know you are a merchant ship, but do you have a spare cabin, captain?"

"As luck would have it, we have one unoccupied cabin, Mr. Benton." He accepted the bag of coin and tucked it inside his coat. "You must join me at the captain's table later this evening. I am curious to learn what urgent business brought about this unusual method of coming aboard." He paused and grinned at Nick in a conspiratorial manner. "Unless, it is of a private nature, of course."

"Nothing too out of the ordinary, captain." Nick hoisted the duffel to his shoulder. "I am meeting a close relative, someone I am most anxious to see again." He saluted then followed a crewman down the companion ladder to the lower deck where he was shown to his cabin. Wondering which compartment accommodated his wife and Annette, he inquired casually, "Do you have many passengers, sailor?"

"We a merchant ship, sir," replied the man. "Cargo pays our passage. Only two gents from Virginia and a pair of ladies going to visit relatives. One of 'em's a real looker but the old man don't allow no fraternizing with any ladies that cross with us—especially with the likes of that one. She be a highborn lady if I ever sees one. Even her companion be an uppity sort."

Nick almost laughed out loud when he pictured Annette warding off the unwanted attentions of any forward member of the crew with one frigid glare. This time he was grateful for the protection her presence had probably offered Christina thus far.

"You must go to the officer's mess without me, dear. The mere thought of food is enough to sicken me further." Annette smiled wanly from her prostrate position on her berth, once again the victim of the motion of the sea. Her features were pinched and her voice weak.

"I don't like leaving you alone Annette," argued Christina. "I could order a meal brought to me here and secure a pot of tea for you. Perhaps that would make you feel a bit better."

"No, no! I couldn't keep even a drop down. It would be best if I took nothing until I get my sea legs—possibly tomorrow. You go on, I would rather suffer alone."

Christina smiled and gave in, remembering

their last voyage. Annette had languished in misery upon her berth in the small, stuffy cabin of *The Madelaine* until—No! She pushed the memory of Nick out of her mind. Turning to the small closet, she removed a solemn black gown of rustling taffeta. Its unadorned high-necked bodice and long sleeves would serve her purpose well. She had worn it for her grandparents' funeral and it would be appropriate attire for her role as a bereaved young widow. She and Annette had agreed on at least one point about this voyage. Widow's weeds would protect her from any undue advances from the male passengers as well as disguise her identity.

She supposed that Nick must know by now that she had left Briar Park and disappeared. He was probably searching for her but she dismissed the idea that he might be worried about her. He was probably glad to be rid of her. She had spent almost two weeks in London trying to secure passage for America and hadn't stopped worrying that Nick would find her until the *Annie Lynn* had reached the Channel. She couldn't go back to him now, not since she had discovered that she was carrying his child. She finished fastening the hooks at her back and adjusted the bodice, frowning at the sight of her swollen breasts straining against the black taffeta. So far, the only signs of her pregnancy were her increasing voluptuousness and a slight queasiness in the mornings.

It had been Annette's aunt who had immediately identified Christina's continual morning malaise as a sure sign of pregnancy, having

bore five children of her own. Both older women
had tried to convince her that she should forego
her trip to America and return to Larkhollow to
await the birth of her child. Christina had remained adamant about her decision to go to
Brian Tremayne. She placed a hand over her
still flat stomach where a small life was growing, a life created by Nick and herself. At first,
she had felt victimized, sure that the child was a
male, the Benton heir she was expected to provide according to the terms of her marriage
contract. Then she had felt relieved, relieved
that in a matter of months she would have
fulfilled her obligation and therefore would not
have to remain as Nick's wife. However, recently her feelings of resentment had changed to
those of maternal protectiveness. She would
never give this child up—never! She would give
him all the love she had wanted to give to his
father, a man who did not love her but the one
man she would love with all of her heart for the
rest of her life.

Had her mother felt this way about Brian
Tremayne? Had she continued to love him all
those years, even after she had been wrongfully
told he was dead? Would Tremayne remember
Elizabeth and accept Christina as his daughter?
What could she expect from a man who didn't
even know of her existence and had been led to
believe that her mother had turned to another
man?

Christina hoped that her real father would
accept her, help her establish herself in a new
country. If he did not—She gave herself a little

shake and turned to the mirror, brushing her hair into a tight chignon at her nape. Securing the last pin, she resolved that if nothing else she would have the satisfaction of meeting her father, finding out what kind of man had sired her. Hopefully, she could then rid herself of the disgust she felt thinking herself the daughter of Benjamin Bristol.

Casting a sympathetic smile at her companion, she left the cabin and was met in the passageway by Captain Muldane. He escorted her to the dining compartment, tucking her arm into his protectively as they approached the large round table where three gentlemen were already seated. Keeping her eyes demurely downcast, Christina barely glanced at her fellow passengers as they rose politely to greet her.

"Gentlemen, may I introduce Mistress Barker, who has graciously consented to dine with us even though she is in deep mourning, having suffered the recent loss of her husband." He introduced two gentlemen and explained that they were American merchants returning to Virginia. Each nodded respectfully. The remaining man stood a step to one side, his back slightly turned away and his face averted until Muldane introduced him. "And last, a countryman of yours, Mistress Barker. Mr. Nicholas Benton."

She froze at the sound of his name, then found herself staring into the penetrating gray eyes of her very much alive husband. She began to sway, but before she could fall, Nick stepped forward and took a firm grasp on her elbow.

"Allow me, madam. Won't you sit by me?" Steely fingers tightened their grip on her arm and drew her into the chair placed beside his at the table. Unable to breathe, Christina sat paralyzed, feeling Nick's presence beside her through every pore. She could not think, could not move. She was terrified of what he might do now that he had found her. How could he have come aboard this ship without her being aware of it? How had he discovered that she was one of the passengers? She thought she had covered her path well, telling no one but Annette and her aunt of her intentions. Would he make their relationship known to the others? Denounce the story she had woven about herself? She felt a sickening thud in her stomach, knowing he would find some way to make her miserable.

While the others began congenially conversing amongst themselves, she and her husband sat silently. Christina did not dare look at him, fearing the rage she was sure she would see on his face. She attempted to eat the food that had been placed before her, but as the speaking silence stretched between them, she was continually aware that Nick's eyes were relentlessly roving over her quaking form, his piercing gaze was stabbing into her like a blade. Why didn't he say something? At first, she had feared what he might say, but now, she thought she might scream if he didn't say something—anything to break the excruciating tension that was like a tangible cord strung tautly between them. He continued his cold perusal, staring at her as if he were looking inside her soul, setting her teeth on edge while she waited for him to make the first move, her brain trying to calculate what action he planned to take and be ready for it.

"Forgive me, dear lady." His voice when it finally came was low, iced with the sarcastic fury that raged slightly beneath the surface but was apparent only to Christina. "But your name is familiar to me. I am certain I may have known your husband. Might I ask how you *lost* him?"

Her mouth dropped open and she groped for words, her trembling fingers closing frantically around the stem of her wine glass. Captain Muldane read the pallor on her face and interpreted her hesitation to be a sign that the death of her husband was still far too painful for her to discuss. "I understand the poor man, Alexander Barker, died of a sudden illness not long after he and Mistress Barker were wed."

"What a tragedy, mistress," intoned Nick, his gray eyes enlarged beneath his raised brows, taken aback by the captain's explanation of his alleged death. He digested the statement, then recovering with remarkable speed, countered, "Why—I *did* know him. We were quite close at one time. He was a fine man. A fine man, indeed. You must be deeply grieved." He stared pointedly at her face, waiting complacently for her to say something. His expression was expectantly polite, but his mouth was twitching and an amused glimmer had replaced the cold rage she had first read in his eyes. It was as if her lies had perversely amused him and he couldn't wait to hear how she intended to go on with the preposterous tale she had concocted.

Squirming, she stammered, "I—I am." She turned slightly away, her distress very real, but not for the reasons Captain Muldane and the other passengers might suppose.

Thoroughly enjoying her agitation, Nick offered, "Please accept my condolences for your great loss. I must say this news has come as a tremendous shock, as you might well guess. Surely your husband spoke kindly of me, madam. Nicholas *Benton*. Does that name have a familiar ring to it?"

Having taken more than enough of his less than subtle jeering, her temper sparked to life, giving her false courage, the bravado she needed to thwart him. Turning her gaze back to him, she said in a voice that trembled weakly, "Perhaps he did once mention you, sir. Possibly in one of his more lucid moments." She dabbed daintily at her eyes with her napkin as if she were brushing away tears. "It pains me to tell you, but as his friend, you have a right to know." She took a deep breath as if gathering courage— as indeed she was. "The end could not have come too quickly. Those of us close to him were glad to see him go, for his illness sadly affected his mind. By the time of his death, he was a hopelessly demented creature not knowing his own identity or the identity of those around him. It nearly broke my heart—" A brittle sob escaped her lips and she rose quickly from the table.

Placing the back of her hand to her forehead,

she lamented, "Gentlemen, you will have to excuse me. The memory of those last days pains me and I must return to my cabin in order to compose myself." She turned and ran from the room, rushing through the narrow passageway to escape the ominous sound of hard leather boots fast gaining on her from behind. She reached for the handle of her cabin door but before she could open it, he was there, spinning her around to face him.

"Just what are you doing on board this ship?" he demanded, all traces of amusement gone from the face held inches away from her own. She could feel his breath against her skin, shuddered as his hands clamped down firmly on her shoulders. She could do nothing but stare up at him, her eyes the deep boundless green of a tumultuous sea. "I'm waiting, madam," he spat out.

"I might ask you the same question," she returned gamely, gulping when his lips went tight and his jaw clamped shut.

"You are coming with me!" He reached for her wrist and began dragging her back down the passageway. "I will get your explanation in the privacy of my cabin." He propelled her with him, not giving her a chance to do anything but keep her balance as he dragged her through the narrow passage. He stopped before a cabin door, opened it and thrust her inside, locking it behind them before turning to face her. "I realize that we did not part on the best of terms, but proclaiming my death and immigrating to another country is a bit extreme—even for you."

She backed away from him, her eyes widening as he stalked her. "Do you have any idea how worried I have been about you?" He posed his first question, steadily advancing as she retreated farther and farther into the compartment. Eventually, she was left with no more space to withdraw, her back pressed against the paneled bulkhead as his deep baritone reverberated around her, his next query coming like the swift stab of a double-edged sword. "Where in hell have you been?" The punishing voice grew louder and louder with each question until the final explosion. "I could strangle you for what you have put me through in these last weeks!"

Words could not come and she stood mute, trapped by the wild flare of explosive color in his dark pewter eyes. His sensual lips were thinned, the deep lines beside his mouth far deeper than she remembered. Transfixed by the barely leashed power in him that she feared would soon career out of control, she panted like a small animal caught in a snare. In the next instant, he had pulled her to him and crushed her against his chest. His mouth crashed down on hers, grinding her tender flesh against her teeth. The tension in his body gathered force as his arms tightened around her. It seemed as if he meant to forge her body into his flesh, melding her against every unyielding sinew, forcing her to feel each virile muscle.

"God!" He lifted his lips. "I thought I had lost you." When the kiss resumed it had gentled, as if he were refamiliarizing himself with her taste, drinking in the nectared essence of her mouth with a craving which he could no longer deny himself. It was a thirst which Christina needed to satisfy within herself as she clung to him, helplessly parting her lips and melting against him.

Chapter Fourteen

Nick rained kisses over Christina's face, her eyes, her cheeks, her neck before returning to savor the sweetness of her lips. Each adoring caress was an insistent pull on her senses. His hands roaming over her, the elemental male fragrance of him permeating her entire being, his kisses drugging her—all combined until all thought of denying him fled. There was no other man who could take his place, no other who could transform her into this soft clinging counterpart to his masculinity.

"Oh, Christina." He questioned in a roughened voice, "Do you hate me so much you planned to put an ocean between us?"

"No, Nick—No," she dissented, no longer sure how she ever could have wanted to put *any* space between them. All she wanted to do at this moment was return his touch and continue to delight in the wonder of the sensual homage he was paying to her. She yearned to answer the desperate longing she felt within his body with her own urgent need.

She leaned toward him, seeking his mouth with her lips, her hands quickly unbuttoning his waistcoat and slipping inside his ruffled white shirt to feel his warm chest. She had dreamed of touching him like this every night since leaving Larkhollow. Their kiss was a mutual exchange of longing, not given or taken but a splendorous gift relished equally by them both. She protested when he brought their embrace to an end, taking her wrists and pulling her hands away from him.

"I can't take much more from you, Christina," he growled, his voice thick with raw desire. "There must be no more deceptions. You won't leave me again, I can't—" A sharp rapping sounded at the door, interrupting the breathless words that seemed to be wrenched from deep inside him. Christina could not credit the meaning of his words and actions. He had not been relieved that she had not returned to Larkhollow. He had actually worried about her. Could that concern mean that he cared for her? She wanted to ask him to explain himself but his expression reflected only the annoyance at the continued pounding on the door.

Paying no attention to his disheveled appearance, Nick strode across the cabin and savagely opened the door. His eyes burned with irritation until he saw the older uniformed man waiting for him outside. "Captain?" Nick asked in a tightly subdued voice.

Captain Muldane stepped into the compartment, sweeping the room with an all-encompassing gaze until he found Christina. Then confusion entered his hazel eyes, which began darting back and forth from Christina to Nick. "Mistress Harcourt was concerned when Mistress Barker did not return after the evening meal. I came to see if you knew of her whereabouts, Mr. Benton. You are all right, ma'am?" The probing question was for Christina, but upon registering her deshabille, wrinkled clothing, flushed features, and loosened hair Captain Muldane's gaze switched to Nick. His brows narrowed disapprovingly as he noted Nick's unbuttoned waistcoat and shirt and equally flushed features.

Christina raised a shaky hand to smooth her hair away from her face and looked to Nick for reassurance, hoping he might offer a plausible explanation for their seemingly indecorous behavior. It was fairly obvious what the older man was thinking. Blood rushed to her cheeks as she stared at her husband, but he did not move or indicate in any way that he would explain. He was lounging indolently against the bulkhead with his arms folded across his chest, a picture of studied nonchalance except for the expression in his eyes. The gray eyes she knew so well were riveted on her face, registering no anger or amusement at the situation, but an unwavering expectation. He was asking her to make a choice, waiting for her to decide their future. For the first time in her involvement with him, she was being given the power to determine her own fate. She could either choose to acknowledge her relationship to him as his wife or denounce him; and she knew if she did negate their relationship, he would let her go. She sensed it and the thought of living without him for the rest of her life was horrifying. No matter what the problems were that remained unresolved between them, no matter how unsure she was of his feelings toward her, she knew that she loved him. The recent moments she had spent in his arms had convinced her that she was as irrevocably tied to him as ever with sensual bonds she could not hope to escape—didn't want to if she could. What had he said at Larkhollow? "Your bondage shall last for a lifetime." She was willing at last to begin her servitude.

"I owe you an apology, Captain Muldane," she began in a clear voice. She heard Nick's sharp intake of breath and pressed on. "This man is my husband and as you can see, he is very much alive. I am Lady Christina Benton." Her eyes traveled to Nick's face and when she saw what could only be relief written there, she had the courage to continue. She explained to the captain that she and her husband had had a lovers' quarrel and that she had run away from him. After a few more minutes of explanation, the man was convinced that she was telling him the truth.

He turned to Nick with an understanding light in his eyes and a sympathetic expression on his ruddy face. "Now I understand your eagerness to secure passage on my ship," he teased. "This lovely lady was the personal business you mentioned, the relative you were most anxious to join." He smiled broadly at Christina. "I don't blame you, lad. Don't let her get away from you again."

Nick pushed his shoulders away from the wall, shrugging complacently as he hooked his thumbs in the waistband of his black trousers and grinned in triumph. "Milady will have no need to deny our relationship again." He came to stand beside her and immediately slipped a possessive arm around her waist, drawing her close to him. "I have learned my lessons well and I don't intend to do anything that might drive her away from me."

With shining eyes, Christina beamed up at Nick's face and their exchanged look was too intimate for the captain to misunderstand. "Since all is resolved, I shall leave the two of you in privacy." He touched the bill of his hat in salute to them both and walked to the door.

After the captain had left, offering to explain things to Annette, Nick swept Christina into his arms and proceeded to take up where they had left off before their untimely interruption. She stiffened in his embrace and turned her face slightly away, placing her fingers over Nick's lips to prevent him from kissing her. "No," she said in a soft voice. "We have too many things that need to be said and when you kiss me I can't think." She was grateful to see a look of understanding come over his face as he loosened his arms, allowing her to step away from him. She crossed the cabin to sit down on a chair, needing to put some distance between them in order to voice the necessary questions that had to be asked and explain why she had done what she had.

Following her lead, Nick took a seat upon a velvet covered bench located below a porthole. "Alright, Christina." His voice was low and he clasped his hands between his knees and leaned forward, resting his forearms on his thighs.

"Thank you for allowing me the freedom of choice just now." She concentrated on a spot beside his head so she wouldn't be affected by his entrancing eyes centered on her face. "That was the first time since Bristol dragged me away from Briar Park after mama's death that I have actually had any control over my own destiny. You gave me the power to decide for myself. Do you understand what that means to me?"

Immediately, he stood up. "Oh Tina, I know you have been through a lot. I do understand, believe me—" He took a step forward but she waved him back to his seat.

"No, Nick," she called sharply. "There is so much more I want to say and it would be easier for me if you would stay where you are."

Reluctantly, he sat back down. "Go on, I will listen to anything you want to tell me."

At first her explanation was hesitant but with Nick's gentle urging, she poured out every detail of what had transpired from the time of her mother's death to the startling revelations of her grandfather's letter. "So you see, Benjamin Bristol is not my real father," she announced with some satisfaction. "That is why—that is why—" She couldn't go on, her throat was aching and the turmoil inside her was making her feel ill. Before she could voice any more of her emotion-packed explanation, tears slipped from beneath her lashes and began to slide down her pale cheeks. "I—I have to go to Brian Tremayne. He has to know that there is no reason for him to hate my mother for marrying Bristol and I want to meet him. I had hoped—" How could she tell him that she had hoped that an unknown planter might provide her with a safe haven? That, as Nick had feared, she had planned to put an ocean between them. But, it had not been because she hated him, but because she loved him and feared that he despised her.

Nick's deep voice, full of tenderness and sympathy, cut into her painful reverie. "Come here, my princess." He held out his arms as if he knew her inner torment and wanted to console her. He remained seated, again giving her a choice. He made no attempt to force her to cross the room and that gave her further proof that he had indeed changed his opinion of her, that he felt something for her besides desire. Her sobbing contained a mixture of tentative joy and raw overwrought emotion, but with only a small hesitation, she ran to him and allowed him to take her in his arms. He drew her down upon his lap, holding her like a child. He gently stroked her hair and waited for her to finish crying out her inner anguish against his shoulder. Comforted by his touch, she was at last able to complete her astounding story, telling him how she had spent the time since her grandparents' funeral and accepting his condolences. Her last words were laced with bitterness. "Benjamin Bristol did his best to destroy my entire family."

She lifted her head to look at Nick and found him shaking his head, the muscles of his jaw tense with suppressed rage. "And mine as well. I *will* destroy him, Tina—for you and for Michael!"

"Your brother?" she asked, watching as a cold hatred doused the warm flames that had filled her husband's eyes.

"Bristol has much to answer for," he acknowledged tautly and began to explain. It was then her turn to provide solace and sympathy as he relayed the details of his young brother's death. In a broken voice, he explained the estrangement that had developed between himself and Sir Albert and why he had been driven to free spirited men from Bristol's clutches. He told her that Tony and Jackson were on a voyage to commandeer another of Bristol's ships and that he hoped to virtually destroy the man as soon as they landed in England again.

"No wonder you hated me," she stated in an unsteady voice, barely able to trust that he did not hate her any longer.

"I never *really* hated you, princess," he reassured, forcefully. "It was my only defense against my own frustrations and resentment. Like you, I did not enjoy having my future determined for me. My marriage to you should have been my own idea, not my father's." His lips curved into a smile and his eyes began sparkling, the cold abated by warm flames. "You said that I was a demented creature toward the end, but where you have been concerned, I've been demented since the very beginning."

It was a great relief to be able to laugh together. Impishly, she grinned up at him, flashing a cheeky expression. *"Usted es loco, capitán."*

Seeing her dancing turquoise eyes, his laughter joined hers. "I have never met a woman like you—Teresa, Anne, Christina, Harris, Bristol, Barker, Benton. You are more women than I shall need in a lifetime."

She felt the change in atmosphere, and in him. Amusement and shared laughter had been replaced by a keen desire. Her eyes which had glittered with mischief only moments before mirrored the warmth in his. "And you are many men—Nick Barker, Lord Nicholas Alexander Benton."

His hand came up to cup her chin, the blunt fingers gentle as they lifted her face. There was no way to hide what she was feeling and she returned his gaze steadily. "Will you let me love you, Christina?"

Wordlessly, she nodded, her affirmative answer written in the softened sheen of her passion-shadowed eyes, there in the slight provocative parting of her pink lips.

He stood up, taking her with him cradled in his arms as he crossed the compartment. Large portholes, framed in shiny brass, lined the mellow dark-stained oak panels of the sleeping alcove. Left open to capture the breeze, the round windows allowed a fragrant tang to drift over the dark green velvet coverlet on the berth. A colorfully designed ottoman rug covered the dark waxed oak floor before the bed and the intricate threadwork was highlighted by the soft glow from a dutch pewter hurricane lamp. Nick lowered Christina's feet to the rug and bent down to remove her slippers. A liquid warmth spread through her as he began rolling her silk stockings down her legs. His fingers were warm at the soles of her feet and excitement curled her toes. When her feet had been bared, he stood up and with shaking fingers pulled the pins from her hair, letting it cascade to her waist. One by one he released the fastenings of her gown. "You look nothing like a widow," he teased tenderly, easing the black taffeta over her shoulders to reveal the lush creamy flesh swelling above her black lace-edged chemise. He proceeded slowly, enjoying each new sight exposed to his devouring eyes, and appreciating her increasingly more rapid breathing as he removed her filmy undergarments until she stood in naked splendor before him, her bright auburn hair her only adornment.

"I have dreamed of seeing you like this again for what seems like years," he breathed, his eyes molten gray as they traveled lovingly from her face to her full breasts, down the pearly flesh of her stomach to the curve of her hip and along the tapered perfection of her legs. She felt his visual caress as if he were actually touching her, and stood proudly before him as he praised her beauty with soft words and admiring eyes.

Reaching out, she began to undress him in

turn, sliding his evening coat from his broad shoulders, removing his waistcoat, then unwinding his cravat before concentrating on releasing the pearl studs at the front of his shirt. She drew the white sleeves off his arms, delicately passing her fingertips along the dark hair of his forearm to his wrist and raising his hands to her lips to kiss the top of each. He stood quietly, enjoying her pleasure in unclothing him as much as he had enjoyed the pleasure of undressing her. When she had loosened the buttons of his trousers, she slowly lowered them and herself to the rug, bending her head in a worshipful pose at his feet when her bronzed sun god was revealed in his glory. She lifted her eyes, slowly raising to a standing position but refamiliarizing herself with each lithe muscle of his body. "I *am* glad you are not dead, Nicholas," she whispered, lifting her arms to his wide shoulders and meeting his burning look. "Very glad I am not truly your widow."

He bent down to pick her up, one arm going beneath her knees, the other at her back as he laid her down upon the forest-green spread and adjusted her gleaming amber tresses across the pillows. Entranced by the adoration in his flickering sterling eyes, she held out her arms for him to join her, breaking out of his hypnotic gaze only long enough to return it with her own visual caress of his long, muscled physique. His manhood rose beneath her heated look and she was enraptured by her own womanly powers that could ignite his desire as hotly as his potent virility set a fire inside her. She called to him, softly, "Come to me, milord."

She beckoned to him with parted lips, her extended arms displaying the tight fullness of her swollen breasts, their rosy tips erect and urgently waiting for fulfillment. The heavy weight of his body when it covered hers satisfied something primeval inside her. He rolled to one side, taking her with him as she arched against his male hardness and their lips met to appease the painful starvation they both had suffered— long, deep, soul-rendering kisses that went on and on and on.

"I crave the taste of you," he groaned, swiveling full length on the bed until his head was at her feet. Beginning with her toes, he trailed a line of nibbling kisses, nipping up the satiny length of one leg while her hands sought and found him. His groan and hers came together as his lips and tongue worshiped at the juncture of her thighs while her mouth caressed him. His grazing lips traveled down her other leg, then he shifted his position and he was once again beside her. Lifting her hand, he gazed into her eyes as one by one he suckled her fingers, then turned her palm and placed his tongue in the center of her hand. "For weeks, I've thought of nothing but you and this," he drawled huskily. "Worshiping your body with mine."

With the tip of his tongue, he began at her wrists and fashioned a sensitized path all the way to her shoulders. "Oh Nick—" Christina moaned with pleasure, moving restlessly, seek-

ing and finding him with her lips and hands,
pressing kisses across his chest. He grazed the
feminine curve of her shoulder with his teeth
until he reached the hollow of her neck, nibbling
up the sensitive cord while her lips burned
against him and her fingers ran through his dark
hair. She clutched his head as his enticing kisses aroused her to a breathless mass of anticipa-
tion. At her ear, he probed with his tongue and it
was almost as much a possession as the greater
one to follow.

His fingers pushed away the wispy strands at
her hairline to give his lips access to the road he
meant to take across her face. He reversed every
exciting movement he had taken until the tip of
the last finger on her other hand was pulled into
his mouth. Unable to withstand another second
of his caresses, Christina mindlessly reached for
him, pulling him against her. "Oh Nick, please.
Now," she moaned, frenziedly running her fingertips down the strongly developed muscles of
his back. Her fingernails raked lightly down his
spine and along his pantherish hips until her
hands flattened over his firm buttocks and she
kneaded insistently, telling him that she wanted
him, was ready to receive his surging hardness.

His hands cupped the rounded flesh of her
quivering bottom, moulding the shapely contours as once again his mouth sought hers. His
tongue plunged inside, accompanied by the si-
multaneous thrust from his loins and at last, she
was filled. Velvet and steel, he moved within her
and she received him, adored him and enclosed
him in the moist, soft cavern of her femininity.

Man and woman, they took flight together, soaring on the passion-feathered wings of rapture that carried them away. They reached the top of their intimate world, for the first time holding back none of the newfound emotions that heightened their velocity and lifted them even higher and beyond.

The cool mist of sea spray that coated their feverish bodies brought them slowly back to reality and their presence in the dimly lit cabin. Nick raised up on one elbow and began closing the portholes, eventually having to sit up to reach the last one. "It's getting colder," he remarked, lying back down beside his wife.

"Not here." Christina pulled the tangled bedding from beneath her and scooted under the linen. Nick joined her beneath the blankets, pulling her into the shelter of his arms, his face in her hair.

"Have I ever told you that you are as wild as the moors and I can smell the heather when I hold you in my arms?"

"Have I told you that you are as untamed as the sea?" she returned, softly. "It's as if I embrace the ocean every time we make love." She tilted her head and looked at him and they exchanged equally foolish grins, each inordinately pleased with the other.

Was now the time to tell him that he was going to be a father? Christina asked herself as Nick reluctantly left the berth to turn out the lamps. She wanted to selfishly gather each second of the past few hours into herself, hardly daring to believe it had all happened. Would the announcement of her pregnancy destroy the happiness they had just shared? Did she dare trust these new feelings she had? The thought that the child she carried might resemble the magnificent male who bounded back to the berth thrilled her, but when he slipped beneath the covers all thoughts of their child were swiftly replaced by a flaming desire. She turned to her husband and succumbed to the fiery need his touch inspired.

Chapter Fifteen

"How dare you attempt a voyage of this length in your condition!" Nick strode across the cabin to confront Christina. "That is my child you are carrying, madam, and I won't allow your reckless nature to jeopardize his health."

"Annette," pronounced Christina, resentment and rage replacing the tentative joy she had felt since reconciling with her husband. "She had no right to tell you I was with child."

"How else was I to learn that you are carrying my son?" Nick demanded, his features harsh and his flinty eyes striking sparks. "You obviously had no intention of telling me. If I had not wondered why your luscious breasts were suddenly spilling out of your gowns, I would be in ignorance still. You are lucky that the ever vigilant Mrs. Harcourt explained your lack of decorum in terms I find acceptable. I was beginning to think you enjoyed displaying your increasingly ample charms to those ogling idiots in the dining hall!"

"Why you despicable oaf!" Christina railed against his accusations and ran to the small closet, swept the gowns from the rod with an angry flourish of one arm. "I won't stay here and listen to another word of these insults. I shall be rejoining Annette without delay." She began walking toward the door. "I shall send someone for the remainder of my things."

"Don't force me to do something we will both regret." Nick stepped in front of the door, effectively barring her way. "You won't be taking one step out of my sight until you deliver me with a healthy son. If you won't behave as a responsible adult, I will take matters into my own hands. Nothing is going to happen to the child you carry—my heir."

Bristling with fury, he was a formidable opponent and one which Christina knew she could not hope to best, but her rage was as great as his and mounting with each autocratic word he uttered. "I knew it!" she exclaimed. "Why do you think I have not told you about our child? I knew you would react exactly like this. I fooled myself into thinking it was *me* that you cared about, but I can see now that I mean nothing when compared to the precious Benton heir. Well, it is my body, Nicholas Benton, and I shall go on doing whatever I wish without asking permission from you. As for displaying myself to other men, I shall do that too and hope I can find one who will appreciate me for myself and not the child I carry!"

His reaction to her threat was far greater than she had expected and her fury was rapidly replaced by awestruck terror. Nick's face washed of all color except for the violent gray tempest alive in both eyes. His hands clenched into fists as if it took a mammoth effort to prevent himself from striking her, and the look on his face robbed her of speech. "Step away from the door, Lady Benton. *Now!*"

Christina obeyed, instinctively knowing she had gone one step too far. She had threatened much in anger, much that she had not meant. She held her gowns in front of her breast, a flimsy shield to ward off the physical danger she greatly feared was only seconds away from descending upon her. "You wouldn't dare touch me!" she breathed, praying her statement was true, her green eyes so wide that they engulfed her face.

"Then don't say another word," he said, turning his back on her to lock their cabin door. He replaced the key in his waistcoat and strode belligerently to the porthole, pulling it open and taking great gulps of air as if the room was short of oxygen. She watched him from her place on the opposite side of the cabin, slipping quietly into a chair as he fought to control himself. She was convinced that he had no greater reason than she to be angry. Her rage was a living thing inside her, her disappointment at learning he seemed to care more for the unborn child she

carried than for its mother filled her with a
wracking pain. It was only the imposing size of
him, the physical superiority he had over her
that kept her from challenging him, berating
him further.

They had enjoyed a few lovely weeks of shared
passion with Christina thinking it was far more
but always Nick had been considering the possibility of her conceiving the Benton heir. Now, he
believed her guilty of flaunting her body in front
of other men. Was that the sort of thing a man
could believe about a wife he loved and respected? No, he did not respect her anymore now
than the day he had married her—probably
never would. He was not capable of love! He
wanted only what he believed belonged to him.
Well, she didn't belong to him or any man!

It seemed like hours, but couldn't have been
more than a few minutes before Nick turned
back to her, walking slowly across the polished
floor, his boot heels tapping against the hard
surface the only sound in the cabin. Slowly he
lowered himself to a nearby chair. "No woman
or man has ever made me more angry than you."
He held up his hand to prevent her jumping in to
defend herself. It was only the crusted frost in
his voice that prevented her from doing exactly
that. She tightened her lips and stared sullenly
at the floor as he went on with his speech.

"I jeopardized years of hard work to come
after you, making a total fool out of myself in the
process. From now on you will obey me. We will
go to your father's plantation and you may make
your peace with him, but when I decide it is time

to go back to England, I won't hear a word of protest from you. And, if I decide that we must remain in Virginia until the birth of your child, you will have no voice in the matter. Your continued good health is my greatest concern. I have taken quite enough from you, my dear wife, and I will take no more."

Christina recovered from the fear she had experienced. She had no intention of allowing anyone to take complete control of her life again. Knowing how much Nicholas and his father desired an heir, she knew that she had the perfect means to determine her own fate and keep Nick from continually interfering in it. If she did not stop his domineering commands she would exercise that means. He would be too fearful for the well-being of his precious heir to chance calling her on a bluff. In an imperious voice, she began with her own commands. "And, I have taken quite enough from you! I am not a member of your crew that you can order about. I have no intention of answering to you for every decision I make. I will go where I wish and speak with whom I wish and I will even wear what I wish!"

"Madam, you go too far!" Reaching out he grasped her wrists and pulled her out of her chair. Rather than cowering under his blistering stare, Christina glared back at him, defiance glittering in her turquoise eyes.

"Harm me and you harm the heir you care so much about."

He released her instantly, his arms falling to his sides, his fists tightly clenching and unclenching. "I won't abuse you, but I can lock you in this cabin and prevent your going anywhere without my permission."

"If you lock me in, I'll not eat!"

"What?" His brows rose incredulously.

"You heard me." She lifted her chin with disdain. "My good health and that of your child will be determined by *your* good behavior for the remainder of this voyage. I am going to visit Annette and I shall not return until you have regained control of your temper!" Regally, she lifted her skirts and walked gracefully to the door, turning to face him with an outstretched palm. "You have the key, I believe."

Struggling in impotent rage, a vein throbbing at his temple, Nick stared at her. She *was* stubborn enough to do exactly what she said, refuse to eat until he gave in. He knew it and was at a loss as to how to deal with it. He needed to think, needed time to develop a means to regain control of his willful wife without jeopardizing the babe she carried. He was too angry to think straight and it would take cool logic to outsmart her. He reached into his waistcoat and pulled out the key, walking to her side without speaking. Stopping inches in front of her, he reached out and yanked her bodice up over her burgeoning breasts, laughing humorlessly at her affronted face, then turning away to unlock the door. He stood to one side, bowing and grandly gesturing with his arm for her to pass. "Go to Annette, milady. But, you cannot starve to death in one night and you shall share my bed for the remainder of this voyage."

"I shall not allow you to touch me ever again!" Christina vowed as she swept through into the passage, quickening her steps to put distance between them.

"I consider this a minor skirmish," his voice followed her. "Enjoy your temporary victory."

Christina spent the remainder of the day closeted with Annette, berating her friend for informing Nick of her condition and denouncing her husband for his dictatorial attitude. Annette calmly explained that she had only defended Christina's virtue by revealing her condition. "My dear, he errantly believed that you had your gowns purposely altered to display an unseemly décolletage. I was forced to tell him of your delicate condition to relieve his unfounded suspicions."

Still angry, Christina paced back and forth giving vent to her ire by describing Nick and all his actions in the least complimentary terms she could think of. Annette's usual unruffled demeanor was shaken a few times by the language Christina used to describe "that lowest of all men—my husband." Having exhausted her supply of derogatory remarks, Christina continued her pacing, slamming one small fist into the palm of her other hand continually as if it were Nick's face she was abusing. At length, Annette decided that Christina had vented her anger long enough. "Child, you must stop. It will do neither you nor the babe any good if you carry on like this."

Annette's admonishment, though coached in a gentle tone, was more than Christina could take and she dissolved into tears, throwing herself across the berth and sobbing, "He doesn't care about me! All he wants is his son. He has only made love to me to assure himself of that !"

"Oh Tina! I'm sure that he does care most deeply. Look at his actions. He left his ship and followed you, leaving his business behind. If he did not care about you, he would still be in England."

Between sobs, Christina cried, "No, no! It was only his pride that brought him here. I am a possession and nothing he owns is allowed to escape him before he deems it necessary. He will not let me go until I produce a child."

Nothing Annette said could make Christina change her mind and finally, the woman enveloped her in her arms, rocking her until exhaustion took hold and Christina had no more tears to shed. Annette convinced her that she needed to rest and at last Christina complied, laying her head against the damp pillows until she fell into a restless slumber. As soon as Annette was certain that her charge was soundly resting, she left the cabin to seek out Nick.

Nursing a large tankard of rum, Nick gruffly barked for Annette to enter after she shrilly announced her presence outside his door. Already much the worse for drink, he didn't stand up when the woman swooped into the compartment, descending on him like an outraged broody hen. Astounded that the matronly woman would dare to confront him, his mouth dropped open as she pressed his shoulder down and forced him to remain in his chair. Poking his chest with an extended forefinger, she commanded his attention. "Young man," there was another poke from the bruising finger. "What did you say to that child to bring about such distress? Have you no concern for her well-being? She shall lose that babe if she must endure any more such abuse from you."

"It is my concern for her condition that prompted me to confront her," he defended, not a little discomfited by the continued harrassment of the harridan looming over him. His reactions were slowed by the large amount of alcohol he had consumed since Christina had stormed out of their cabin, and he seemed incapable of rousing himself from the chair long enough to escape the scathing indictment of Christina's champion. He had already accused himself of more despicable things than those Annette was now damning him for, and her wrath only increased his self-proclaimed guilt. He winced beneath the scornful probing of Annette's blue eyes, grudgingly admitting out loud that she could not make him feel any worse than he already did. Choosing his words carefully and speaking slowly lest his benumbed tongue and lips cause his words to slur, he began. "What can I do, mistress? I cannot reason with her. I tell her I love her and she threatens to go to some other man."

"When did you tell her you love her?" Annette demanded, only slightly soothed by his remorseful expression. She had no sympathy for the dull flush that came up in his cheeks in response to her question.

"You are overstepping your position, mistress."

"My position is not the issue here, young man. I care for Christina with all my heart and I will not have you or anyone else upsetting her like this." Annette plunged on, outrage fueling her courage. "I don't care what you may think of me. Dismiss me if you will, but I am compelled to speak my mind. You have treated that sweet lamb disgracefully since the very beginning when you kidnapped her. I shall not stand by and allow you to abuse her time and time again. If you really care for your wife, it is time you used the intelligence you were born with and convince that dear child that you adore both her and your unborn babe. It is unfortunate that I was forced to give you the news of your heir's forthcoming before you declared yourself. Now young man, what do you intend to do?" Annette fixed him with an intent stare, seated herself across the table from him and disdainfully moved the bottle of rum to the side.

Dumbfounded, Nick straightened his shoulders. Feeling like a schoolboy faced with an outraged master, he was no more prepared to deal with Annette Harcourt than he had been with Christina. In the years since Michael's death, he had not voiced his true feelings to anyone but his father—and that was only recently. He had honed his ability to hide his emotions but somehow a slender, redheaded female, more girl than woman, had broken past his defenses and left him feeling more vulnerable than he had felt since his young brother had died. He had prided himself on his ability to remain in control of every situation, but from the beginning of his relationship with Christina, he had little or no control. He behaved like a boor, almost afraid of what the little wisp of femininity could make him do, could make him feel. Forgetting the barriers that normally existed between the ranks of society, he let down his guard and spoke the truth to Annette.

"Perhaps I have not actually spoken the words, but I do love her." His voice was little above a whisper, his gray eyes were lifeless. "What can I do?"

Pleased by his chastened behavior and admission of his love for Christina, albeit reluctant, Annette relaxed and softened her expression. "To begin with," she suggested in a gentler tone, allowing a faint smile to play at the corners of her thin mouth, "you cannot bully the girl. She must be wooed gently. Remember that she has spent the last three years cloistered behind the walls of a convent, away from those she loved."

"She's never behaved meekly with me," Nick was stung into saying. "She always speaks her mind."

"And have you behaved as a refined gentleman?" Annette mercilessly queried. "A convent education does not mean she has no spirit. I am only saying that she has had little experience dealing with the outside world, let alone a man like you. Despite this background, she has a rare courage. It is important that you not crush her spirit. In addition, the poor child has no one."

"She has a husband."

"Yes, but she believes that you consider her no more than a possession. Perhaps you should spend less time satisfying your baser instincts and more time proving your worth, showing your wife how much she means to you."

"I could have shown her that if she had returned to Larkhollow where she belongs!" Nick's alcohol-hazed mind was beginning to clear, his words less slurred, but just as belligerent.

"That's just the point, milord. When she lost her grandparents, milady lost the last people on earth whom she believed truly loved her. Can you understand how important it is for her to seek out her real father in the hope that the love she lost along with her grandparents might be replaced by his? The Lord knows she never received anything from that vile creature who claimed her. She also has the need to redeem her mother in Brian Tremayne's eyes, for he was led by Bristol to believe that Elizabeth Harris had betrayed him. Family honor is not unique to the Bentons! The Harrises have a fine tradition to uphold and though their title may not be as lofty as yours, it is a family name to be proud of and one that dates back centuries to the Saxons!"

Annette stood up but smiled down at Nick for a brief moment before returning to her stern demeanor. "Since Christina is the only one who is still unaware that you are thoroughly besotted with her, I suggest you carry on in a more sympathetic manner until she recognizes what is readily apparent to everyone else. Good eve-

ning, milord." She swirled away from him with
her back ramrod straight and marched to the
door, gone as abruptly as she had come. The
door closed behind her retreating form before
Nick could recover from his complete and utter
astonishment.

Besotted? Is that what he was? Nick poured
himself another neat measure of rum and sat
dejectedly back in his chair. It was a most
disturbing thought that all but Christina could
take one look at him and see exactly what mala-
dy had beset him. He feared that there was no
cure for his affliction. He gulped down the remaining contents of his stein and refilled it.
"Ensnared!" he groaned, an increasing shroud
of self-pity encased his senses. "I am bound
hand and foot to a beautiful woman no bigger
than a sprite who can defeat me with one show
of tears!" He saluted the porthole with his drink,
took a gulp of rum, then made a toast to a host of
castigating spirits who seemed to be crowding in
on him. He watched bleary eyed as they all
shook their fists at him, chastising him for his
brutish behavior toward the gentle maiden with
the large innocent blue-green eyes. Annette, his
father, even a faceless planter from Virginia. He
got up from his chair, swaying as he lurched
toward the berth, tossing aside his tankard in
order to drink straight from the bottle.

It was growing dark inside the cabin and it
was time for him to retrieve his wife as he had
promised, but for some reason the thought of
dragging her protesting form back with him in
order to salvage his pride seemed wholly unpal-

atable. The sea of disapproving faces that swam before his eyes convinced him to wait. "I have rights," he growled, his surly speech steadily becoming more slurred. "Sheez not the angel ya'll think." He closed his eyes, a frown marring his forehead as he fell across the pillows. "Sheez mine," he declared pettishly, then passed out on the berth.

It was well past dinner when Christina finally had gathered enough courage to re-enter the compartment which contained her personal belongings. She had begged Annette to retrieve her things but Annette had adamantly refused, telling her that it would be far wiser to settle matters with her husband without any outside interference.

"I don't know what good this will do," Christina declared to herself as she placed her hand against the door before pushing it open. "He never listens, only judges and decides for himself what is best for me." With a spurt of rebellion, she walked resolutely into the cabin coming to a full stop when the alcoholic vapors reached her nose. Nick lay spread-eagled on the berth, fully clothed and reeking of spirits. An empty bottle of rum was clutched possessively in one hand, the other flung over his brow. One long leg was half off the bed, his booted foot resting at an uncomfortable looking angle on the floor. He was loudly snoring, something he had never done before.

Her resentful expression changed and became quizzical. The evidence of how he had spent the day could not be hidden. He had drunk himself

into oblivion. While she had sobbed her heart
out, he had drowned his frustration in spirits,
probably having a jolly good time while he did it!
If the mere smell of the alcohol permeating
every niche of the compartment didn't make her
stomach lurch, she would consider downing a
few measures herself. Hadn't old MacDougald
once told her, "A wee dram of good scotch
whiskey is good fer wot ails ye." She giggled to
herself at the memory of MacDougald's occasional unsteady gait—a result of imbibing in
more than the "wee dram" he advised.

Wrinkling her nose, she crossed to the porthole and opened it wide. The fresh sea air helped
to dissipate the lingering odors in the compartment and also provoked a restless movement
from the figure sprawled on the bunk. Nick lost
his grasp on the empty bottle and it toppled off
the bunk and rolled across the cabin floor to rest
against the opposite wall. His foot slipped, upsetting his precarious balance and before Christina could prevent it, his limp body slid off the
berth onto the hard floor.

Christina covered her mouth to keep from
laughing out loud at the ridiculous picture her
husband made trying to get comfortable on the
rug. He began to mumble and before she could
stop herself, she knelt down beside his supine
form.

"Christina—" he moaned weakly, but she
could not tell if he were calling for her to come to
him or spurning her within some stuporous
dream. She reached out her hand to prod him
awake but his voice gained strength. "Go way,"

he slurred, throwing one arm away from his body, dismissively.

"Fine!" She jumped back to her feet. "Don't worry, I'm leaving as quickly as I can." It took her only a few minutes to gather up her nightclothes and the personal things she would require for her morning's toilette. She marched to the door, slamming it sharply behind her until it rattled on its hinges, gratified when she heard a loud groan from the other side of the door.

Chapter Sixteen

IT WAS A CLEAR DAY, THE BLAZING SUN REFLECT-
ing a myriad of dancing beams across the green
swells of the Atlantic. Nick hung his head over
the side, taking a death grip on the rail as the
glare bored into his aching red eyes. His stomach lurched, matching the steady rise and fall of
the deck beneath his unsteady feet. No invective
could be harsh enough to convey his agony. For
the first time since he had signed on as a mid-
shipman in the Royal Navy, he was wretchedly
seasick. "Let me die!" he implored to any saint
who might be listening. Vowing never to touch
another drop of the demon rum, it took every
ounce of his control to retain the remaining
contents of his stomach.

"Land ho," a sailor's hail from the crow's nest
sounded as loud as the shrieking call of some

vengeful bird of prey intent on warning his
helpless victim before descending to capture it
in his strong sharp talons, talons that seemed to
be ripping at every nerve in Nick's body. Lifting
the heavy weight of his pounding head, Nick
gained his first view of the American shore. The
two capes which guarded the entrance to Chesapeake Bay lay on the horizon. At the sailor's call,
a cheer echoed across the decks as the crewmen
joyously began proclaiming the end of their voyage. Several agile sailors climbed the rigging for
a better view of the distant shore.

Laying his head upon his folded arms which
rested atop the rail, Nick valiantly tried to shut
out the exuberant shouts resounding around
him. "None to soon, I would judge." Mr. Jerome
Withall, one of the Virginian merchants who
had traveled across with them, joined Nick at
the rail. "Your first voyage, sir?"

"No." Nick cleared his throat, "but my first
wife." Momentarily, the large middle-aged gentleman looked taken aback by Nick's strange
remark, but then his round face broke into an
understanding smile. He patted Nick companionably on the shoulder, ignoring his wince.
"You'll live, my boy."

A charming feminine laugh captured both
men's attention. Christina stood further down
the rail, a rapturous smile lighting her face as
she pointed to the sky where a host of gulls were
swooping and diving to the sea. Annette stood by
her side, a grateful smile curving her lips. "At
last." Christina gazed longingly toward the dark
mass of land on the horizon, retied her high-

crowned straw bonnet which was festooned with yellow ribbons, then buttoned the short cloak she had slipped over her light piqué day dress. She turned questioning eyes on Captain Muldane when he came to stand beside her. "That be Cape Henry and Cape Charles, the gateway to the Chesapeake and the James River. It won't be long now before we set you down at the common wharf near the Tremayne plantation. You won't have any trouble securing transport to their land. As I told you before, Whispering Willows is a well-known place on the James. The Tremayne's have lived for generations on the banks of the river. By late tomorrow evening, you shall be welcomed by one of the finest families in the Old Dominion. Pardon me for asking, ma'am, but are you kin to the Tremaynes? You bear a striking resemblance to that clan."

"I have come for an answer to that question," Christina explained, her anxious expression readily apparent. "I was told by someone in England that I might be related to the Tremaynes."

"Whatever the case, you won't be turned away," the captain reassured. "The Virginians pride themselves on their hospitality. It hardly matters if you are a blood relative or not, for they will claim you as their own with hardly a question asked."

Christina doubted it was going to be that simple. There were few men who would receive an unknown woman, alleging to be his daughter, without questioning further. Did she dare hope that eventually Brian Tremayne might accept her as his own? Maybe she shouldn't have attempted this voyage without sending prior notice of her identity. Maybe her father would not want to be reminded of his relationship with the young English beauty, Elizabeth Harris, who had promptly married another as soon as Tremayne had sailed for his home.

Captain Muldane answered a call from his first officer, tipped his cap to Christina and strode away across the deck to the forecastle. Christina turned back to the sea, fully aware that Nick was moving slowly toward her, one of his hands never leaving the rail as he walked unsteadily to her side. She remained silent, perversely enjoying the green tinge she had spied surrounding his mouth, and the deep furrow of his brow, caused by what she felt was a well-deserved pain. She smiled slightly when she saw an unmistakable shudder course through his body, delighted that for once he was not the self-assured, over-confident male animal. "Your concern for my well-being is hardly admirable, madam," he remarked testily, grasping the rail with both hands as soon as he came to a stop beside her.

"A man who resorts to drink to solve his problems merits no admiration," she retorted, her lips twitching as the sound of her voice deepened the crease between his brows. She felt only a slight twinge of guilt that she was adding to his extreme discomfort. Didn't he deserve to suffer? He'd made her life miserable for the past weeks! "Is this sudden illness of yours solely from the amount of rum you consumed or are you suffering from the rolling swells? Up and down, back and forth." She drew the words out slowly in a voice that matched the rolling pitch of the waves, not caring that her description of the sea motion was increasing his nausea and was a childish retaliation. Unable to stop herself, she continued to heap abuse. "Perhaps a large breakfast would be of help. I believe you missed the dinner bell last evening. The cook has prepared some very good pork sausage this morning. Its salty smokey taste is a perfect accompaniment for a thick hot gruel."

Nick's lips tightened and his coloring turned a sickly green as he glared at her dramatically solicitous face. She couldn't resist laughing when he turned his back and rushed to the nearest open hatch and disappeared. She was left to her own devices for the remainder of the day.

That evening the *Annie Lynn* sailed slowly in the sinuous waters of the James. Less than eight miles separated Christina from her father's plantation. Before the passing daylight blotted her view, she had gotten a disturbing impression of what she might expect to find at the Tremayne plantation. The desolate ruins of countless plantations dotted the landscape along the river, decaying fences, fallow fields, and crumbling outbuildings were the rule, rather than the exception. Was it likely that the Tremaynes had somehow escaped the ruination that had plagued these other families? She could only hope that she would find her father's home in better repair than some of the decrepit estates she had seen thus far. Mr. Withall had appointed himself her guide and had pointed out the remains of the Jamestown settlement and explained that the ruination she viewed along the shore had been caused by the soil exhaustion, and many of the planters being too stubborn to change their ways and practice conservation, crop rotation, and contour plowing. Those planters had simply abandoned their tidewater lands and moved inland to the more fertile Piedmont region. He related that those who had accepted the advice of men like Thomas Jefferson had continued to prosper. Christina forced herself to believe that Brian Tremayne had been prudent with his land. Withall continued to expound upon the many contributions his country's third president had made in the area of agriculture, describing a place named Monticello as being a showplace of provident care.

She descended the companionway for dinner with her mind awhirl with foresighted agricultural practices, but heavily occupied with thoughts of her American family and their possible adverse reaction to her presence, no matter what the condition of their plantation. The captain had informed her that Brian Tremayne was master of his plantation, but the estate also supported his widowed mother and his younger brother's family. She rebuked herself for not considering the possibility of being confronted with more relatives than just a father. It was strange to contemplate the possibility of meeting a paternal grandmother and several other relatives.

Her husband was waiting for her at the table, looking recovered from his morning's malaise. He was freshly attired in a single-breasted tail coat and dark trousers, his cravat neatly tied at his throat. He stood upon her entrance and gallantly pulled out a chair for her. "Good evening, my dear," he offered politely and bestowed her with a brilliant smile.

Taken aback, Christina gracefully took her seat. "Good evening. You are looking well." She gave him a slight frown conveying her suspicion of his solicitous attention, but he merely nodded briefly in acknowledgement, then dipped his spoon into the soup which had been placed before them by the steward. Annette and the two gentlemen from Virginia were engaged in conversation with Captain Muldane, and Christina made a good show of appearing to listen to the captain's narrative about the city of Richmond. All the while, she was conscious of her husband's presence at her side, the deliberate brush of his thigh against hers as he shifted in his chair. Had he given in to her demands to do as she wished or was he planning some new method of bringing her to heel?

"Will you be accompanying me to my cabin this evening, milady?" he asked, conversationally. "We do have several things that should be discussed before we disembark tomorrow."

Immediately, her eyes narrowed on his face, but he seemed to have no ulterior motive in mind. "I have done some thinking," he continued blithely, "and I realize why you must seek out Brian Tremayne. I commend you in this, Christina, but as your husband, I would have liked to have been informed of your plans."

"I will agree to speak with you later this evening, Nicholas, but I want you to understand that I shall not remain the night. My view on that subject has not changed."

"As you wish." He looked away and began speaking to Mr. Withall.

Later that evening, they were together in Nick's cabin, seated at opposite ends of the long low sofa. "You look very becoming in that gown, Christina. I appreciate the concession you have made to my sensibilities." Nick's eyes complimented her choice of gown and especially the concealing chemisette she had tucked into the low décolletage.

"I have borrowed this from Annette. I had not realized that my gowns were unseemly." Christina fingered the silky material at her throat. "I was unprepared for the changes in my figure and have none but the gowns in my trousseau to choose from."

"I shall rectify that matter as quickly as possible." Nick was doing his best not to insult her as he had done the previous day. "There must be seamstresses in Virginia."

Of a similar mind, Christina wanted to change the subject and asked, "What is it you wish to discuss?"

"Had you thought beyond your arrival, Tina?" He studied her face to find out if she had given any thought of what might be in store for her. Seeing confusion register in her lovely eyes, he offered, "Since I am here, perhaps you would consider relying on me to assist you. You will be dealing with a stranger who might very well turn out to be as much a scoundrel as Benjamin Bristol." He inwardly cursed himself as soon as his words were out. Christina's wide-eyed confusion had rapidly turned to fear, and he knew his ill-chosen words comparing her biological father with Bristol had hurt her. Why was he constantly hurting her when all he wanted to do was protect her, hold her close—love her? With steeled determination he fought the urge to pull her into his arms. It was too soon, he reminded himself. She didn't trust him, with probable cause, at least in her mind.

Christina's long fingers fluttered uneasily in her lap. "I—I don't know what to expect," she admitted defensively. "I have to believe that my mother would not have given her love to a man anything like the one she married. He—he just has to be worthy of my mother," she stammered and tears threatened to fill her eyes.

"That's just it," he pressed gently. "You don't know what he is like or even if he will acknowledge you. I suggest we put our differences aside and confront whatever we may find tomorrow together." He leaned closer, smiled, and reached for her hand, taking it tenderly in his own and softly stroking her chilled fingers. "Agreed?"

Christina acknowledged to herself that he was right. She hadn't thought beyond her need to meet Brian Tremayne and clear her mother's name. If it wouldn't have been so difficult to admit, she would have liked to tell Nick that she was grateful he was with her. Even if his reasons were not the ones she wanted, she knew that Nick would make certain no harm would come to her.

She looked squarely into his eyes for the first time since entering the compartment. She saw there what appeared to be genuine concern and a willingness to help her. Could she dare believe he felt more than a solicitude for the mother of his child? Could he ever understand what had driven her across the Atlantic to seek out a stranger? His strong fingers were delicately caressing her skin, but it was a touch of reassurance, not a caress meant to ignite her senses until she was helpless to any thought beyond the sensual pull she always fought against when near him. The warmth and strength conveyed by his touch on her fingers was relaxing, a sensation she had never felt in his presence. She wanted to reach out and by some means physically grasp onto the peaceful companionship they were sharing at this moment, find a way to secure it, thinking it only temporary, and possibly only in her mind. That was what she wanted with this man, both the security and the excitement of his touch. She saw a flicker of something more in Nick's eyes. She was becoming increasingly more uncomfortable gazing across the space at him—and he, at her. The meaning of the expression in his eyes eluded her and she quickly convinced herself that it was part of an act to gain her easy compliance with his future dictates. "Are you no longer angry with me, Nicholas?" she queried, thinking if she reminded him of the vicious argument they had had yesterday, he might put aside his disconcerting show of husbandly concern.

"Don't you know yet that we shall always strike sparks off one another?" Nick slid closer to her, lifting one arm to place along the back of the sofa while his other hand went on toying with her fingers. "Like it or not, you are my wife and I cannot turn my back on you when you might be walking into a situation fraught with trouble. You have shown me that I have no choice but to allow you to continue with your plans but I would like you to concede that I have a right to be involved."

Of course, she thought sadly, the right of a father to protect his forthcoming heir by insuring the well-being of its mother. "I have no idea how long this might take," she answered stubbornly. "Perhaps my father will want me to spend a fair amount of time here in America so that we may become well acquainted."

Damnation! Nick thought to himself. He had sensed her withdrawal from him. He had seen a hint of trust in the depths of her gaze, then as if a curtain had been drawn she had quickly withdrawn the trust and was once again wary. He would have to guard every word and action. But how long would it take to gain her trust, and how long before he could return to captaining the *Libertine Lady* and finishing what he had vowed to do—ruin Bristol!

"How long do you plan to stay?" he inquired, but there was a sudden edge to his voice.

"As long as it takes," she insisted, waiting for the inevitable explosion of his temper. When it did not come, she turned her surprised face to his. "That is agreeable to you?"

"I know that I must be patient with you." He looked grim, his eyes traveling past her to some distant place. She suddenly understood the trend of his thoughts. Selfishly, she had not considered what her precipitous flight might have done to upset his plans. Indifferent to the very real quest he had undertaken to destroy Bristol, she had not even asked what her headlong flight across the sea had done to his long well-thought-out battle with his enemy.

"Were you near to ruining my—Benjamin Bristol?" she asked, a stricken expression freezing her features.

"Very near," he acknowledged, shrugging as if it did not matter, when she knew very well that to him, it had been all that mattered since the time of his young brother's death.

"I am sorry," she apologized, deeply regretting her rashness. "You can take the next ship back to England. I—I didn't think of what my plans might do to yours, I didn't expect you to accompany me." She had made a mess of things, but from her point of view, Nick himself had to shoulder his share of the blame. If he hadn't treated her so abominably, insulted and demeaned her, alternately making love to her to satisfy his lust then lashing out at her with his vile temper, she might have thought to consult

him. She still believed that he had only followed
her aboard this ship because he could not toler-
ate a wife who dared to run away from him,
dared to defy his commands. Wasn't his reaction
to her pregnancy proof that he had no love for
her, but was only interested in his heir? She
knew that he still desired her, it was there in his
speaking dark eyes, but how would he feel when
she was swollen with child, grossly misshapen
in the late stages of pregnancy? He won't even
desire me then, she silently railed, wishing to
recall her apology until he offered one of his
own.

"You are very young," Nick stated, not realizing that his reference to her youth only increased
the black thoughts she was rapidly gathering up
against him inside her head. "We have until the
Libertine Lady docks in Richmond to settle this
matter of your father. I will not leave you behind
in America. Will you concede that perhaps I
know better than you what must be done?"

"Because of your great age?" she reproached,
knowing that she had little other choice that
would not make her appear like the immature
fool he believed her to be.

"I am not in my dotage, but maturity and
experience have improved my judgment." He
grinned beguilingly, and as usual, she couldn't
resist him. She smiled back and stood up to
leave, needing to put space between them in
order to retain any semblance of control.

"Very well, Nicholas. For now, we shall proceed in the way you have suggested." She
walked to the door, gratified by the thwarted look

on his face. She wondered if he might call her back, beg her to spend the night with him, but when he did not and allowed her to walk, unimpeded, out of the cabin, she didn't understand her own disappointment.

As soon as the door closed behind his wife, Nick began to pace. He contemplated taking up with another bottle of rum, but the last vestiges of his previous night's bout lingered to remind him of his folly. Every part of him had wanted to keep her with him. He ached to hold her in his arms throughout the night, but knew that if he hadn't let her go, hadn't given her the freedom she so wanted, he might never convince her of his love for her. Hopefully, there would be other times when he might be able to prove that desire was only part of his feelings for her. Women were an illogical breed—especially his woman! He wondered if it were going to be possible for her to separate her passion from the love he hoped to inspire in her. He knew it was impossible for him to do it at the time, but women were no doubt not as inherently sensitive as men! He lit a cheroot and continued his pacing, alternately cursing and blessing the fates that had brought Christina into his life. Life had been simpler before he met her, of that he was sure. But he was just as sure that he would never let her out of his life again.

The old Negro retainer who had offered to be outrider for the English newcomers to Virginia rode a plodding mule a few yards ahead of the hired carriage Nick had obtained from the poor

inn which had been located near the common
wharf. Nick had to pull sharply on the reins
several times to keep the sway-backed horse
which pulled their rude equipage from stopping
on the muddy road to enjoy a leisurely bite of the
dark foliage that canopied the rutted lane. A
thick cloud of mosquitoes seemed intent on following them every inch of the way, buzzing and
droning incessantly as they ignored the swatting
hands of the perspiring threesome who occupied
the ancient carriage. Whenever a slow-moving
bovine decided to investigate their progress,
Nick, Christina, and Annette were forced to
endure a lengthy halt at which time the bloodthirsty insects became more emboldened in
their attack. Eventually, their guide would knee
his mount into motion and take his stick to the
rump of the stubbornly complacent beast who
blocked their path.

"How much farther?" Nick called after one
particularly long delay. "My wife and her companion cannot take this heat much longer."

"Weez almos' thar, cap'n." Silas turned on his
mule without haste to drawl in an agonizingly
slow manner, "Spect we'll see the front gates
'fore too long."

"What did he say?" Christina asked quietly,
wiping her forehead with a white lace-edged
cambric handkerchief.

"God knows." Nick slapped irritably on the
reins. "I thought this was an English speaking
country but I was obviously wrong. I haven't
understood a word spoken since stepping foot on
this godforsaken land. Even the birds seem to fly

like they have all the time in the world to reach the ground."

As if to prove Nick's statement, a slowly descending swallow arched in a deliberate curve toward the river, circling and circling before landing gently on the sedgy bank. "See what I mean?" Nick spat in a disgruntled tone. "Oh Lord, there's trouble if I ever saw it." All occupants of the carriage stared uneasily at the view before them.

A rickety wooden bridge tilted drunkenly across the slow-moving creek that traversed the road. A loud chorus of bullfrogs greeted the noisy clatter from the mule's iron shoes as Silas nonchalantly rode across the rotting planks. "Wait up, man," Nick shouted, bringing their horse to a halt before crossing. "I don't think that thing will hold our weight. Perhaps the women should walk across in case I end up in that mud hole."

"Aaaw cap'n, why the ole Apple-bug bridge 'as been here longer'n me. I 'spect it'll hol' one more wagon." Silas didn't bother to look back, assuming they would follow as he slapped the rump of his mule and continued on at the same sluggish pace.

"Hurry up, Nicholas," Christina pleaded as the gray mule went around a curve and passed out of view. "We might lose sight of him."

"Please do," Annette reiterated from the rear seat, where she sat like a swooning damsel, fanning her reddened face with a handkerchief.

"Several turtles have already passed the man," Nick quipped, but decided to take Silas at his word. As the Negro had said, the bridge lasted through one more wagon and a few minutes later they caught view of the mule and its rider a short distance ahead of them. Silas was also accurate in his estimation of their imminent approach to the gates of Whispering Willows, and all the occupants of the carriage let out a loud sigh of relief when the man slid off his mule and went to unlatch the heavy iron gate.

"Ah'll be movin' along, folks," he informed them with his indistinguishable mumble. "Gots to visit my kin up the road a piece."

Nick immediately withdrew a few coins from his purse and hopped down from the carriage to pay the man, amazed when his dark face crumpled into an affronted frown. "No, no, cap'n, wouldn't do for me to take nuthin' for hepin' folks new to these parts." While Nick stood in confusion, knowing he had unwittingly offended the man, the Negro got back on his mule and went on his way, whistling a low tune off-key. Nick and Christina exchanged puzzled looks as Nick got back up on the seat and prodded their reluctant horse to proceed through the gates.

Freshly laid white gravel was spread between two wide brick pillars of the drive, leading away from the ostentatious iron gate toward a rolling grass clearing. The gravel road meandered up a gentle incline where several stacks of chimneys became visible through the neatly planted rows of lombardy poplar. As the carriage made the top of the hill, a pack of yapping dogs arrived to escort them the rest of the way to the main house.

Christina gasped with pleasure when the many-windowed edifice of brick came into view. The stately mansion, composed of two low wings reaching out from a double-storied center, had the dimensions of a castle. A white painted wooden porch spanned the entire front of the imposing façade, matched by smaller enclosures off the two wings. A mass of shrubbery shaded by several old willow trees hid the supernumerary buildings which were situated to the rear of the mansion. Christina could see the stables and several other white painted structures which made the homestead look more like a prosperous settlement than one man's family seat. The surrounding grass lawns stretched for miles, only ending at the banks of the James where a mantel of pine and dwarf oak guarded a series of narrow inlets. Before she could take in the full magnitude of the entire estate, a liveried servant stepped down the wide front steps of the main house and smiled a polite greeting as he offered his hand for the reins of the carriage.

While the carriage rolled away toward the stables, Nick, Christina, and Annette stood nervously facing the house, none of them quite sure what to do next. Before they could offer any opinion, the large walnut door opened and two small boys, looking to be about seven and eight years old, bounded down the steps toward them, shouting a boisterous greeting. They were followed by a pretty young woman in a flowing blue silk dress, her snapping blue eyes alight with welcome. "Come in, come in out of this awful heat," the woman called, not hesitating an instant as she descended the worn steps and reached out for Christina's arm, tucking it beneath her own as two more adults walked through the door to stand on the wide veranda. Christina looked frantically over her shoulder at Nick, only to see him being dragged along by the two little boys who had each grabbed one of his hands. Annette followed behind looking uncharacteristically bewildered.

"My, my aren't you a pretty little thing," a white-haired woman declared delightedly from her place at the top of the steps. "The lemonade is cool and we'll have you'all feeling comfortable straight away." She held open the door, calling to someone who she must have thought was being decidedly tardy in appearing to greet the newcomers. "Son, we have callers. Get out here and say hello."

Christina thought that these people who were bestowing such an effusive welcome must have been expecting visitors and had mistakenly assumed that they were the awaited guests, but she was immediately proved wrong when a well-dressed gentleman with auburn hair and green eyes stepped across the veranda. He waited for Nick and Christina to mount the steps then came forward with an extended hand. "Nathaniel Tremayne, sir," he introduced himself. "This is my wife, Lena, and those two rascals holding your hands are our boys, Davey and William." He turned to the elderly woman at his side and said decorously, "My mother, Claire Tremayne.

Welcome to Whispering Willows. And you are—"
He lifted an inquiring brow, showing nothing
but a pleased interest in learning their identity.

"Nicholas Benton, Mr. Tremayne," Nick returned with considerably more aplomb than
Christina was feeling at the moment. "And I
would like to present my wife, Christina, and
her companion, Mistress Harcourt."

"Upon my honor, you are from England!"
Nathaniel exclaimed to the others who proceeded to demonstrate their delight, asking a barrage of questions that no one was given the
chance to answer.

"You must forgive my family, sir." A deep,
resonant voice rose above the din. "They are
unused to receiving guests who have traveled so
far. I am Brian Tremayne and I bid you and your
womenfolk come inside before these curious
magpies completely tax your patience."

Chapter Seventeen

CHRISTINA'S THROAT LOCKED AND SHE WAS UN-
able to move or speak as she came face to face
with the man who had sired her. Brian
Tremayne stood before her, a tall well-
proportioned man, displaying all the assurance
and dignity of a landed gentleman. Young looking for his years, he had a thick mane of dark,
waving russet hair, deep-set blue-green eyes,
and a ruggedly lean face. Christina instantly
registered the resemblance between herself and
the commanding figure framed in the doorway.
Did he see it too? Or was she merely imagining
something that really wasn't there? The moment that she had thought about for weeks was
now upon her and she could think of no appropriate way of stating why she had come. She,
who had demanded control of her own destiny,

was quaking at the first opportunity to show herself as a capable woman, able to handle even the most delicate of situations. Anxiously, she looked to her husband for assistance, thankful for his encouraging nod. He took hold of her elbow and drew her along with him as they went to meet her father.

"Nicholas Benton, sir. My wife, Christina, and her companion, Mistress Harcourt. Before we accept your kind hospitality, there is a matter of grave importance that must be discussed in private. Is there somewhere we might talk?"

"Certainly," Brian returned smoothly, intelligent green eyes surveying Nick's face before passing to Christina. He smiled kindly into her eyes and led the way into the house, telling his family to offer refreshment to Annette while he spoke with Nick and Christina. Upon entering the house, Christina felt the immediate drop in temperature. A cool breeze passed through the central hall, coming from the open French doors at the back of the wide corridor. Dark-paneled walls brought a shadowed relief from the glare of the afternoon sun out of doors. Nick's firm grasp on her arm was reassuring and she was able to contain the rising panic that threatened to overtake her. They were ushered into a large study at the back of the house. Paneled in poplar, the greenish-white walls lent an air of freshness and life to the otherwise masculine room. Brian asked them to be seated in two high-backed leather upholstered chairs. He seated himself behind a large writing table facing them, his figure framed by the large map of

Virginia which hung on the wall behind him. Christina remained silent, curiously studying the contents of the room, the heavy volumes of richly bound books which lined the shelves, the nautical charts, and various paintings which stood out on the walls, while Brian and Nick made mundane small talk as they waited for a young Negro houseman to serve them with cool glasses of iced nectar. Soon after, Brian stood up and closed the double doors leaving the three of them alone in the serene atmosphere of the study.

Twisting the cords of her reticule with nervous fingers, Christina tried desperately to think of some way to open their conversation. Nick gave her an understanding nod, then turned to Tremayne. "Sir, my wife and I must impart information that will surely come as a great shock to you. I would like to assure you that whatever your feelings on the matter, we will abide by them and have not come to cause injury to you or any member of your family." He turned back to Christina, giving her an encouraging smile.

Nervously clearing her throat, Christina began, "I am afraid that there is no subtle way to prepare you for what I am about to say, Mr. Tremayne. I would only add to my husband's assurance that we do not intend to cause you any distress or embarrassment. My mother was Elizabeth Harris. She died more than four years ago, but I have recently learned that though she married Benjamin Bristol, he was not my father." Unable to continue without gauging Brian's reaction to this information, she bit her lip and clutched the mellowed arms of the chair. She looked across the table, directly into the eyes of Brian Tremayne, blue-green eyes, so similar to her own. He had gone slightly pale beneath his dark tan, but indicated that he was waiting for her to continue, reserving judgment until he had more information.

Reaching into her reticule, Christina extracted the thick envelope that contained her grandfather's letter. She held it in her hands for a moment. "Perhaps this will better explain why I am here." She stood slightly and extended the envelope across the table. Brian looked at her uncertainly, but slowly extracted the sheets of parchment and began to read. While they waited for him to absorb the contents, Nick stood up from his chair and went to stand by his wife, placing a comforting hand on her shoulder as the silence became profound.

The soft ticking of a large floor clock measured the time until Brian looked up from the papers, an anguished expression on his face as he rasped, "You *are* my daughter." The parchment flittered to the top of his desk as he let go of it and stood up, turning his back in order to hide the moisture gathering in his eyes. He stared out the leaded window, clasping his hands behind his back as he looked past the flowing James River to an isolated English moor where he had once lain with a beautiful young girl who had been meant to share his life. "I loved her very much," he whispered, not turning around. "How did she die?"

Choked with a renewal of grief over the loss of her mother, Christina murmured softly, "We were out riding and mama fell—her neck was broken—"

"And you, child? What became of you after you lost your mother?" Brian swung back to her. "Did Bristol treat you as his daughter?"

Nick sensed that Christina was unable to talk and offered the information that she had immediately been sent to a school in Spain where she had remained until their marriage. "It is my understanding that Bristol had no love for either his wife or her child and that they did not live together except for the months prior to Christina's birth. My wife has suffered greatly at his hands. Perhaps now you can understand why she has come to see you. It was important to her that she convey her mother's innocence and that for all those years, Elizabeth never forgot you. I hope that you can find it in your heart to forgive an old man who thought he was doing what was best for his only child. Bristol's misdeeds are legion. I can assure that justice shall be served one day soon."

Awkwardly, Brian crossed the room to Christina's chair and reached for one of her hands. "Words are not adequate to explain the emotions I am feeling at this moment. I see your mother in you and for that reason alone, I would love you." He pulled her up from her seat and exchanged a questioning look with Nick, who immediately released his hold on his wife. Brian slowly and gently enveloped his daughter into his arms. "If only I had known of you, I would never have left

England without your mother." Father and daughter held each other for the first time and together shared a grief for the lost years, their love for Elizabeth Harris and the new love they felt for each other.

After some time, Brian released her and brushed the tears from her eyes with his own handkerchief. "I would be honored to claim you, Christina. I assure you that no member of this family will raise an eyebrow at the circumstances of your birth. But you? Will you be uncomfortable? Can you face what others beyond this plantation might say?" He turned his gaze toward Nick. "And you, Benton, will a public declaration that your wife is my bastard daughter affect your regard for her?"

Without a moment's hesitation, Nick responded. "Sir, for reasons of my own, I am greatly pleased that Christina is not Benjamin Bristol's daughter. As for being your 'bastard,' I shall not regard her any differently. Our association is brief, but I sense that you are an admirable man. However, were you not, it would make no difference in my regard for my wife."

Brian acknowledged Nick's words and accepted them with a slight smile that conveyed approval. He turned his gaze back to Christina. She looked up into his face and saw nothing but acceptance and love. There was no disgust, anger, or resentment, only an animated sparkle from the turquoise depths. Shyly she lifted her wet lashes and beamed up at him. "I am honored to be accepted as your daughter and would not fear it being public knowledge. I would be proud to be recognized as your daughter, Mr. Tremayne, no matter the circumstances."

A heartily amused chuckle greeted her response. She looked quizzically at her father. "Christina, my dear daughter, I do believe that we should agree on some form of address other than 'Mr. Tremayne.' Legally, Bristol may be your father, but in all other ways you are mine. Would you give me the pleasure of hearing you call me papa?"

"Oh yes—M—Papa."

A wide grin brightened Brian's face. "Thank you, daughter." Keeping a possessive hold around her shoulders, he turned to the young man hovering a few feet away. "In my new role as parent to this lovely young woman, might I look upon you as my son-in-law?"

"I am astonished at your congeniality, sir," Nick admitted. He offered his hand once more and the two men greeted each other as if for the first time, but with a strength born of their mutual concern for Christina. "Although it might seem to you that you have had enough revelations for one day, there is more. I believe in being totally honest from the beginning." He grinned and chuckled at Christina's look of total bewilderment. "Christina, it might be wise to tell your father of the additional role he will be forced into in the not too distant future."

Gray eyes traveled to the as yet nonexistent curve of her stomach, and Christina finally understood what her husband was talking about. A becoming blush rose in her cheeks as she shyly admitted, "I am with child—Papa. You shall soon be a grandfather as well. I—I hope you do not mind."

"Mind?" Brian ejaculated. "How could I mind learning that my love for your mother has resulted in a continuing line of new life? We have much to discuss, so many years to catch up on but there is a roomful of people outside, consumed with curiosity." He escorted Christina to a comfortable sofa, gesturing with his hand for Nick to be seated near his wife, then suggested that they wait in the study until he had informed the rest of his family of the information he had just obtained. "Do not worry that the news will settle badly, my dear. They know how greatly I suffered over Elizabeth and will be more than happy to share in my newfound joy over you. If the truth be known, I have shown a remarkable distrust of the fairer sex which has troubled my poor mother for years. To learn that Elizabeth did not play me false has given me back something I thought I had lost forever. I will always be grateful to you both for destroying the poisonous thoughts that have plagued me." He hesitated with his hand on the door knob. With a twinkling grin he added, "Fortify yourselves, my mother can be quite overwhelming at times and this is definitely one of those times. She has wanted a granddaughter to spoil for years, but alas my siblings have produced only sons." He took careful note of Christina's confused expression. "You have met only the Tremaynes of Whispering Willows. Nat and I have a sister, your Aunt Elaine, who lives with her husband and ever-increasing brood of young rascals on another plantation. I promise not to thrust them upon you for another day or so." With that announcement, he left them.

Less than a half-hour later, the study door burst open and the petite white-haired lady who had greeted them upon their arrival bustled into the room and headed straight to Christina. Given no chance to say a word, Christina was quickly pulled into another emotional embrace. "I knew immediately that you were kin," Claire Tremayne said brokenly, between joyous sobs. "A Tremayne can recognize their own and you, my dear child, possess the red hair and wonderful eyes of my ill-tempered sons, along with their father before them. Perhaps my great-grandchild will take after this handsome young man who has brought you to us."

Claire was immediately followed by Nathaniel, Lena, and the two small boys, Davey and William. Christina was overwhelmed by their rambunctious and totally sincere welcome, overcome by the immediate acceptance of her into the family. The renowned Virginian hospitality was undoubtedly true if this group of people were any example. She and Nick were drawn into the dining room where a resplendent table laid with several large platters of food was set up for their dinner. Given places of honor near the head of the table, they dined on ham and roast mutton, a diversified mixture of poultry, and a profusion of products from the garden. Sweetmeats and pickles were placed in several spots along the white linen table cloth along with oysters and crabs in an abundance of different dishes. Although Christina could barely touch a bite of her meal, the rest of her newly discovered family seemed to have vigorous appetites. All but her father, who enjoyed exchanging conspiratorial looks with her, and grinned at the mound of food still heaped upon his plate in comparison to her own lack of appetite. Nick did justice to the feast, lightening the atmosphere by telling stories of his experiences on the sea, leaving out the more colorful details of his background and the less than honorable profession of pirate he sometimes took upon himself. Young William was enthralled, asking so many questions that finally his mother told him he was being impolite. Christina found it awkward to call these people by the legally incorrect family titles they requested she use. Her "uncle" Nathaniel and his wife, Lena, were less than ten years older than she. They settled on addressing each other by their given names. But she was comfortable in referring to their children as cousin and had no trouble calling Claire grandmama.

After a few hours of pleasant conversation filled with questions and explanations, Nick annoyed Christina by informing the Tremaynes that his wife's delicate condition was reason for an early retirement. Having difficulty keeping her eyes open, she had little choice but to accept the solicitous attention paid to her, and a short time later she and her husband were ensconced in a large guest chamber in the east wing. It had been assumed that being a married couple she and Nick would expect to occupy the same chamber. Neither were willing to raise any speculation by insisting on separate accommodations.

Wanting to lighten the sudden tense atmosphere between them, Nick mused, "That bed looks large enough for far more than the three of us." He ignored the dubious look on his wife's face as she drew a long white nightgown from her trunk.

"The three of us?" she asked peevishly, not understanding his reference to a third occupant.

"It doesn't matter." Nick quickly sensed that his reference to their child was not something she could joke about after the emotional upheaval she had experienced. "Let me unhook your gown for you, Tina, you look almost ready to drop. It has been a very long day and I am concerned that you have overtaxed yourself."

Turning her back on him, Christina struggled with the hooks at her back until she had to admit defeat and submit to his offer of help. She stood quietly while his fingers fumbled with the row of fastenings, but quickly moved away as soon as he had finished, and slipped out of her dress and underthings. A cloud of white cambric fell over her head and settled on her shoulders. She raised surprised eyes, lined with fatigue, to Nick's smiling face. "I thought I'd complete my duties as your maid. Sit down on that bench and let me brush out your hair." Too tired to argue, Christina moved to the satin-pillowed low bench placed before a beautifully inlaid dressing table, and allowed Nick to remove the pins and begin to brush her titian tresses with long, slow strokes. His touch was gentle but impersonal, and the action so relaxing that soon her eyelids began to droop and she only faintly registered that Nick had scooped her up in his arms and gently placed her in the bed. The down-filled embroidered comforter was drawn up over her shoulders and she felt a soft brush of his lips across hers before completely giving herself up to sleep.

Hours later, she awoke only slightly to the unfamiliar chiming of the great cabinet clock that stood in stately dignity in the first floor corridor of the main part of the house. Her head was resting on Nick's shoulder and she could feel his breath fanning her forehead. One of his arms was under her shoulders and the other rested lightly across her waist. His even breathing indicated that he was sleeping, but his arms tightened when she attempted to move away. Without a further attempt to extricate herself from his intimate embrace, Christina's eyes closed once again and slumber overtook her.

Chapter Eighteen

"YOU DON'T UNDERSTAND, NICK! MY PEOPLE have chosen, to a man, to remain under my protection. These people have no other place to go!" Brian's deep drawl boomed from the outside as he and Nick returned from an afternoon of riding.

"You could send them back to their homeland?" Nick bellowed, just as forcefully.

"That would be ridiculous! They have been in Virginia for many generations and have adopted so many of our ways that they would be helpless to survive. I will say again, if you would but listen this time, I personally abhor the institution of slavery and I have offered freedom to any Negro who has wished it. I might remind you that it was the English who first introduced this

271

practice to my homeland, and it is practiced in your own country!"

Christina looked embarrassed at her husband's continued arguments against her father's ownership of slaves. Sensing her distress, Claire dropped her embroidery in her basket and joined her granddaughter on the sofa in the parlor. She patted Christina's hand. "Now, now, dear. I've heard this argument before. Your father used to have it with his father. Those two men will argue it out for a few more hours over their afternoon toddies until they reach some sort of understanding. In the time that you have been here, I've come to know both you and Nicholas. It will take him only a little longer before he realizes that he and Brian have more than a great love for you in common. Brian has spent a large amount of time arguing against slavery in the state legislature. He has already drawn up the papers of manumission for all our people and they know it. Whispering Willows has always treated its people fairly and not split up families as some of our neighbors do. Your father has raised the ire of many planters by insisting that the slaves be allowed to marry." She gestured to Lena to hand her the small reed basket that held her embroidery and after carefully rethreading her needle with a strand of silk, continued explaining Brian's viewpoints on slavery. The women had spent the afternoon chatting while their nimble fingers flew over the squares of linen in their laps. "Our plantation produces well, and with far fewer workers than those of our neighbors because of the respect and fair treatment your father gives his people. However, do not fault your husband for stating his beliefs." A twinkle appeared in the sharp blue eyes of Claire Tremayne. "I know that my son is thoroughly enjoying these heated discourses with your husband. It won't last much longer today, for it is almost dinner time and Brian wouldn't dare continue the discussion during the meal. He may be master of Whispering Willows but I am still mistress of this house. No disagreements are allowed during dinner or the evening's activities." She paused to give Lena a mischievous wink.

"My husband is also quite outspoken," Lena laughingly proclaimed, her soft lilting voice matching the pixielike impishness in her blue eyes. "But I must admit that your Nicholas is a fair match for our Brian. My brother-in-law takes his position quite seriously and I think he is a bit amazed that anyone would question his integrity."

"Nicholas can be most disagreeable," Christina replied, wincing as the raised voices on the veranda grew even louder. "I do wish he wouldn't antagonize papa. After all, we are guests here."

"Christina, dear! It grieves me to hear you call yourself a guest," Claire admonished. "You are family and so is that sweet boy you have married."

The words were out before Christina could stop them, "Nicholas is no sweet boy! He has a terrible temper, demands his own way, and is extremely autocratic!"

"Oh fa, child. All men are like that sometimes. Nicholas is no worse and far better than most!" Claire chided kindly. "That he cares so deeply for you is proof enough that there is a gentle side to his strong nature. Your well-being is his constant concern, darlin'."

Christina was instantly overtaken by an utterly spontaneous flood of weeping, an unreasonable show of emotion that occured with increasing frequency as her pregnancy progressed. She despised this show of weakness, yet couldn't seem to stem the copious flow of tears. Whenever she thought of her husband's reasons for professing concern for her, she succumbed to self-pity. "He does not care for me, but for the child I carry." She completely broke into sobbing. "No one knows how little merit I have in his estimation."

Annette, who had been quietly assisting Lena with her tapestry in a far corner, rose to come to Christina's aid, but Claire's raised hand stayed her. A sharp look from the elderly lady's blue eyes indicated that all others in the room should quietly excuse themselves, with the understanding that nothing that had transpired thus far would go further. Claire immediately framed Christina's tearful face with her hands, hands that were softly delicate, but firm at the same time. "Child, child, don't go on so. It's plain as the nose on your face that that boy loves and worships you. Whenever you are in the same room, his eyes never leave you. Whenever possible, he is at your side watching out for your welfare. Only last night when your eyes were drooping, he carried you to bed as if you were the most precious thing in his world."

"That wasn't for me," she exclaimed, brokenly. "It's the Benton heir, I carry that is so precious to him."

"Darling lamb, all women in your condition think from time to time that nothing is so important to their husband as the child they carry. For some reason, we seem to wallow in self-pity and use the slightest little thing to feel sorry for ourselves. However, I do believe there is more amiss here. Whatever it is can be righted by the love you feel for each other. I have lived a lot of years, seen a lot of young couples, and I have never seen a man who loved his wife more than your Nicholas loves you—or for that matter a wife who loved her husband more."

"But grandmama, you don't understand. He—he never wanted to marry me!" Claire pulled Christina into her arms and rocked her like a small child, gently patting and soothing as Christina related everything about her relationship with her husband from their first meeting on board the ill-fated *Madelaine,* through their forced marriage and Nick's pretended amnesia, and ending with their arrival at Whispering Willows. If the older woman was shocked at anything that her granddaughter revealed, she did not show it, but rather continued to hold her and listen.

"My darlin' girl, you may have had a most unusual start in your married life, but no matter what has gone in the past, it is in the past and you should leave it there. Any man who would follow his wife across an ocean, insure her comfort and safety with every passing minute, is not a man who does not care. Perhaps it is you who have misjudged his feelings." Claire brushed a few damp strands of hair from Christina's forehead, produced a dry handkerchief, and dabbed at the tears on her granddaughter's face. "You are young and much has happened to you, but it is time you accepted the role of wife and mother. I want my great-grandchild to be born into a loving family, which won't be the case if you allow this estrangement to go on much longer. You are a Tremayne and we do what needs to be done before it's too late. You love him and he loves you, it's as simple as that."

"You think I should go to him?" Christina queried, not wanting to believe that her grandmother was so advising. "Admit that I love him with all my heart and hear him laugh in my face?"

"He will do no such thing," Claire retorted impatiently. "Give him a chance to let him show you how he feels. What is there to lose—unless you are not ready to leave your childhood behind and become a strong woman, a match for a man like Nicholas Benton."

The call to dinner came before anymore could be said. Seated beside her husband, Christina watched him carefully, looking for signs of the love her grandmother thought so clear to everyone else. Yes, he was polite to her, even gallant. He seemed consistently concerned for her comfort. His chair was pulled as close as possible during the meal and he seemed to find every excuse to touch her. Did this mean he loved her? Since coming to Whispering Willows he had made no attempt to make love to her, until she was sure even the desire he once felt for her had died. Yet, he tenderly held her in his arms every night. During the day, his attentions were purely platonic, there were never the sensual innuendos that had marked their conversations in the past.

By the time the rich desserts had been passed around the table, Christina had mentally gone through all the evidence and had reached no concrete conclusion. When the family removed themselves to the drawing room for tea and coffee, where Lena entertained them nightly at the pianoforte, she was no closer to a decision. Nick sat down beside her on the claw-footed love seat, one arm draped along the back of the carved rosewood frame, his hand resting lightly on her shoulder. When Brian and Nathaniel gathered around the instrument and joined their voices to Lena's playing of "The Rose Tree in Full Bearing," Nick used the occasion when all attention was focused on the entertainers to move closer and press a quick kiss on the top of her head. It was a light caress but sent a shiver down Christina's spine and a yearning through her body for so much more from him. Maybe grandmama is right she thought, and vowed that she would find out when they were alone. She gave thanks that they had been given a room so isolated from the rest of the household. She turned slightly and nestled her back against

Nick's chest, leaning her head on his shoulder. His hand, that had rested so lightly on her shoulder, slid down her arm and clasped her fingers. With a boldness fanned by her own desires, Christina moved her free hand to cover Nick's where it lay on his knee and he shifted his position in order to lower his head near her ear.

"Christina," he whispered, his warm breath probing the sensitive spot just behind her ear and the resonant vibration in his voice making her squirm. "Is this an invitation for more than lying passively in my arms, tonight?"

A heated flush spread from her neck up to her face and she was too embarrassed to answer his question as her eyes widened. She looked about the drawing room to ascertain if the others could possibly have overheard him. No one was paying the slightest bit of attention to them. Brian and Nathaniel continued their duet, while all the ladies, including Annette, were showing their enjoyment by giving their smiling entertainers encouraging nods and rounds of applause. Christina nearly jumped from the love seat when Nick's lips slid down her neck and began nibbling on her shoulder, bared by the wide décolletage of her gown. He murmured against her skin, with a twinkle in his eyes, "I'm waiting for an answer."

She whispered back, "Wait until later, Nicholas. Stop it or I'll join grandmama and Annette on the other sofa." He immediately straightened, muttering something about his discontent that the evening might drag on for hours before they could gracefully excuse themselves. She almost laughed aloud at the exaggerated look of pain he gave her.

With a dramatic glissando ending with a resounding chord, Lena finished her playing and Brian chose to invite his brother and Nicholas to join him on the veranda for juleps and cigars. Nick gave Christina's hand a squeeze and pulled her tighter against him before releasing her and rising slowly to his feet to accompany the gentlemen outside. Christina watched him exit the room and sat staring at the empty doorway until Lena touched her on the arm, "Christina, more tea?" Christina turned to look at her aunt, registered the questioning look in her wide blue eyes and realized that she had spoken more than once before Christina had heard her.

"Oh—oh yes, thank you," she stammered and reached for her empty china cup resting daintily in its saucer on the rosewood candlestick table at her elbow. It was then that she saw that the others were watching her and she flushed as deeply as she had moments before when Nick had been practically making love to her on the small settee. There were knowing smiles upon the faces directed toward hers and she was grateful that she could turn her attention toward the silver teapot in Lena's hand. She was saved from any further scrutiny when the boys, Davey and William, burst into the room bubbling over with the exciting news that their spaniel, Cassandra, had presented them with six little puppies. As was their usual habit, they had disappeared immediately after the meal to

check on the faithful Cassandra, as the puppies'
birth had been anticipated for days.

In unison, they gave a description of each of
Cassandra's offspring, each too excited to wait
for the other to finish a sentence before cutting
in to add his own comments. "And ol' Isaac says
we're supposed to let Cass rest now," Davey
announced with William nodding his head in
solemn agreement, both little boys finally wind-
ing down. "We can all go see her tomorrow
morning, right after breakfast, mama," William
added with the unthinking confidence of his
tender years that everyone would want to. "How
early is breakfast?"

Lena managed to usher the little boys out into
the waiting arms of their nanny with the information that the quicker they were bathed and
into bed, the sooner morning would come and
they would be allowed to go back to Cassandra's
side. For once, there were no squalls of protest at
the prospect of going to bed. Each little grubby
boy raced ahead of their puffing smiling nurse,
convinced of the wisdom of their elders—if only
this time.

A cool breeze drifted up from the river, flowing
slowly beyond the deep rolling lawn in front of
the mansion. An occasional owl could be heard
in the distance as the men puffed silently on the
"segars" Brian had extracted from his coat
breast pocket. Iced silver cups of minted whiskey were offered by one of the housemen to the
men sitting quietly on the reed chairs scattered
on the wide veranda. Nick breathed deeply of
the scented evening air, smiling as he recalled

the two youngsters' excitement. The men had
been treated first to the breathless announcement of Cassandra's delivery. He was deep into
a futuristic picture of animated little boys having Christina's beautiful blue-green eyes, full of
the same exuberance for life, cavorting on the
lawns of Larkhollow when the sound of gravel
crunching beneath the hooves of a rapidly approaching horse brought all three men to their
feet.

The rider pulled his mount to a stop at the
corner of the veranda, threw the reins carelessly
over the hitching post and rapidly advanced
toward them. "I've a message for one Nicholas
Benton. The gentleman who sent it said it was of
some urgency and that I should find Mr. Benton
here."

Nick stepped forward, thinking it news of the
Libertine Lady's arrival in Richmond. "I am
Nicholas Benton." The man quickly produced
an envelope from his pocket and handed it to
Nick. Startled to see his name written in an
unfamiliar hand, Nick stared at the missive,
then broke the seal and extracted the letter. He
scanned the contents, stiffening when he spied
Benjamin Bristol's signature.

*So Nicholas Benton, alias Nick Barker, I
have at last identified my nemesis—my
very own son-in-law. I trust you are happy
with your gain in the bargain I entered
with your esteemed parent. The extra ships
enabled me to capture your infamous ship
and all its crew, but it is you I want and*

*shall await your arrival in the captain's
cabin on board the* Libertine Lady. *Come
alone or you will forfeit the lives of Anthony Carstairs and Jackson Fry—*

The letter went on to give Nick the location of
his ship and specific directions on how to board.
Nick visibly paled, crumpled the paper into a
tight ball in his hand, then walked toward a
giant live oak where he smashed his fist against
the rough bark. "Damn," he swore beneath his
breath and stared out across the misty river.

"Nick?" Brian inquired at his elbow. "Is it bad
news?" Nick dropped the wadded paper into
Brian's hand and went on staring sightlessly at
the hazy shores of the James. "You can't go
alone," Brian stated after reading the message.
"You'll be walking into a trap and Bristol might
have already killed your friends."

Nick turned steely determined eyes toward his
father-in-law. "I have to go," he returned in a
quiet voice. "Would you have me walk away
from men who have risked their lives for me in
the past?"

"No, of course not," Brian remarked angrily,
"nor would I like to see my daughter become a
widow! I'm suggesting that you accept our help
in this matter and together we will find a way to
save your friends as well as confront Bristol."

"I can't involve you and Nat in my battles. You
could both be killed."

"As could you. My God, man! I have as much
reason to hate Bristol as you. You've told me of

his blame in the death of your young brother, must I remind you that he robbed me of the woman I loved, years I could have found happiness, years of watching our daughter grow into womanhood?" The two men argued back and forth for several more minutes until Nathaniel joined them and suggested they continue their discussion further from the house so as not to alarm the women. Nick's frustration at his helplessness grew with each step away from the large manor, but he continued to adamantly deny Brian's offer of assistance, continually pointing out the danger while Brian just as adamantly argued his right to be involved.

Christina and the other women heard the men's raised voices but couldn't discern the words. Claire commented that they must be arguing over slavery once again and assured all present that they were undoubtedly enjoying their heated exchange. Christina sat uneasily back in her chair and tried to pay attention to the conversation going on around her. Claire was giving another humorous description of her daughter Elaine and her brood. Christina had not met her father's sister, despite having been at Whispering Willows for several weeks. Word had been sent to Elaine and an excited response had been returned almost immediately, but with Elaine's regrets that she could not come for a visit until she finished nursing her children, five young boys ranging in age from two years to eleven, through the chicken pox. It seemed that the childhood ailment had started with the eldest and was determined to run down through all Elaine's offspring. Her letter had conveyed the same warmth and exuberance that Christina had come to recognize as a Tremayne family trait, and Christina was looking forward to meeting her aunt.

She managed to nod and smile at the appropriate times, but Christina's mind was elsewhere. She kept casting furtive glances at the doorway, straining her ears for the sound of approaching footsteps. When her grandmother announced that it was time for bed, regardless of the men's ill-mannered desertion for the evening, she followed the others to the central hallway and lit a taper to take to her chambers, agreeing that whatever the "menfolk" were doing it did not merit the "womenfolk" losing sleep over.

Once inside her bedroom, Christina was struggling in vain with the hooks at the back of her gown when she heard a soft knock at her door. Thinking it was Nick, she fairly ran to open it, curious as to why he might knock before entering. She was unprepared for the small army that awaited in the narrow corridor. Several of the housemaids stood with pails of steaming water while three of them struggled with a dainty porcelain tub. The first white-aproned girl softly drawled, "Ol' Mistruss sen' us heah. She say you be want'n a maid an' a bath." She smiled shyly, her beautiful large brown eyes waiting for Christina's approval. "Iff'n you like, Ah'll be yo' maid whilst yo' is heah at the Willows. Ol' Mistruss say she sorry she di'n think on it 'fore this." Christina silently thanked her grandmother for her thoughtfulness and gave the entourage permission to enter.

Within minutes, she was comfortably immersed in the warm water scented with rose petals, while the young girl busied herself carefully seeing to Christina's discarded clothing and silently laying out a nightdress on a bench near the tub, along with a large towel. She seemed to understand that Christina was unused to the presence of a maid and instinctively knew that it would be best to allow her new mistress to take her bath without assistance. Christina luxuriated in the warm water, letting it relax her tense body, until it began to turn cold. She toweled herself dry and slipped into the soft lace-edged gown and matching peignoir, then seated herself before the dressing table and started to remove her hairpins.

Soft brown hands began to assist her and an equally soft voice accompanied them with, "Ah is to brush out your hair, Miz Christina." Christina complied and the girl, Naida, very capably took over the remainder of Christina's nightly toilette, having stopped her melodic crooning only long enough to answer Christina's inquiry of her name.

By the time her new maid had left her, Christina had relaxed and curled up in a chaise lounge beside the long window at the front of the room to read a small volume of poetry that Lena had given her. She fully expected Nick to enter within a short time, but as the minutes passed, her relaxed mood changed to one of anxiety, then anger. The latter two emotions warred as she began pacing the large aubusson carpet that covered most of the center of her bedchamber. The taper she had brought from the main hall had guttered in its holder and she had been forced to light another from the tin candlebox that hung on the wall before Nick finally returned.

"I thought to find you soundly sleeping. Are you all right?" His voice was quiet as he shrugged out of his coat and loosened his cravat.

All her anxiety for his well-being drained away with his casual entry and unhurried preparations for bed. Temper rose within her. "Am I all right? I might ask you the same! Where have you been? How could you go off for hours with no explanation? The last I knew of you, you were loudly arguing some point with my father. For all I knew, you and he had finally come to blows in some outer region of the plantation!" Her questions and accusations fell in torrents and her voice steadily grew more shrill as she came to stand in front of him.

"Christina, I'm sorry if I worried you. As you can see your father and I did not come to blows." He reached for her and pulled her into his arms. "Come, where is my beautiful young wife who flirted so outrageously with me earlier? I must go to Richmond tomorrow and I would like to take that memory with me." He attempted to relax her stiff back by gently running his hands up and down her spine and molding her against him, but she pulled away.

"Richmond? Why are you going there?"

"The *Libertine Lady* has docked and I must go see to her." He pulled her back against his bared chest.

"Does that mean you will want to go back to England soon?"

"Not necessarily, I think we can certainly stay a while longer. I just need to see to my ship and men." His hands continued their mesmerizing movement across and down her back and she relaxed against him, relieved that he would not force her away from her new-found family.

"May I go? I would like to choose some lengths of fabric and perhaps commission a seamstress to make some dresses for my increasing figure." Nick stiffened, startling her when he curtly answered, "No!"

"Why not? It was you who were so concerned about my appearance. I should think you would be happy that I am conceding to your wishes." She leaned her cheek against his chest, breathing deeply of the scent that seemed so much a part of him, a mixture of tobacco, sandalwood, and his own unique scent.

"It's business, not pleasure, Christina. You will stay here where you will be sa—" He stopped himself from completing the sentence and inwardly cringed. Would this be the last time he would hold her in his arms? Would he never again be able to feel her soft body pressed to his, breathe in the scent of her silken hair? He tightened his embrace as if he could indelibly imprint the feel of her upon himself for eternity.

She sensed the strangeness in both his tone

and the hold he had around her. "So I'll be what? Why are you so against my going with you? I can do my shopping while you do your business."

"No, Christina!" His voice was too sharp, too emphatic, his arms too tight around her. Something was very wrong!

She wrenched herself away from him and stared up into his face. His expression was one she couldn't identify, something she had never seen before. "What is wrong, Nicholas?"

He looked into her beautiful face, filled with question, all traces of her previous anger gone. All he wanted to do was make love to her for what little time might remain to them and not worry her about the desperate business he must attend tomorrow. With a sinking sensation, he read her determination to receive an answer. "All right, I'm not going to Richmond. You do have the right to know where I am going." He led her to the chaise, sat down and pulled her into his arms, determined to find a way to dispel her fears. Calmly, he disclosed the contents of Bristol's letter, along with his plan of defense, making light of the danger. He put a finger across her lips to quiet her and smiled, promising he would return safely and as quickly as possible.

"Oh Nick, he'll kill you!" she cried, tears rolling down her cheeks. "You can't go, I won't let you."

An engagingly boyish smile spread across Nick's handsome features. "Not long ago, that would have brought you great pleasure, sweetheart. Dare I hope that you have acquired some slight affection for a man who adores you?"

"Nick, I—I," she faltered, but remembered her grandmother's lecture. She was a Tremayne. She was a woman, not a schoolgirl any longer. "I—I love you." The whispered words were barely off her lips before Nick pulled her against him and fastened his lips over hers. His tongue demanded entry and Christina opened to him as desperate for the taste of him as he was of her. Her arms moved up around his shoulders, clinging desperately as he shifted on the floral chaise and pressed her down beneath him, his mouth moving over hers hungrily. His hands caressed her as if memorizing her every curve.

"I've waited a long time to hear you say that," he rumbled from deep in his chest. "I think I wanted those words from you since you tried to bash my head in with a candlestick, maybe even before that." He raised up, supporting himself on his elbows, to look down at her face, a face softly illuminated by the flickering taper stuck in a wall sconce. "Oh, Christina, I must have been the world's greatest fool to ever think I didn't want you for my wife."

"And I also, for ever railing against having to marry you," she said huskily, reaching up to frame his face with her hands. Would this be her last night with this man? This man she loved with all her being. He pulled her up with him, crossed the room and loosened the ribbons at her shoulders, the soft fabric of her nightdress whispered to a heap on the floor as her fingers flew to the fastenings of his trousers.

They sank together onto the downy mattress of the wide European post bed, their nude bodies merging in mutual yearning and desperation, hoping that this night together would carry them through whatever lay ahead.

Chapter Nineteen

BULLRUSHES GREW UP ALONGSIDE THE RAM-
shackle wharf, camouflaging the weathered
timbers of the dock that had buckled up over the
lazy green water of the James. Out in the deep
channel, the *Libertine Lady* rode the gentle
swells with regal patience, becalmed by the
absence of wind, anchored for the planned revenge of Benjamin Bristol. Nick pushed aside
the cumbersome grapevine which swung between the thick stand of tulip poplar and cypress
along the river bank, oblivious to the swarms of
dark insects, the playful chatter of gray squir-
rels, and the indolent water snakes that explored
the narrow brook gliding toward the river. All he
had to do was walk across the twenty-odd yards
separating him from the decaying pier, board
the small boat Bristol had left for his use, then

row toward his ship. He waited for the signal that would tell him it was time to step out from his hiding place, taking another look through his spyglass to scrutinize the armed men stalking the decks of his ship. Several of them were standing at the rail, keeping a close watch on the pier for his arrival. Benjamin Bristol was not among them, but Nick had no doubt that his enemy was below decks, probably enjoying a snifter of his best brandy.

He pulled a timepiece from his waistcoat to remind himself that a few minutes error in timing could ruin his risky plan.

A small flat-bottomed riverboat being poled by four bare-chested Negroes came into view on the river. Rounding a bend, they were singing a river chantey in low mellow voices, the rhythmic cadence drifting on the slow moving waters. Nick moved his glass from the riverboat to the *Libertine Lady*, smiling when the interlopers on board his ship paid scant attention to the approaching craft. Minutes later, another small vessel, a sleek-lined sloop, sailed into the channel from the opposite direction. Riding low in the water, it was heavily laden with huge barrels, most likely a profitable cargo of grain being taken to Richmond to be ground into flour. Upon sighting another flat barge floating around the bend with a hogshead of tobacco secured to its deck, Nick replaced his spyglass in his pocket and stepped into the clearing which stood between him and the pier. He did not look in any direction but straight ahead, carefully sidestepping the mucky sedge along the banks until he reached the dilapidated dock. He strode purposefully along the decaying planks, nimbly vaulting across the jutting gaps in the wood as he neared the waiting launch. He untied the ropes, jumped from the dock into the boat, then took his seat and adjusted the oars in their locks until they dipped into the river.

Pulling on the oars, he did not take long to reach his ship. A thick line of hemp was thrown down to him which he grasped with both hands. He climbed up the rope, planting his feet against the hull as he ascended higher with each outward swing. As expected, he was greeted immediately by Bristol's boarding crew. He stood silently, contemptuously waiting for them to search him for weapons, trying not to wince when his arms were jerked roughly behind him and his wrists were bound securely.

"Ye're goin' below, ye pirate scum," one of Bristol's watchdogs proclaimed, laughing gleefully between an overabundance of yellowed teeth. "Our leader's waitin' to teach ya' a lesson, laddie. They call me Foolish Harv but I knows not to toy with my betters. Master Bristol ain't a forgivin' man."

Nick didn't bother to respond to the jibe, stepping forward when he felt the sharp jab from a long-barreled pistol jammed against his ribs. He was escorted by four men, two in front of him, two at the rear, as he went down the hatch and was prodded toward the captain's cabin. He was violently shoved inside, the momentum carrying him to a place before the table where Benjamin Bristol sat dabbing his lips with a white napkin. "Over there." Bristol ordered, his deadly pale eyes glittering with irritation. "He's not worth the interrupting of my meal."

"Where's my crew, Bristol?" Nick inquired as he was physically assisted into a straight wooden chair and tied securely to his seat. At a nod from Bristol, the man called Foolish Harvey backhanded Nick across the face, splitting his lip.

"You'll speak when the master tells ye'."

"Huddelson!" Bristol called, and immediately thereafter a short bald man dressed in a floral coat and striped breeches came into the cabin. He stood expectantly to one side of the door, waiting further orders. Bristol nodded toward the wardrobe, rising from his seat, then reaching out a bejeweled hand to take a final sip from a large silver wineglass.

Licking the salt taste of blood from his lip, Nick watched in stoic silence as Bristol was helped into a brocade coat. Bristol lifted his head and his manservant retied the flamboyant lace cravat beneath his flabby chin. Huddelson handed his superior a long silk scarf, and the bile rose in Nick's throat when the reward Huddelson received for his services was an effete pat on one cheek.

"Now then," Bristol walked slowly across the room, running the thin scarf through his fingers. "Lord Benton," he jeered, "to discover that the blight on my enterprises was also my son-in-law came as something of a shock. Tell me dear boy, what possessed you to foolishly attempt my financial ruin?"

When Nick refused to answer, Foolish Harvey took a tight hold in his hair and forced Nick's head back. "He's talkin' to ye', pirate!" Harvey reminded sarcastically, releasing his hold on Nick's hair with a vicious forward thrust of his hand. "Answer 'im!"

"Let us say I had a vested interest," Nick made no attempt to deny that Nicholas Benton and Nick Barker were one in the same. "I came Bristol, so now do you intend to release my crew as promised?"

A crafty look came into the gray eyes, and Bristol's men enjoyed a loud gale of laughter at what they thought was Nick's expense. Play along! Nick told himself, let them think I am even more a fool than they expected. "What have you done with them?" he asked, struggling against the restraints that held him, a frantic expression twisting his features. "You cursed devil! You promised they would go free upon my arrival, unarmed and unaided."

"Calm down dear boy, you will see that they have fared decently in your absence. Your first officer is a bit bruised and that burly mate has been taken down a peg or two but they are none the worse for wear. You would have envied the counterattack I staged to overtake them. They boarded my ship but instead of the skeleton crew they expected, they got a brigade of armed sailors portraying the bonded men they had been led to believe were aboard. Very clever of me, don't you think?"

Nick glared at him, giving the impression that he was consumed with anger and appalled at the trick Bristol had played upon his unsuspecting crew. "When I discovered that Nick Barker was not aboard," Bristol continued, relaying the story with an increasingly dramatized tone, "I was greatly distressed. But when a puny sailor relayed the information that you had sailed with your wife to Richmond, I realized where you had gone and I had the means to bring you to me."

Nick's eyes darkened to angry smoke. "I trust that that sailor is now safely stowed in the hold."

"Indeed!" Bristol laughed, as if Nick had told him some amusing joke. "As are all the others who thought they could escape my bondage. Valuable cargo, every one of them." He walked to the walnut chest against the wall and picked up a gold box, scooping a dab of sickeningly sweet pomade onto his fingers and rubbing it into his hair. "Tell me Benton, how did you find Brian Tremayne? Did he welcome his pretty bastard with open arms?"

"My *wife* was greatly relieved to discover that her sire was not a perverted swine, yes," Nick declared, barely flinching at the immediate open-handed swipe he received across the face for his slight. "Tremayne has learned who caused the breach between himself and his intended, and I do not doubt he will seek vengeance for that travesty and exact payment for your other crimes."

The momentary uneasiness that crossed Bristol's beefy face was swiftly covered by another burst of raucous laughter, mimicked at once by the other men in the room.

"As you are punishin' 'im, pirate?" Foolish

Harvey snickered, looking to Bristol for approval.

Whether or not he would have received it was a matter for conjecture, as a sharp rap on the door interrupted them. Upon Bristol's order, Jackson Fry and Tony Carstairs were pushed inside the cabin, followed by a thick-chested crewman wielding a musket. Chained together at the ankles and manacled at the wrists, they were roughly forced up against one wall.

"Two of your most loyal officers," Bristol grinned, enjoying the sight of Nick's clenched teeth and provoked glare. "The three of you will fetch a handsome price in the West Indies. Your ship will come in handy to replace those vessels I have lost at your hands. If I had known all those years ago that the mewling runt who expired in my arms was your brother, Benton, I might have connected you with the vengeful pirate who has plagued me for the last few years. Unfortunately, your father shall not hear of your fate at my hands for no one suspects my presence here. As I once did with Tremayne, notice that the *Libertine Lady* went down at sea with all hands shall be dispatched to your wife. I have no more need of that chit as my daughter so I shall leave her in the bosom of her newly found family to grieve." So caught up in his narrative, Bristol did not hear the silent entry of another man into the cabin.

"But she will not be grieving for her husband, sir, but rejoicing at the downfall of the despicable animal who treated her so abominably."

"What's this?" Bristol snarled, turning to face

the intruder. The sight of a gleaming pistol pointed squarely at his heart mottled his pasty complexion, but he could do nothing but stare as the room was swiftly invaded by ten Negro men as intimidating as their leader. Armed with pistols, knives, and clubs and flanked by Nathaniel, the men commandeered Bristol's crew's weapons. Brian eyed Bristol with disgust, commanding the immediate release of Nick and the two members of his crew.

"Bless the saints!" Jackson exploded when he was free, quickly moving to Nick's side. As soon as Nick's bonds were released, Jackson wrapped both arms around Nick's chest and gave a mighty squeeze. "I knew you wouldn't be as great a fool as I took you for when they hauled me in here."

"Thanks," Nick grinned, impatiently shrugging out of his mate's hold. He cut Tony's grateful declarations short with a curt gesture.

Bristol swayed in his belligerent stance, wheezing like he was suffering from an attack of apoplexy. He backed steadily away from Brian's weapon and eventually came to a stop backed up against the bulkhead.

"He is mine," Nick declared, striding across the cabin to Brian. "He has admitted that Michael's death can be laid on his head. I have waited years for this, Tremayne."

"What pleasure would you gain by killing the effeminate swill?" Brian asked, pointing at the sniveling figure cowering against the far wall. "That fop has never held a weapon so how do you intend to end his life? If you murder him, will you be able to live with it?"

"He killed my brother, ruined your chances with Elizabeth and denied you your child. You can ask if I will feel any guilt over killing him?" Nick was incredulous. He had waited, plotted, thought of little else but this moment when he would confront his enemy. "Hand him a sword, let him die as he deserves."

"Very well," Brian went to take down the blades mounted on the wall, "My concern is certainly not for him." Looking bland, Brian patiently held out a sword for Bristol who reluctantly took hold of it. He then brought the second weapon to Nick, ordering his men to clear the room of its other occupants. When at last it was only the three of them inside the cabin, Brian sat down at the table and poured himself a glass of wine. "Be quick about it Nick." He lifted his glass. "Our womenfolk are waiting for word and your wife is in no condition to worry overlong."

Slowly, a perplexed frown creasing his forehead, Nick approached his enemy. Bristol looked nothing like the pompous autocrat who had gleefully recounted his loathsome exploits only minutes before. Shaking, the man could barely bring his sword to a level stance, eyeing Nick like a cowardly weasel faced with a predator. A dribble of spittle frothed on his protruding lips. "Please," he begged, shutting his eyes as Nick began circling his wrist, plotting his first thrust.

Getting no response, Nick tried to provoke

Bristol into battle, flicking the end of his blade to
jab encouragingly at the shiny waistcoat buttoned over his paunchy waist. Nothing! The
man had no intention of defending himself. His
sword slipped out from his shaking fingers and
rolled away across the floor as Bristol collapsed
in a slobbering heap at Nick's feet. In frustration, Nick glanced over at Brian who lifted his
brow as if to say, what did I tell you? Pressing
his lips together, Nick lifted one boot and thrust
Bristol's supplicating figure away from him.
Cursing loudly, he threw his sword across the
room. "Damn you, Tremayne. You knew I
wouldn't be able to do it."

"Not a man of honor like yourself," Brian
agreed, pouring a second glass of wine for his
daughter's excellent choice in men. "It was
almost too simple to take over this ship. Bristol's
crew are a scurvy lot and my men had no trouble
overcoming them and releasing your crew from
the hold. I suggest we charge some of your loyal
men with the pleasurable task of carting Bristol
to the nearest public jail. I believe the usual
course the general court takes in these matters
is a quickly dispatched hanging."

"I might think my newly found father-in-law
is a man of sentimental weakness," Nick picked
up his glass, still upset by the unsatisfying
ending to his quest.

"You might but you won't," Brian laughed, not
even bothering to acknowledge the existence of
his old enemy as Bristol was escorted out of the
room by two of his men. "Show me how well you
master this ship. If we put her to sail we can be

home in far less time than it would take us to man our lowly rivercraft. She seems to be a well-built lady, so let her prove her merit. Let's go on to Richmond and rid ourselves of these vermin."

"I am not sure I am going to enjoy having you as a close relative," Nick retorted, not as quick to dismiss Bristol from his thoughts. His gray eyes followed the broken figure slumped between his burly brown-skinned guards. "I now have an interfering male relative on either side of the Atlantic. Perhaps I should tell you how I came to be your daughter's husband."

"Perhaps you should," Brian confirmed, looking much like the lady in question as his sparkling green eyes came alive with curiosity. "My mother has told me some of it but I was hard put to believe it. It was a lucky thing that she had only a few minutes yesterday to take me aside or it was likely our beefy friend would have had company in the jail."

"My feelings were never in doubt," Nick replied, coming to sit at the table, "But my dishonorable intentions would surely cast dispersions on my character."

Each man took a long thoughtful sip of their wine.

"As I recall," Brian grinned like a much younger man, "I had similar designs on her mother. Odd how such fragile beings can bring down our sex like so many unbalanced pins on the bowling green."

"Very," Nick agreed sagely, and belatedly offered his thanks to Brian for bringing their

involvement with Bristol to its successful conclusion. It seemed incongruous, but he felt no
sense of loss at the way things had turned out.
Justice would be done, but the vengeance would
come by the law. He had more important things
to think about. "Excuse me, Tremayne." He
jumped up from his chair, "I will give orders to
set sail. We should not be wasting time drinking
to our health when our women sit waiting for
news."

"I should have thought of that," Brian remarked sardonically and stood up to accompany
Nick to the deck. "Perhaps the child Christina
carries will be more considerate than his closest
male relatives."

Nick was already too far ahead of Brian to take
notice of his dry wit, shouting orders to his crew
and concentrating on an adventurous future
with his redheaded wife and the laughter they
would share when watching the escapades of
several auburn-haired, green-eyed children.

Christina stood watching the fireflies flit over
the misty shadows on the lawns. Katydids sang
strident lullabies while the nighthawks shrieked
in the moonless sky. Where was Nick? An inner
voice pleaded the same question over and over
again in her mind. Doubt, anxiety, and dread
were contained in each word. Clutching a thin
shawl around her shoulders, she lifted her hand
to the wooden rail of the veranda, staring at the
muted sparkle of the jewels in her wedding ring.

The nighttime air had grown sharp, dew falling in a steady mist to the ground like a shroud.

It was as if the whole world was waiting, breathless with apprehension, fearful with weeping, waiting for some word that the men who had left Whispering Willows before dawn would return safely. The gray haze which coated the stagnant air was like a pall, a pervading gloom matched only by the three women who tried to see past the gathering mist. From the white wooden cabins below the hill, a lonely song could be heard, sung by the black women of the plantation who were also waiting for news of their men.

"Come Christina," Claire ordered quietly, the steady creak of her wicker rocker marking the time. "Sit on the swing by Annette. Lena is bringing out some brandy-laced coffee. I think we could all use some about now."

Reluctantly, Christina turned away from the rail and her view of the river to take her place on the veranda's wooden swing.

"Why aren't they back?" she asked fearfully, biting her lower lip to keep back the tears. "If anything happens to him, I don't know what I will do."

"Soon child," Claire reassured, her voice more firm than her feelings. "My son will not let anything happen to your husband. They shall take care of that Bristol person, then return to us. A man like that will deserve whatever they give him."

Annette swiftly echoed Claire's assurances but Christina was not convinced.

"He's a dangerous man, grandmama," she reminded. "He wouldn't think twice about killing Nick or my father." She broke off suddenly as Lena came out on the veranda carrying a tray of small cups. Her pale oval face was streaked with tears and Christina knew that Lena was as desperately afraid as she was. She did not want to add to the woman's fears so she stopped discussing Bristol.

"I do hope Nathaniel thought to take a warm coat. The mist is descending and it will be cold on the river." Lena handed each woman a cup, her reedy voice quivering. "Perhaps you should retire, mama. This damp air is not good for you."

"Don't coddle me, Lena. I won't close my eyes until our men arrive safely and you know it. Josie brought me a rug and this hot drink will warm me. Now settle yourself down like a good girl." Claire sipped from her cup, resting back in her chair as her eyes drifted out over the grounds.

They sat silently after that, each woman lost in her own thoughts, until a loud splash as if a heavy weight had been dropped in the river was followed by the deep male voices they had all longed to hear.

"It's the *Libertine Lady!*" Christina cried happily, leaning far over the veranda rail to see the billowing white sails through the trees. "Thank God!" She flew down the steps, the shawl slipping from her shoulders as she ran toward the river and Nick. Her skirts went flying, a white blur in the darkness, her auburn hair flowing freely behind her back.

"Come back," Claire shrieked, afraid that her granddaughter might stumble and fall in the darkness before she reached the plantation docks. "Have a care child. Your man is not going anywhere but here."

"It's them," Christina called back, "I can see Nat and Papa—Nicholas?—Nick!" she shouted, a hysterical fervency making her voice sound unnaturally high. She got her first view of the dock as a plank was quickly lowered, and ran faster when the men began parading off the ship. Where was Nick? Had they come to tell her that he had not survived their encounter with Bristol? It was difficult to discern one man from another as they walked en masse up the hill, breaking into two groups as the Negro men went to greet their wives and families. One figure—two—then several tall male forms began striding swiftly toward the manor house.

"Nick—Nick!" Christina cried, joy replacing the initial terror she had felt until she spotted him walking between Jackson and Tony a few feet behind her father and Nat. She raced across the wet grass which separated them, throwing herself into the familiar strong arms she had feared would never reach out to hold her again.

"I was so afraid," she sobbed, her fingers rapidly tracing the planes of his face, running down his neck and over his shoulders to assure herself that he was actually with her and all right. "Thank God—Oh, Thank God," she repeated over and over again, unaware of the concerned expressions exchanged over her head between her husband and father. It was right that Nick should lift her into his arms, cradling her against the hard strength of his chest, right that he should hold her shivering body lending her the warmth and security she so desperately needed. "I—I," She couldn't tell him how greatly she had feared he would not return to her, could do nothing but wrap her bare arms around his neck, fiercely clutching him as if she never meant to let him go.

"Hush love, hush," Nick spoke harshly in her ear, quickening his step. "You are shivering with cold. It was foolish to come out here to meet us. Think of the babe, Tina."

Think of the babe? Was that the first thought that had entered his mind when he spied her running toward him, all the love and concern she felt for him shimmering in her eyes? Her tears of joy were swiftly replaced by an icy despair, the shivers he thought caused by the cold night air were actually from the shock of hearing him state what she had known all along. The child would always come first in his heart, even after what they had shared together last night and many nights before.

"You could have fallen." Nick tightened his hold and she could feel the taut anger in him.

"I—I'm sorry." Her muffled apology was given into the damp material of his coat as she stiffened in his arms.

He muttered something savage under his breath but before she could replay the harsh words in her head, they were walking up the veranda steps where Lena, Claire, and Annette stood waiting to greet them. Strangely, Nick did not replace her back on her feet, a strained expression on his face, as Brian and Nat introduced the two crewmen from the *Libertine Lady*. Brian began relaying the events that had transpired since they had left the plantation.

"Forgive me." Nick's voice interrupted Brian's narrative, "My wife is in no condition to listen to our recount of the tale. I am taking her inside to our chambers before she takes a chill."

"I want to hear—" Christina started but the words died in her throat upon seeing the blaze of fury alight in Nick's eyes. Thin lipped and angry, his expression was violent and her green eyes opened wide. "Let me down," she cried, beginning to squirm in his arms, her temper soaring to match the anger she sensed in every sinew of the man who was holding her. She was not a child to be carted off to bed and nothing— *nothing* had happened to jeopardize the health of his precious heir!!

"Excuse us," he pronounced tersely, his jawline tight with determination. Without waiting for their compliance, Nick carried his wife away from the family and into the house. When she began struggling in earnest, he merely adjusted her more securely against his chest, keeping a dominant hold on her small form as he strode toward the east wing.

He kicked open the door of their chambers, using his shoulder to close it behind him, then walked over to the bed and sat down. He retained his hold on her as he began unbuttoning her gown. Speechless with temper, Christina said nothing as he stripped every stitch of clothes from her body. When she was naked, he grabbed a soft flannel sheet from the bed and used it as a towel to rub down her skin.

"I am perfectly all right," she snapped when she was finally capable of speech, crying out when he again lifted her into his arms and walked purposefully to the tall bureau which contained her clothes. He pulled a long white nightgown from a drawer and grimly, silently, lowered it over her head, ignoring her mutinous glare. Without uttering a word, he turned over her wrists and fastened the tiny pearl buttons of her sleeves. "Are you now satisfied that you have taken proper care of the babe you are so worried about?"

"I don't know," he growled. "Do you feel properly cared for?" Grabbing one of her wrists, he propelled her behind him to the bed, jerking back the covers and swinging her off her feet to place her lightly across the mattress. He then drew the blankets over her body, leaving only her stunned face uncovered.

Her mouth gaping, green eyes showing her shock, she asked, "What did you say?"

He began tucking the blankets around her body as if she were a young child with the chills. "I love you, Christina," he ranted loudly. "Every stubborn willful inch of you, and if you won't take care of yourself, I'll damn well do it for you. I've spent a hellish day and half the night thinking of nothing but getting back to the woman I love and what do I find when I step one foot on the ground? You, stumbling blindly in the dark, wearing nothing but a thin gown, wet clear to the bone."

He didn't notice the tender, joyful smile which began on his wife's face and grew wider and wider as he continued his furious tirade. "I'm damned well not going to lose you to pneumonia when I've thought of nothing else but keeping you with me for the rest of my life!"

"Oh my darling, Nick," Christina cried, an enveloping warmth invading every bone. "You do love me." She wanted to hold the words to her breast as if she could actually touch them. "It's not just the baby, is it?"

He stared down at her flushed face, the harshness draining from his features as he read the love for him there in her eyes. He brought his hand to her forehead and gently brushed her hair away from her temples, his gray eyes hiding none of his feelings. "Little love, nothing would have any meaning for me without you. I plan on bringing several more Bentons into the world but it is their mother who can bring me alive, drive me to drink, and fuel my temper."

"That is hardly a romantic thing to say to me," Christina protested softly, suddenly quite secure in his love even so far as to be able to return his teasing. "I believe I fuel more than your temper, milord."

His most audacious pirate grin was her reward, the smile of the adventurous sea captain who had first stolen her heart. "Far more, Tina."

With a swift glance of regret he stood up from the bed, but she was quicker and caught hold of his shirt before he could move away. Her fingers nimbly worked loose the buttons on his shirt, her laughter full of irrepressible joy as his chagrined expression became one of deep sensual hunger. His gray eyes were molten with longing and he could see that his wife was no longer suffering from the cold. He tore at his clothes as she, as swiftly, removed the nightgown he had so recently pulled over her head.

In seconds, he had slipped beneath the covers, his naked body clasped to hers. His mouth sought and found her soft lips, sought and found and explored with infinite pleasure. They were engulfed in a torrential storm of delight, moving as one as they reveled in the tumult of sensations that they alone could create. He guided her from one tempest summit to the next until she did not know how much higher they could climb and could only hold on while returning his tumultuous strength with the velvety power inherent in every woman who is with the man she loves.

When at last they recovered from the shudders of passion, the gauzy mists had lifted, and locked together they watched the first beams of morning light filter through the netting over the open windows.

"I never believed this day would come," Christina murmured, sleepily nestling her head more comfortably against her husband's shoulder. "I shall love you forever, Nicholas."

"Forever is not nearly long enough for the love we share, princess," Nick whispered, and settled her soft body possessively closer against his hard length. "Not nearly long enough."

HISTORICAL ROMANCES

Breathtaking New Tales

of love and adventure set against history's most exciting time and places. Featuring two novels by the finest authors in the field of romantic fiction—every month.

Next Month From Tapestry Romances

REBELLIOUS LOVE
by Maura Seger

EMBRACE THE STORM
by Lynda Trent